PRAISE FOR JACI BURTON AND HER NOVELS

"Jaci Burton's stories are full of heat and heart."
—#1 *New York Times* bestselling author Maya Banks

"A wild ride."
—#1 *New York Times* bestselling author Lora Leigh

"Jaci Burton delivers."
—*New York Times* bestselling author Cherry Adair

"One to pick up and savor." —*Publishers Weekly*

"Jaci Burton's books are always sexy, romantic and charming! A hot hero, a lovable heroine and an adorable dog—prepare to fall in love with Jaci Burton's amazing new small-town romance series."
—*New York Times* bestselling author Jill Shalvis

"A heartwarming second-chance-at-love contemporary romance enhanced by engaging characters and Jaci Burton's signature dry wit." —*USA Today*

"Captures everything I love about a small-town romance." —Fresh Fiction

"Delivered on everything I was hoping for and more."
—Under the Covers Book Blog

"A sweet, hot, small-town romance." —Dear Author

"Fun and sexy." —Fiction Vixen

TITLES BY JACI BURTON

• • • • •

THE

Accidental

NEWLYWED

GAME

JACI BURTON

JOVE
New York

A JOVE BOOK
Published by Berkley
An imprint of Penguin Random House LLC
penguinrandomhouse.com

Copyright © 2022 by Jaci Burton, Inc.
Penguin Random House supports copyright. Copyright fuels creativity, encourages
diverse voices, promotes free speech, and creates a vibrant culture. Thank you for buying
an authorized edition of this book and for complying with copyright laws by not
reproducing, scanning, or distributing any part of it in any form without permission.
You are supporting writers and allowing Penguin Random House to continue to
publish books for every reader.

A JOVE BOOK, BERKLEY, and the BERKLEY & B colophon
are registered trademarks of Penguin Random House LLC.

ISBN: 9780593439630

First Edition: June 2022

Printed in the United States of America
1   3   5   7   9   10   8   6   4   2

Book design by Alison Cnockaert

THE *Accidental* NEWLYWED GAME

CHAPTER

· · · · · ·

one

AFTER EIGHT HOURS of workshops and networking and smiling—dear God, so much smiling—Honor Bellini desperately needed a stiff drink.

The conference for wedding planners had been amazing. She'd learned a lot and had met great people from all over the country. But she'd talked so much her throat was raw, she had taken so many notes her fingers were cramped and her brain was oh-so-tired from being filled with information. All she wanted was a double margarita, some dinner and then bed.

The bright lights and jingling bells of the casino beckoned as she walked through the lobby of the Bellagio, but she resisted easily. She loved a lot of things about visiting Las Vegas. Gambling wasn't one of them. There were plenty of casinos back home in Oklahoma, so gaming had no lure for her here. But the shows and the shopping? Totally different experience, and she'd spent much of her free time the past three days soaking up the sights, taking in some shows and browsing through stores, even if she had done it alone. Not that it had bothered her to go by herself. She was, after all, pretty great company.

After putting her work stuff in her room, she tucked her hotel key card in her purse and went downstairs, heading toward the bar lounge in the lobby. It was surprisingly quiet and uncrowded, and a pianist was playing soft music. She found a seat and a server came over right away. She ordered a Cadillac margarita, then relaxed against the oh-so-comfy cushioned chair and people-watched, as both tourists on vacation and people dressed for business walked by.

Vegas was a busy place that catered to both the party people and the business types. Everyone could have fun here, even if you had to slip in your fun on a work trip, like Honor was doing.

The server brought her cocktail. She thanked him and took a sip. It was delicious and very strong, exactly what she needed. If she could kick off her heels this would be perfect, but she'd settle for an excellent marg for now.

Her attention was drawn to a guy standing at the registration desk right outside the bar. Even though she could only see his back, she easily recognized his dark hair and the way he walked. Plus, she would know that fantastic butt anywhere, even though he was totally off-limits—first, because he was her sister's ex-fiancé, and second, because, well, see number one.

She pulled her phone out and sent a text to Owen Stone, just in case she was wrong.

Where are you right now?

The guy at the front desk pulled his phone out of his jeans pocket and typed.

Vegas. What's up?

Her lips curved as she typed a reply.

I'm in the bar across the lobby. Turn around.

He pivoted and she waved. She caught his thousand-watt smile as he waved back, struck by the flash of heat she felt.

Okay, that was probably the tequila hitting her. It couldn't be because she had just seen Owen. They'd practically grown up together. He had once planned on marrying her sister. The wedding hadn't happened, of course, but that was beside the point.

And, sure, Owen was hot. So very hot. And, sure, hadn't she always had a thing for him, even before he'd dated her sister Erin? Who wouldn't, with his good looks and incredible body? But once Erin had decided to date him, Honor had stepped back and marked Owen off her list forever.

But now? Now her sister was happily married to Jason, and Owen was . . . was . . .

Well, what was he, exactly? He looked amazing since finishing up his cancer treatments last year. He'd gained his weight back—and a lot of muscle, too. He looked healthier than ever. And hot.

Had she already thought about how hot he looked? How his polo shirt fit snugly against his broad chest? How his jeans looked so incredible on his hips? And had he somehow gotten taller? No, that couldn't be right. And that hair. She had a thing for dark, slightly tousled hair that was just made for a woman to run her fingers through.

Oh, my, God, Honor. Calm yourself before you ooze right off the chair.

He finished up at the front desk and walked over while Honor sipped her drink and watched him, happy to see someone from home while she was so far away from it.

That's what it was. She was happy to see someone from home. She wasn't at all ogling all his hotness or anything.

She stood and they hugged.

But did he have to smell so good?

He sank into the chair next to hers. "This is a surprise. I can't believe you're here."

"I can't believe *you're* here. Are you staying at the Bellagio?"

He nodded. "I've been around all week, actually."

"Me, too. How have we not run into each other?"

He shrugged. "No clue. What are you here for?"

"A conference for wedding planners. I just finished up today."

"Yeah? Was it good?"

"It was awesome. I learned a lot. I not only picked up amazing tips from the speakers but also from my fellow wedding planners. My head is spinning with new ideas."

"That's great."

The server came over and took Owen's drink order, then disappeared.

"And you?" she asked. "What brings you to Vegas?"

He stretched out his long legs. She absolutely would not stare at the way his jeans fit so nicely tight against his thighs.

"Craft brewers conference," he said. "Kind of the same thing as you, only with beer."

She laughed. "And was yours good?"

"Yeah, it was great. I picked up new ideas for brewing quality and maximizing efficiency, and learned a ton of new governmental rules that gave me a headache, and some tips on growing my business."

Their server brought Owen his beer. He immediately took a long swallow.

"When do you leave?" he asked her.

"Not until Sunday. I wanted some downtime while I had the chance."

"Yeah, it's not like you take a lot of time off, with weddings happening every weekend at the vineyard."

"Very true."

"The family's holding down the fort for you this weekend?"

"Yes. And I hired an assistant to handle things for me."

He cocked a brow. "*You* hired an assistant? You let someone else take the reins?"

"Funny. Erin and Brenna are there to manage everything. Besides, Mae can handle it."

Owen looked at her. "You hired Mae Wallace? The one who's been a bridesmaid in all those weddings? And was almost a bride herself?"

She nodded. "She knows as much about weddings, planning weddings and being in weddings as I do. Probably more than I do."

"And about how to cancel a wedding."

"Which wasn't her fault."

"No, it wasn't. At least you won't ever have to host a wedding for the asshole that cheated on her."

"Not at Bellini Weddings, we won't. He will never be welcome on our property."

"I'm glad you have her to help out."

She lifted her glass. "I'll drink to that."

He tipped his glass to hers. After she took a couple long swallows, he asked, "What are you having?"

"Cadillac margarita."

"Strong stuff. Though if you're gonna drink that you might as well do shots. End of the week and all, celebrate big."

She laughed. "Oh, sure. While you're having beer."

"Hey, I meant *we* could do shots. It's been a long week and my head is filled with government regs and beer formulas."

"My brain is on overload, too. Which is why I ordered a double."

He signaled for their server and ordered them both shots of some top-shelf tequila. Their server brought the shot glasses over with a smile, then left.

She looked at the golden liquid, then over at Owen. "I'm not sure it's such a good idea to do shots on an empty stomach."

Owen shrugged. "One shot. Then we'll go get something to eat."

"That sounds like a fabulous plan."

She had planned on eating alone, then going up to her room.

Instead, she was going to have dinner with Owen. Hot Owen.

No. Friend Owen. That was all.

It was going to be fun.

CHAPTER

......

two

Owen PRIED ONE eye open, and even that hurt. He closed his eye again, figuring it had to be the middle of the night. Except sunlight kept blasting his face.

He was dead. That was it, he had to be dead. No, wait. If he was dead, why would he feel this bad?

Where the hell was he and who dropped a bomb on his head last night?

He heard a moan. A moan that definitely hadn't come from him. He grimaced and forced one eye open again, trying his best to focus. All he saw was a blurry form in the bed next to him.

Okay, there was a person, and based on the moan, it was a woman. But who?

Eyes fully open now, he took a good look, then cringed. There was no denying that gorgeous head of brown hair with streaks of auburn. He couldn't remember much from last night, but he knew he'd been with Honor Bellini. And that was Honor's hair, and Honor's naked shoulders, along with Honor's naked back. And as she rolled over, the sheet drifted down, revealing Honor's naked—

He quickly pulled the sheet up, though if they'd already—

Did they already? And if they had, why couldn't he remember?

What the hell did they do last night?

Maybe his bedmate had a better memory than he did.

"Honor," he said, keeping his voice soft and low.

Her reply was a sexy low moan and a stretch, which only made his balls tighten in response.

He cleared his throat. He tried again, this time a little more forcefully. "Honor, wake up."

"Mmm. Headache. Go away."

He'd like to go away. But as reality came more into focus he realized he didn't know where they were, since this wasn't his hotel room. And based on the décor and the unfamiliar view out the window, this wasn't their hotel, either. He wasn't about to get dressed and leave her there alone.

She finally rolled over to face him and he saw the same pained expression on her face that he'd had when he first woke.

"Ow."

"Honor."

Then her eyelids peeked open. "Owen?"

"Yeah."

She shot up in bed. "Owen! What are you doing in my bed?"

"This isn't your bed. Actually, it's not my bed, either. I'm not exactly sure where we are."

She pulled the sheet up tight and clutched it like a favorite blanket. "What? What happened last night?"

"I was hoping you might remember."

She frowned and rubbed her temple. "I remember tequila. Shots. Lots of them. And then a club and dancing and more drinks. And not much after that."

His lips curved as memories of bright lights and moving hips came back to him. "Oh, right. Dancing."

"Stop smiling, Owen. We are naked in bed together."

Which to him wasn't a bad thing. But from the look of horror on Honor's face, to her it was. "I'm sorry. I don't know what happened. We got toasted and obviously fell into bed. I guess it happens."

"It does not happen. Not to me."

"It's not like I do this every weekend, either."

She blew out a breath, sending one of her curls sailing in front of her face. He so wanted to reach out and tuck it behind her ear, but he didn't think that would be a good idea right now.

"I need to go to the bathroom," she said. "Would you turn around?"

"Sure."

He flipped over on his side and waited until he heard the bathroom door close. He rolled over and stared up at the ceiling, lacing his fingers behind his head. It was then that he felt the metal on his finger. He lifted his hand and saw a thin band of gold encircling his left ring finger.

Huh.

His left ring finger.

His Left. Wedding. Ring. Finger.

Ohhhh, fuck.

He heard Honor's scream coming from the bathroom at the same time the realization hit him. He threw the sheet off and barely had time to climb into his boxer briefs before she pulled the door open. She was wrapped in a towel and waved her left hand in his face.

"Tell me this isn't what it looks like," she said.

He gave her an apologetic look and held up his left hand. "It might be?"

She shook her head. "No. It's some joke. It has to be."

"Even drunk, we wouldn't do that, would we?"

"Of course not."

"But we should check just to be sure. I mean, if we got married, there'd be paperwork, right?"

She pointed her finger at him. "You're right. There would be." They both scrambled over to the desk, where all their clothes were piled up. Underneath their clothes and her purse was a bag from Chapel of the Bells wedding chapel.

They looked at the bag, then at each other. Honor grabbed it and pulled out the contents. There was a veil along with candles and an envelope. She handed the envelope to Owen, who opened it and stared at the contents before focusing his attention on Honor.

"We got married last night."

Honor put her hand to her mouth, dropped the bag, ran into the bathroom and shut the door. He walked over and tried the knob, but it was locked.

He was pretty sure he heard vomiting.

This for sure wasn't the way he pictured his honeymoon going.

CHAPTER

· · · · · ·

three

AFTER EMPTYING HER stomach of whatever she drank last night, Honor felt somewhat better, but she desperately needed a shower. She also needed to talk to Owen, to figure out what happened and what their next steps should be. But a shower had to come first.

Okay, sure, she was probably avoiding that conversation by showering, but the hot water made her feel a little more human, even though she felt naked as all get-out after last night with Owen. And well, she *was* naked. But at least she was a bit more refreshed, and ready to face him. When she opened the door, she saw her clothes all neatly folded sitting right outside the bathroom door.

"Owen?"

There was no answer. Had he left? He wouldn't do that, would he? Not without talking to her.

She grabbed the clothes, climbed into yesterday's underwear—yuck—and her now-wrinkled dress and went to dig her brush out of her purse, then combed out the tangles in her hair. She might look a wreck and she might be in yesterday's clothes, but at least she was clean. If only she had a cup of coffee.

The door opened and Owen walked in carrying a bag and two cups of coffee.

"I figured we needed coffee and carbs, so I got us bagels."

She sighed in relief, though whether it was for the coffee or the fact he hadn't left her, she wasn't sure, but she didn't have the mental capacity right now to figure it out.

She was married. To Owen. How had that happened? Where had their brain cells been when they'd decided *that* was a good idea?

Before they figured it out, she pulled the top off the coffee and took a sip, realizing Owen had added double cream—just the way she liked it. How had he known?

"Thank you for this."

He dug into the bag and pulled out a bagel, handing it to her. "You're welcome. Are you feeling all right?"

"Much better now, thanks. Where are we, by the way?"

"The Sahara, which apparently is close to our wedding chapel."

She grimaced, her stomach rolling. She took a bite of the bagel, hoping if she ate something it would prevent her stomach from revolting again. "What did we do last night? Other than getting drunk and married?"

She didn't ask the sex question, figuring there was enough on the table to deal with right now.

He swallowed a bite of bagel and shrugged. "Hell if I know, Honor. I vaguely remember us doing a few rounds of shots at our hotel, then heading out and hitting some clubs. Did we ever eat anything?"

"I don't remember dinner. That was probably our downfall."

"Yeah. It's been a long time since I drank like that. Like maybe since my misspent youth. I'm really sorry."

"It's not your fault. I went along for the ride. And the wedding, too, apparently." She ate another piece of bagel, though for some reason it wasn't making her feel better.

"I should have done a better job taking care of you. That's on me."

She hated seeing the look of guilt and remorse on his face. "Not everything is your fault, Owen."

"Yeah, but I already screwed up big with Erin. And now you. This is becoming a trend, and not a good one. I'll fix this."

"No, *we'll* fix this. We'll . . . I don't actually know what we'll do, but we'll do something."

"We should get an annulment, I guess."

Ouch. "Can we do that?"

"Sure we can. I mean, I think we can. I don't know the rules of annulments. I also don't know what happened last night, but it's not like we were engaged or in love or anything. It was a drunken mistake. An annulment should be easy, right?"

Nothing like getting married and dumped all within a twenty-four-hour period.

Or less.

Stop it, Honor. He's not dumping you. You're not even a couple.

She finally nodded. "An annulment should be easy. Then it's like this whole thing never happened."

The look of misery on his face mirrored her own discomfort.

"I guess that would be the best thing," he said. "It took your family a long time to forgive me for what I did to Erin. I can't imagine how pissed they'd be if they found out I got you drunk and married you."

That gnawing pain in her belly was becoming less about the hangover and more about feeling as if she'd just been wedded, bedded and shed.

The trouble was, she couldn't remember anything about last night, so she'd missed the entire wedded-and-bedded part.

And didn't that just suck?

"Now what?" she asked.

"I don't know. I guess we head back to our hotel. I don't know about you, but I could use a shower and a change of clothes. And a more substantial breakfast."

She liked the change-of-clothes idea. "You're right. We'll probably think more clearly if we eat something."

They grabbed their things and headed out, got in a taxi out front and rode in silence back to the hotel.

Honor wondered what Owen was thinking. Was he panicked, hoping they could end this whole marriage thing as soon as humanly possible? He sure seemed to have a lot of regrets.

For herself, she was mainly . . . numb. She stared down at the gold ring circling her finger, then glanced over at Owen's hand. He hadn't yanked the ring off and stuck it in his pocket—at least not yet—so that was something.

When he reached over and took hold of her hand, the shock of sensation nearly had her jumping out of the back seat of the taxi. She forced herself to remain still as she met his gaze.

"It's all going to be okay, Honor. I promise."

He didn't let go of her hand, and she forced herself not to react to his touch, though it was hard not to, because her entire body was reacting with a surprising blast of heat.

What exactly had happened between them last night?

And why couldn't she remember?

What a disaster. She was never touching alcohol again.

CHAPTER

......

four

OWEN HAD HOPED that getting back to his hotel room and taking a hot shower would clear his head. Unfortunately, the shower offered him no clarity, but at least he was cleaner now.

He did know the one thing he wasn't going to do was abandon Honor and let her think he wanted to get away from her. In fact, that was the furthest thing from his mind. If he was honest, he wanted to stay close to her.

This whole debacle was confusing as hell, coupled with the fact that he couldn't remember how it had all come about, or what had happened between doing some shots and waking up in a strange hotel room, naked. And married.

At least he'd married Honor. If he was going to get married, he couldn't think of any woman he'd want to be with more than her. Which was kind of a fucked-up realization since he'd once been engaged to Honor's sister Erin. And that hadn't turned out so well.

Then again, circumstances had been different.

Excuses, excuses, Owen. You bailed. You got scared about your cancer diagnosis and you bailed.

He sucked in a breath, determined not to rehash past mistakes. Instead, he got dressed and went downstairs to the lobby to meet Honor. He saw her at the entrance to the restaurant, waving at him, so he walked over to meet her.

"There was a line, so I thought I'd go ahead and get in it," she said.

"Good idea."

She had a lot more color in her face now, and she'd changed into black leggings and a black-and-white tee, along with tennis shoes. Owen noticed she still wore her wedding band. Then again, so did he, though he had no idea why. They'd both agreed to an annulment.

That pang in his stomach had to be a combination of hunger and hangover.

They finally got seated, and both ordered coffee and orange juice. Owen picked up the menu. "I want to order everything," Honor said. "I think my body is trying to tell me something."

He looked up from the menu. "Yeah, it's telling you we forgot to eat dinner last night."

"And drank too much."

"And ended up married."

She sighed and shook her head. "I still can't believe that either of us would have allowed that to happen. We're both so levelheaded."

He laughed. "Tequila, Honor. The evils of tequila."

"The shots were your idea."

He gave her a critical eye. "I said one round. I might not remember everything, but I'm pretty sure the second—and third—rounds were your idea."

"Were they?" She frowned. "I don't remember that part."

Their server came over and they ordered their food. After he left, Honor said, "My stomach rumbled just ordering."

"Same." He sipped his coffee and then took a long swallow of orange juice.

"So, what are we going to do?" she asked.

"I don't know. I thought today I might take a drive and see some of the desert sights. You want to come along?"

She cocked her head to the side. "That wasn't at all what I was asking."

"I know what you were asking, Honor. But until I get a full load of carbs and protein, I'm just not prepared to give it a great deal of thought."

"That's fair." She sipped her coffee and flipped through her phone, and then after a long fifteen minutes of awkward silence—something Owen had never suffered with Honor before—the server brought their breakfast.

They both dove into their meals. Over food they talked, though it was mostly about innocuous things like what they'd done while they were in Vegas, both of them tiptoeing around the disaster of last night.

He devoured everything on his plate, and in the end he felt a lot better. His headache was gone and that gnawing ache in his stomach had disappeared.

Ever since his cancer diagnosis he'd taken good care of his body. He drank beer, but he hadn't indulged in hard liquor much at all. Until last night, anyway. He didn't know what had made him suggest doing shots with Honor.

Bad judgment, obviously, something he thought he'd gotten past. Apparently not.

And now, once again, he was going to have to pay the price for making a reckless decision. And Honor was going to have to pay that price, too.

When would he learn his lesson? When would he stop hurting the Bellini women in his life?

CHAPTER

· · · · · ·

five

OKAY, SO OBVIOUSLY doing impulsive things with Owen was going to be a standard.

Over breakfast they decided that instead of taking a desert drive, they'd check out of the hotel and just drive all the way home to Oklahoma. They figured it would give them plenty of time to talk things through and make a plan for ending their marriage. Owen had contacted the rental car company and made arrangements to drop the car at the airport in Oklahoma City. Then they'd packed up and checked out.

Honor was so happy to get out of Las Vegas and focus her attention on the incredible scenery all around her. The sun shone brightly on the desert landscape, which made her feel as if they were driving past spikes of various golden hues.

So here they were, driving along the highway, just her and her new husband.

She couldn't help but fiddle with the gold band on her finger. She had a husband. She was married. Sure, it had been a drunken impulsive thing, but it was still a legal contract. She'd laugh if the whole idea of it weren't so ludicrous. And life-altering. And just a tiny bit panic-inducing.

They had planned to discuss it over breakfast, but they hadn't. In fact, neither of them had said much of anything. Hunger and hangover had taken precedence, and they'd both mostly eaten in silence. She figured they'd talk about it on the drive. But so far, they'd been in the car for an hour and a half and Owen hadn't said much of anything other than pointing out interesting landscapes.

But, finally, he pulled over onto a vista where people were taking pictures. They got out and she stretched, arching her back, realizing her muscles were sore as if she'd had some major workout the day before.

Or maybe the night before. She eyed Owen, wondering just what exactly had transpired between them last night. Sex didn't typically make her muscles feel as if she'd done a huge workout, so just what kind of sexual calisthenics had they engaged in? She'd been in too much of a panic this morning to survey the hotel room to see if her ass prints were on the hotel room window or if her handprints were on the bathroom mirror. Had they done it in the shower? On the chair? Up against the wall? Owen had some fine lean muscle. She'd just bet he could hold her nicely up against the wall while he—

"Honor. Did you want to get some pics?"

She cleared her throat—and her mind of hot sex visuals. She'd been staring off into space. "Oh. Sure. Yes, definitely."

Good God, woman. Where is your head?

Back in the wedding-night hotel. Naked, and doing dirty things with her husband, obviously.

She scanned out over the incredible scenery and took a few quick photos, but her mind was elsewhere. They got back into the car and she buckled her seat belt.

"Are you okay?" he asked.

She looked over at him and smiled. "I'm fine."

It wasn't long before they reached the canyon where they were going to take a short hike. Owen had suggested it this morning to break up the monotony of driving. And, since they were driving, they might as well enjoy the beautiful area they were driving through.

She saw no reason to disagree with that.

They'd ordered a picnic lunch to bring along, so Owen grabbed it and they started walking. She was glad she'd worn her tennis shoes. She'd rather have her hiking boots, but they weren't going to do any tough-terrain hiking, instead planning on just ogling the scenery. And since she was behind Owen, his very fine ass made for some incredible scenery at that.

Really, Honor, control your urges.

Maybe it was all the sex she had last night. That sex she couldn't remember but clearly wanted more of.

But the cliff faces were amazing and colorful and this time she did manage to relax long enough to get some incredible photos. They found a flat spot about an hour in and Owen laid down a blanket that came with their pre-purchased picnic. They sat to eat their lunch. Honor took a bite of her turkey wrap, enjoying the soft breeze blowing around her. The food was good, but there was an uncomfortable silence between them that she didn't care for. She and Owen had always been able to talk—about anything and everything. They'd been friends since childhood. He might have once been in love with her older sister, but he'd been her buddy forever.

Until they'd accidentally gotten married.

"You're quiet," Owen said. "You've been quiet."

She cocked her head to the side. "So have you."

"I've been thinking."

"Me, too." She would not tell him all the things she'd been thinking about—a lot about him. A lot of sex thoughts.

"I guess we should talk about it. The whole 'we're married' thing."

"I guess we should."

He unscrewed the cap off the bottle of water and took a long swallow. Honor wondered what he was preparing to say.

"I think we shouldn't jump into making any rash decisions right away."

She frowned. "What? Rash decisions about what?"

"An annulment. I mean, we don't even know if we had sex. And if we did, what if we didn't use protection? You could be pregnant."

That thought had never occurred to her. "Oh. You know what? You could be right about that. I have an IUD—or I did. I had it removed recently and I was going to wait a few months to let things settle and get back to normal before I had another put in."

He cocked his head to the side and just looked at her.

"I wasn't intending to have sex without protection, Owen."

"Yeah. I get that." He raked his fingers through his hair. "Shit. I always take precautions. And I haven't been with anyone else for . . . a while."

"Neither have I."

"But last night? I can't say for sure since I'm a little fuzzy on what happened between us. And if we did do it, then we should wait to see what happens. But there's also the chemo that I had for my cancer. It can affect my sperm viability, so there's a chance I couldn't get you pregnant anyway."

"What? Really?"

"Yeah. It could take a few years for my sperm to get back to normal, if ever."

She laid her hand on his arm. "Oh, Owen. I didn't know that."

"That's okay. I knew that before going in for treatment, and I left a healthy deposit at a sperm storage place. And this is a really weird conversation to be having with you."

"I know. But still, I'm glad you shared it with me. There's no way of knowing if your swimmers are viable or not, is there?"

"No. I mean, I guess I could do some kind of test or something, if you think that's important."

"No, it's not. Of course it isn't."

She blew out a breath and took a long drink of water, because her throat had suddenly gone as dry as the desert. As if the unexpected marriage wasn't enough, now there was the possibility of an unplanned pregnancy.

She highly doubted she was pregnant since she'd just finished her period. But she wasn't all that regular to begin with. And if she was pregnant, did she even want to have a baby right now? Or ever?

"And what if I was?" she asked.

"Pregnant?" He smiled. "Then I guess we'd have a baby together. If that's what you wanted, of course, since the choice would be yours."

He made it sound so simple, when it was anything

but. The kinds of complications having a baby would bring could be endless.

"Do you even want kids?" she asked.

He shrugged. "Eventually, sure. Yes. I guess. You?"

"Eventually, sure. Maybe. I don't know. It's not the top priority in my life right now."

"Mine, either. But if it turns out you are pregnant, and you decide you want to have the baby, I'm in."

"And we'd stay married? You don't even love me, Owen. Having a child together is no reason for a marriage."

"Probably not, but how about we cross that bridge if and when we come to it? In the meantime, we stay married."

"And, what? Hide it from our families?" She hated lying. She was, in fact, terrible at keeping secrets—especially from her sisters.

"You said you didn't want them to know."

"I absolutely don't want them to know."

"Then we don't tell them. And if you're not pregnant in a month or so or whenever it is that you find out, we get the marriage annulled. Easy, right?"

"Right. Totally easy." Except somehow, she didn't think any of this was going to be easy. "Although I think—and I'm not sure about the legalities of all of this—but if we want to get an annulment, wouldn't we have to start the proceedings for that right away?"

"Shit." He dragged his fingers through his hair. "You might be right about that."

They both went silent, but then Owen said, "We could start the annulment process. Nothing in the legal world turns on a dime. By the time you find out whether you're pregnant or not, we'll at least be in the process. If it turns out you are and we want to stop the annulment, we can."

"Okay, that makes sense. We'll start there and see how things go."

It would be like walking a tightrope, but she could handle it. Maybe.

He leaned forward and took her hand. She felt the spark of his touch all the way to her toes.

"It's going to be okay, Honor. It's not like we did anything that can't be undone."

Right. Unless she was pregnant. "I know. It's just hard for me not to talk to my sisters about everything."

"I get that. But you can talk to me about how you feel."

She laughed. "I think that's a little different, since you're the topic of conversation."

He leaned back and gave her a lopsided grin that was so sexy she almost self-combusted on the spot. "You want to talk to your sisters about me?"

In ways she couldn't begin to tell him. Her emotions and feelings were so twisted up right now. And he still held her hand, his thumb sweeping back and forth over her skin, making her heart beat faster, making her want to touch him, to kiss him, to see if anything felt familiar so she could test her memories from last night. Then maybe she'd know if she had anything to worry about.

"We should kiss," she said, her eyes instantly widening as she realized she'd just verbalized her thoughts.

His brows shot up. "What?"

Now that it was out there, she might as well continue. "Kiss. Make out. I want to see if it'll spark some memory of last night. If it doesn't, and it turns out nothing happened between us, then we don't have to worry about a possible pregnancy."

His lips curved, a slow, sensual smile that made her belly jump. Then he inched closer, curved his hand around the side of her neck and brought her face to his.

"Yeah, we should definitely kiss."

Honor thought she'd prepared herself for this.

She was so unprepared for the onslaught when Owen's lips met hers. She'd expected something sweet. Maybe even tantalizing. Instead, what he gave her was wickedly hot. Incendiary. Knock-her-out-of-her-shoes inflammatory. His mouth moved over hers with purpose, with a deep, desirous need that made her breath catch, made her grab on to his arms and hold on for dear life as he plumbed the depths of her mouth, sucked on her tongue and made the spot at the nape of her neck tingle, a sure sign that she was utterly and unabashedly turned on.

Wow.

And then he laid her back onto the blanket and half covered her body with his, and all his delicious muscle was hers for exploration. She couldn't help but wrap one leg around him and arch, feeling that hard ridge of his erection against her hip.

He groaned. She moaned in response. And when his hand slid along her hip, she had a brief flash of memory.

The two of them lying on a bed in a position just like this. Owen's hand slipping under her dress, his fingers climbing higher. And that same sensation of utter bliss, of anticipation, of supreme desire.

She breathed out, and Owen kissed her deeply, taking her under, where another zap of memory hit her. This time, the two of them were entwined, and most definitely naked. The slide of skin against skin, and all those glorious sensations of him moving against her, inside her. She lost herself in the memory, in what they were doing and in the taste of him now, smoothing her hand over his arm, grounding herself in the feel and warmth of his body.

Until he lifted, and she heard the rustle of footsteps and the conversation of people approaching. He pulled her to a sitting position. She grabbed her drink and took a long swallow.

She looked over at Owen, whose heated gaze seared her. She took a couple of deep breaths to center herself.

"I remembered something from last night."

He gave her a curious look. "Yeah? What did you remember?"

"Just flashes and bits and pieces. But we were on a bed. And definitely naked."

He didn't look upset. Instead he offered up a knowing smile. "I guess the kiss worked."

On so many levels. "I guess it did."

"So we keep the secret for a while, then, huh?"

"I suppose we do."

But keeping this secret was going to be the hardest thing she had ever done.

And this long drive home, sitting next to him, breathing him in the whole way?

Even harder.

THEY'D DRIVEN AS far as Albuquerque before Owen yawned enough times that Honor insisted on stopping for the night.

And, okay, he was tired. He had no idea how much—if any—sleep he'd gotten the night before. Not wanting to chance falling asleep at the wheel, he'd agreed. Honor had looked online and found them a decently priced but nice hotel just off the highway. They'd parked, checked in and gone straight up to their rooms.

Or . . . room, as it turned out. She looked at him as she slipped the key in the door.

"It seemed like a waste of money to get two rooms," she said. "So I got us one room with two queen beds."

He was too tired to argue with her, but after spending the entire day with her gorgeous body twisting and turning in the seat next to him, not to mention breathing in her lemony scent, he was almost at a breaking point. And then there was that kiss earlier that nearly shattered him. Honor had been warm and pliant and she'd made moaning sounds that made his dick hard.

And now she wanted to share a room with him?

Either she hadn't been affected by that kiss at all—which would be colossally disappointing—or, or . . .

Hell, he had no idea. He was so damn tired he couldn't think straight.

"This room seems fine," she said. "What do you think?"

It was a basic room. Not high-dollar, which suited him just fine, but not a dump, either. "Yeah, it's great. I'm gonna take a shower."

"Sure. How about I go get us some cold drinks?"

"Sounds great." He opened his suitcase and pulled out clean clothes, then went into the bathroom and closed the door. He stripped and looked in the mirror, studying his face. No wonder Honor hadn't been turned on by the kiss. Look at him. His hair stuck up all over the place, he had dark circles under his eyes and his skin looked sallow and sunken.

He turned away from the mirror and stepped into the shower, turning the heat up to full blast, hoping it might put some color in his face. Or, if nothing else, it might melt his skin off and he would die and wouldn't have to face the repercussions of his epic fuckup.

He scrubbed and rinsed, then turned the scalding water to a slightly more tolerable level before getting out, drying off and putting on a pair of shorts and a sleeveless shirt. He combed his hair, then opened the door to find that Honor had changed and was wearing pajama pants and a tank top. She'd pulled her hair into a bun on top of her head.

"Drink's on the nightstand," she said. "I took the bed farthest from the door so you can defend me against anyone who might break in."

He laughed. "Good call."

"I'm going to go wash my face. I'll be right back."

She grabbed a small zipped bag and went into the bathroom, leaving the door partially open.

"Holy crap, Owen, it's steamy in here. You must like really hot showers."

He took a long swallow of his soda. "I felt dirty."

She popped her head out the door. "Clearly. It's like a hundred degrees in here."

Her skin was pink and clean. Even without makeup, she was beautiful.

Honor was consistently gorgeous, no matter the situation. She always had been. Even as kids, when they'd been outside, playing in mud, she'd been pretty, her incredible eyes shining brighter than the spring grass.

Dude. He sat up, heard her humming in the bathroom and wondered where this sudden attraction to Honor had come from.

Or was it so sudden? Had it always been there, and he'd been so struck by Erin's flashy smile and glitter that he'd bypassed Honor? If so, shame on him. Because he sure as hell saw it now.

Honor came out of the bathroom and planted a look of concern on him.

"You're frowning. Is something wrong?"

He shook his head. "No. Just tired."

"I was going to read for a bit on my tablet, but if that'll bother you, we can just turn the lights off."

"Go ahead. It won't bother me at all." He turned over so his back faced her.

"Okay. Good night, Owen."

"Night, Honor."

He closed his eyes, but of course now he was wide awake. He could smell her again. Lemony and sweet. He wanted to kiss her, to feel her soft lips moving under his, her body pressed against him.

This was not gonna work.

He rolled over and stared up at the ceiling.

"Owen."

He looked over at Honor. "Yeah."

"Let's talk."

"About?"

"Whatever's bothering you. You're huffing out sighs and tossing around on the bed. You said you were tired. Clearly something's upsetting you."

He shoved up against the headboard and propped the pillow behind his back. "I don't know. I feel like I screwed this all up. First, I got you drunk, then I married you. Then I might have gotten you pregnant. It's like I can't leave the Bellini women alone. I'm always hurting one or another of you."

She laughed. "Do I look hurt?"

"Well, no."

She pushed her covers away and came over, shocking the hell out of him by pulling his duvet aside and climbing in next to him.

"If I were so disgusted by you, I wouldn't have taken this road trip with you, would I?"

"I guess not."

"And I definitely wouldn't have suggested you kiss me today, would I?"

"No."

Her gaze drifted to his mouth, then back up. "That kiss was incredible, by the way. We should do more of that."

"Kind of defeats the purpose of us getting an annulment, doesn't it?"

She shrugged. "Maybe. But our circumstances are a bit unusual, wouldn't you say?"

"Definitely."

"Did you like kissing me today?" she asked.

"Hell yeah."

"Would you like to kiss me some more?"

"More than I'd care to admit." And now he was getting hot and hard and she should get out of his bed because she smelled really good and he desperately wanted to touch her.

Then again, she was technically his wife, and she was smiling at him, and leaning into him.

"Kiss me, Owen."

He started to, but then for some reason he pulled back. "You know, I think we should wait."

"For what?"

He had no idea. Why had he said that? Had he lost his

mind? He wanted to kiss her. What was wrong with him? "For us to figure out what's happening with our marriage. Or nonmarriage. You know, not complicate things further between us."

She sighed. "You're probably right." She eased out of his bed and went over to her own. "It's a good thing one of us has some common sense."

Yeah, right. He could have her naked and underneath him right now, with his cock buried inside her, both of them feeling really damn good. Instead, he had to be the one with common sense?

Fuck common sense. Common sense didn't have any fun.

He was going to regret this.

Hell, he already did.

CHAPTER

......

six

OWEN WAS WORKING in the back of the Screaming Hawk Brewery, checking on the tanks and the brewing process. Everything was going well. So well, in fact, that he was glad he'd decided on this oversized warehouse when he leased property for his brewery, because he was already thinking about expansion. Business was booming, something that surprised him every day.

His craft brewery was his baby, his lifeblood, something he'd dreamed of doing ever since high school. Making this brewery a success had been a dream come true. Being waylaid by his cancer diagnosis had made him panic, hoping that his dream wouldn't crash and burn. But his employees and friends had helped him keep the business afloat during the times he'd been too sick to deal with the day-to-day operations. He'd never be able to repay their kindness.

Now that treatment was over, he had his strength back and he could actually look forward to the future, something he hadn't hoped to think about when he'd been undergoing treatment.

Casey, his brew manager, walked into the back room. "I think the new batch of pale ale will be ready by the end of the week."

Owen nodded. "Looks that way."

"I'd like to try a new Irish ale. I've written up the specs to go over in our meeting. What do you think?"

"I think Finn will love it. So will I. I'm looking forward to seeing the specs."

"Great."

Owen liked that Casey wasn't afraid to speak his mind, or experiment. They'd started out small, but now that they had a steady flow of customers, they also had a lot of client requests for different types of beers, and they kept track of those requests to see what was the most common. Owen kept his eye on the bottom line, of course, but it didn't hurt to branch out. That was how they were growing.

He spent the day doing supply inventory, then took a couple of hours off to go to the gym. After he'd finished his treatment last year, his primary goal was to gain back the weight he'd lost, to get strong again and work on his health. He started eating better, and working out every day—or at least as much as he could. Sure, he'd drink beer—after all, it was his livelihood—but other than that, he took good care of himself.

Except for that wild drunken night in Vegas with Honor.

He paused as he racked the weights, thoughts of Honor creeping into his head. After they'd driven home, they'd gone their separate ways and hadn't spoken since, apart from exchanging a few text messages about choosing a lawyer. But now that the wheels in his brain were turning, he really wanted to contact her.

Hey, our meeting with the lawyer is coming up.

She texted back. Yes, it's on my calendar.

He waited a beat, then typed a response. Why don't we have dinner tonight? We can discuss everything and prepare for the meeting.

He stared at the phone, not knowing what he expected. He knew she was busy during the day, but he saw the dots, so he thought she was going to reply. But then the dots disappeared and nothing came through.

He frowned.

Okay, so this was complicated. He got that. But they were still friends.

And maybe a lot more than that, though the details of their wedding night were still fuzzy in his head.

Finally, a message popped up.

Are you sure that's a good idea?

Damn. Not exactly the answer he was looking for.

He typed a response: I don't know. I like to eat. Don't you?

She replied with a laughing emoji and a text that said, I do like eating. But what if someone sees us? Aren't we doing low key?

He typed his reply: How about my place? I'll cook.

She responded right away: You cooking? This I've gotta see. What should I bring?

Now he smiled and replied with: Just bring yourself. I'll take care of everything else. How about seven?

She replied with: See you then.

He slipped his phone back in his pocket and couldn't contain the grin on his face. Okay, they had a date. Sort of. Or at least they were going to share a meal together, and that was a start. And he'd get to see her, which was really what he wanted.

Now he had to figure out what he was going to cook for her.

He pondered that while he picked up the next set of weights.

"HONOR, ARE YOU even paying attention?"

Honor blinked and looked up at her sister Erin. "Of course I am. The budget for the Meyers and Pearson wedding."

Erin looked over at their sister Brenna, who just shrugged and said, "That was two topics ago."

"Oh," Honor said. "Sorry, I was thinking about something else." Like those text messages she'd been sharing with Owen, and the fact that she'd agreed to have dinner with him. At his place. And why did she feel so ridiculously giddy about that? After all, she was only going to discuss their annulment.

"Honor!"

She jumped when Erin yelled her name. "What? What did I miss?"

Brenna gave her a casual arch of her brow. "Two conversations, apparently, because you've been on your phone and not paying attention. New guy?"

Her eyes widened. "No. Of course not. Why would you ask that? It was just a . . . a new florist I'm working with. Flower things, you know?"

Erin gave her a dubious look. "Flower things make you blush like that?"

"Maybe the new florist is a dude," Brenna said, giving her a knowing smile.

"Ooh," Erin said. "Do tell why the florist guy is making you blush. What did he say in those text messages?"

She pushed her phone to the side and covered her cheeks with her hands. "I am not blushing. And the florist is not a dude. It's just hot in here."

She took a long swallow of her iced tea, hoping to cool down her cheeks.

"It's not hot in here," Brenna said. "Your head hasn't been in the game since you got back from your Las Vegas trip. Is there anything you want to tell us about?"

"Maybe she met a guy in Las Vegas," Erin said, giving her a once-over like she was inspecting her for evidence of I Met Someone Hot disease.

She coughed and put her tea down. "No, there is absolutely nothing I need to tell you about, and I did not meet a new guy in Las Vegas."

Which wasn't a lie since Owen wasn't new. She was dying to tell her sisters everything that had happened. But there was no way she was going to open that ticking time bomb of a secret. And now she was having dinner with him? At his place? Probably not a smart move.

"I have a few agenda items, if we're ready to get back to the meeting."

Honor shifted her gaze gratefully to Mae Wallace, their new assistant and her personal lifesaver, and not just right this moment. With their parents out of the country on an extended and well-deserved vacation to Ireland and Italy, they'd all had to pick up the slack. Brenna was doing full-time duty in the vineyard and winery, Erin was handling all of Mom's duties overseeing the business and Honor was dealing with all the wedding planning for Bellini Weddings. Even their cook and housekeeper, Louise, and her husband, Marcus, the property carpenter, had taken off on a vacation, after much insistence from Mom and Dad. So they were shorthanded all around. Having Mae to assist with, well, everything wedding related had been a godsend. She had helped in ways Honor couldn't begin to list. She'd jumped right in from day one as if she'd been doing this all her life, and Honor was so grateful.

Too bad Mae didn't stick around after hours to cook, because Honor really missed having Louise's home-made meals. Salads and microwave dinners just weren't cutting it.

"What's on your list, Mae?" Erin asked, pulling Honor away from her personal woes about food.

Mae looked at her laptop. "For Friday evening's wedding, I noticed in a flurry of group email exchanges that the mother of the bride and the mother of the groom have gotten—let's just say—more than a little snippy with each other. Now it might be pre-wedding stress, but there also could be some underlying hostility, too. No clue what's going on there, but I thought we should be aware in case we need to run interference on the day."

"Oh," Honor said. "Let me check that." She quickly pulled up and scanned several weeks' worth of group emails for the wedding party, then nodded. "Yes, I see where that could be a problem. Great catch, Mae."

"It looks like way more than just pre-wedding nervousness to me," Erin said.

"Agreed," Brenna said. "More like they hate each other."

Honor nodded. "We'll need to keep those two occupied and separated."

Mae jotted down notes. "I'll alert the photographer as well so he's aware and doesn't position the two moms next to each other during photos."

And this was why Mae was worth her weight in gold.

"Okay, what else?" Honor asked.

"The bridal salon called. Your bridesmaid dress for Alice Weatherford's wedding is in, Erin, and ready for your final fitting."

Erin spouted a smile. "Really? I can't believe I missed that call. I've been so busy with Mom being gone, it must have slipped past me." She started scrolling through her phone.

"Hey, no worries," Brenna said. "Take a minute to call them back so you can book an appointment for the fitting."

"We could all go with you," Honor said. "Our favorite pizza place is in the same area."

"I'm always up for pizza," Brenna said.

"Fine, then. Shoot me your open dates and I'll make an appointment. You, too, Mae."

Mae's eyes widened. "Ooh, thanks. I love pizza."

"I can't believe Alice's wedding is coming up so soon." Brenna leaned back in her chair and blew out a breath.

Erin scrolled on her laptop. "I know. Which makes me so happy that Jason and I got married last fall instead of this spring. If I was trying to juggle my own wedding, plus being in Alice's? Yikes. I don't even want to think about that stress."

"You did the right thing," Brenna said. "Plus, you had a beautiful fall wedding. It turned out perfect."

"Thanks. I think so, too. And speaking of weddings, have you and Finn set a date yet?"

Brenna shook her head. "Right now we're more interested in the plans for the new house. A wedding can come later."

"And how are the plans coming for the new house?" Mae asked.

"Good. We've bought the land, and the architect and construction company are sketching out ideas that we've given them."

Erin grinned. "This is all very exciting, Brenna. I know you can't wait to get out of that one-room house on the property."

"I actually like it there. Plus, I can just walk a quarter mile and be here at the house. But I can't deny I'm super excited about building a house. And having land. And being able to have my own place to plant flowers and vegetables."

Erin looked around at the dining room table. "Before long this place will seem empty."

"Before long?" Honor looked at them both. "It's empty now. When we were little it seemed crowded. Now you're gone, Brenna's gone and I'm all alone here. With Mom and Dad and Louise on vacation, I'm like an old lady wandering around a dusty mansion. All I'm missing is a rocking chair and thirty cats."

Brenna snorted out a laugh.

"Aww, poor baby," Erin said, giving her what Honor knew was fake sympathy.

"I'm sure you're not upset at all about having the entire upstairs to yourself," Brenna said.

Honor laughed. "Okay, that part isn't terrible."

"There really is nothing better than all that space to yourself," Mae said. "I don't know why I even considered getting married. Having to share a room? A closet? A bathroom?" She shuddered for effect.

"I'm sorry that didn't work out for you, Mae," Honor said.

"He wasn't the right one for you anyway," Brenna said.

"That's an understatement," Mae said.

"Having been there with the wrong guy," Erin said, "I will tell you that when the right guy comes along, you'll feel differently about sharing space."

Mae shrugged. "Doubtful. I like my independence. And my huge closet."

Honor laughed, and inwardly cringed at Erin's comment about Owen having been the "wrong guy."

But here she was, accidentally married to Erin's wrong guy. And now she was going to have dinner with him tonight.

What was she thinking?

That you want to see him, that's what you're thinking.

True. He'd been on her mind—a lot—since she'd gotten back from her trip. Maybe having a meal and a conversation about their annulment would get him out of her head so life could go back to normal.

She could use a bit of normal right now.

CHAPTER

· · · · · ·

seven

OWEN HAD SHOPPED, come home and put the groceries away, then headed outside to take care of the horses, cattle and chickens.

When the twenty-acre ranch had come up for sale last year, he hadn't even hesitated. After being stuck in that small condo for so long, he knew he wanted land, and this deal had been exactly what he wanted.

Exactly what he'd needed, too, he thought as he breathed in the air, looked up at the clear blue sky and walked the distance back to the house.

He straightened the place up, cleaned, then showered. He made snacks, got the menu together in his head and then wondered why the hell he was nervous.

Because it's Honor, and you want it to be right.

Yeah, yeah.

He should have a beer, sit down and take a breath. Because it *was* just Honor, someone he'd known most of his life. They'd been good friends long before they'd inadvertently gotten married. She had always been the one he'd gone to when he needed someone to talk things over with. She was his go-to person.

Until their epic blunder. Which didn't mean anything was going to change between them, right? It was all going to work out.

Except that kiss. He might not remember the wedding, but he could remember the kiss, the taste of her, the way she had felt when he'd laid her down on the blanket, the way she'd responded to him. His body still reacted to the memory of it, still tightened as he recalled the feel of her underneath him.

He wanted a lot more of that. Which was so wrong.

Or was it?

The doorbell rang, so he went to answer it. Honor stood there looking fresh and beautiful in a pale green dress, her gorgeous hair blowing in the spring breeze.

"Come on in," he said.

"I realized earlier I haven't been to your new house yet, so I brought you a housewarming gift." She handed him a plant.

He lifted it up and smiled. "Thanks."

"It's a succulent. Don't overwater it but make sure it gets light."

He liked how serious she was about it. "You can help me figure out the best spot for it."

"Okay." She wandered around and surveyed the house.

It wasn't huge, but a lot bigger than the condo he'd moved from.

"I like this house, Owen. I was so happy to hear you bought it from the Gannett family last year."

"Yeah, the timing was right. Though I was sorry

about Lee's passing. He and Vera had put a lot of love into this place, especially the renovations."

She smiled. "I remember all their kids talking about the sweat equity. But they got a few years of enjoyment out of it. It's too bad Lee died so quickly after Vera."

"Yeah. And the kids all scattered about, none of them wanted to keep the ranch. Bad for them, good deal for me."

"It was. And it's the perfect size ranch for you. What is it, twenty acres?"

"Twenty-three."

She nodded as she moved farther into the kitchen. "Manageable. And this kitchen is the perfect size. It's all so open, too. A great entertaining space."

It was one of the first things he'd thought about when he'd come to look at it. He had imagined having friends over, some sitting in the kitchen at the island, some at the table and others spilling out into the living room, but all still connected. It was perfect.

"Not as big as the Bellini mansion, but it'll do."

She set the plant on the windowsill that looked over the backyard. "That's a nice spot where it'll get enough light, I think." She turned to face him. "And we don't have a mansion, Owen. It's just a big house. It seems overly big these days without Erin and Brenna there."

He stepped fully into the kitchen, which seemed even brighter than usual with Honor in it. "I'm sure you miss them."

She shrugged and ran a fingertip over the small island. "Some days. Okay, most days. It's not the same without them there, even though I'm happy for both of them."

"I get it." He moved around the island so he was closer to her. "It won't be long and you'll be gone, too."

She tilted her head back to look up at him, one brow arched. "Is that right? Where do you think I'll be going?"

He shrugged, itching to put his arms around her and pull her close. Instead, he jammed them into his jeans pockets. "I just meant, I don't know, that someday you'll move out." He fumbled for the right words, realizing he was assuming, which made him an ass. "I should shut up."

She laughed and reached up to lay her hand on his arm. "It's okay. I was teasing you."

He huffed out a relieved breath. "I'm sorry. I didn't mean to insult you."

"Why would you think I'd be insulted? I will move out one day. Either I'll decide to get my own place, or I'll get married. Or maybe I'll buy a ranch, too."

Now it was his turn to arch a brow. "You? Buy a ranch?"

She shrugged. "I might want a llama or two."

"I never knew you had a thing for llamas."

"My preference would be unicorns, but those are in high demand. Llamas would do."

He laughed. "Unicorns, too, huh?"

"One should always dream big, Owen."

He moved to the fridge and pulled out a bottle of wine. Pinot grigio, which he knew was Honor's favorite. He popped the cork and poured a glass, handing it to her.

"Thank you."

He grabbed a beer for himself and led her into the living room.

"I imagine you like having the space here," she said as she sat on the sofa. "Along with all the land."

He nodded. "Not the main reason I ended up getting this place, but yeah, having the land is a definite bonus."

She shifted to face him. "What's the main reason?"

"I needed to get out of that condo. It's where Erin and I were going to live together. I needed to move past that part of my life and start fresh. And after my treatments were finished I figured a fresh start all around would be good for me, ya know?"

"I think that was a good choice. So when should I move in?"

He blinked. "What?"

"You know, now that we're married and all, we should probably live together, right? How do you feel about llamas? You do have plenty of space."

He wasn't sure she was serious. "Uh, Honor."

"I'm joking. But it was fun to see your face go all pale like that."

He took a couple of long swigs of his beer, then said, "Dammit, Honor. I do not want to clean up llama shit."

She tilted her head to the side and gave him a curious look.

"What?" he asked.

"Oh, nothing."

It was definitely not nothing, but since she didn't want to give up what she'd been pondering, he got up and went to the kitchen. He pulled out the appetizers he'd made and brought them into the living room.

"This looks tasty," she said.

"It's not fancy. Just some cucumber-and-cheese-stuffed cherry tomatoes, shrimp tarts and a caprese salad."

"They look fancy to me." She picked up a tomato and

popped it into her mouth, then sighed as she swallowed. Before she said anything else, she tasted the tarts and the salad, so he took a couple bites, too. Not bad.

"You are good at this, Owen," she said.

He laughed. "I can follow a simple recipe. There's nothing hard about any of these."

"Still, you went to the trouble to make appetizers and I appreciate it. Most guys I know would throw pretzels into a bowl and call it a day, if they even did that much."

"Then you've been dating all the wrong guys, Honor."

She shrugged. "So I've been told."

"See? Now you're married and you don't have to worry about all those wrong guys anymore."

Her lips curved and she pointed her finger at him. "Ha. Funny. But speaking of us being married, I have a question for you."

"Sure."

"Does it feel weird? I mean, I know we're only technically married, but do you feel . . . I don't know, somehow different? Or is it just me?"

"It's not just you. And it is different. Maybe what we did was reckless, but we still did it. It's not like I'm going to go out on a date with anyone while we're married."

"You won't?"

"Hell no. That would be . . . I don't know, cheating or something."

Her lips quirked up in a smile. "I like that you think that way, Owen."

"Why? Were you going to just go about your business like normal?"

"No, of course not. Though I should probably cancel that date I have on Thursday."

He gave her a deadpan look. "You aren't serious."

"I am totally serious. I do have a date. I just forgot about it. But I'll of course cancel. I wouldn't even think of going out with Stan—or anyone else—while we're married."

He made a disgusted face. "You're going out with Stan Berger?"

"I was." She lifted her chin. "And what's wrong with Stan?"

"Stan's an asshole. Treats women like dirt. Good thing I married you so you don't have to find that out for yourself."

"Like I couldn't have figured that out on my own. What would women do if men weren't around to save them," she said, rolling her eyes.

He leaned back and sipped his beer, figuring this would be one of their men-versus-women arguments. "I didn't say I was saving you, did I?"

"No, but you did intimate that I couldn't figure out whether or not a man was good for me."

"Hey, you're the one who agreed to go on a date with Stan Berger. Has the dating pool for women emptied out or what? He'd be the last one you should pick and you know it."

She lowered her gaze, and oh, man, did he know that look. She was irritated.

"Oh, and now you're choosing the men I date?"

"Well, I am your husband, after all."

She gave him a look and her mouth opened to speak, but then she burst out laughing and said, "This whole conversation is ridiculous."

He was glad her irritation had turned to something

else. He definitely liked that her fuse was short. "Yeah, it is. Because our situation is ridiculous."

She took a sip of her wine, then snacked on more appetizers, studying him while she did. He had to admit he wasn't sure whether he liked her staring at him like that; it made him feel like she was going to find something lacking in him.

"You know," she said after she wiped her fingers with one of the napkins he'd provided. "I can see how this married thing would have its advantages."

"Like what?"

"For example, I can start turning down dates with all the wrong men."

"You could." He definitely liked that idea. He'd watched her date loser after loser for years. And he hadn't liked it at all. Not that he'd had any say in who she went out with.

"Second, you can cook for me."

He laughed, then looked down at the platter in front of them. "This can hardly be considered cooking, Honor."

"Close enough. And third, you can kiss me more often. I really liked that kiss you gave me in Nevada. I was kind of sad when you turned me down in New Mexico."

His stomach tightened, because he sure as hell had no complaints about her third observation. "You know damn well why I turned you down in New Mexico. But if you want to start some kind of kissing routine, I'm game."

"Excellent. We'll start after you feed me dinner."

"There's a bossy side of you I hadn't noticed before."

She lifted one shoulder. "You should have figured that out before you married me."

Also a pretty damn funny side to her, which he'd always known about.

He got up and held out his hand. "Come on. We'll refill your wineglass and you can help me."

"I'd love to. As long as I don't have to cook anything."

He laughed. "Promise."

He grabbed the appetizer plate and they went into the kitchen, where he motioned for her to take a seat at the kitchen island. Then he got out the salmon, brussels sprouts and sweet potatoes.

She looked up at him. "I love all of these things."

"I know." He slanted a smile at her, then cleaned and sliced the sweet potatoes and put them in a pot of boiling water on the stove. He prepped the salmon and laid it in a basket, and sliced the brussels sprouts and poured balsamic vinegar and honey on them before tossing them into the oven.

"Let's go outside," he said, reaching for the basket that contained the salmon.

He grabbed his beer and she took her wine. He held the door open for her and they stepped outside.

It was still spring, but the day had been plenty warm, which made him grateful for the covered patio. He turned on the grill and adjusted the temperature, then took a long pull from his beer, watching Honor as she stood at the edge of the patio and surveyed his land.

"You have so much space out here," she said. "And I love all the shady trees. But there's still plenty of sunlight over on the west side."

"That's where I put my vegetable garden."

"You did? What did you plant?"

He thought about it, doing a mental inventory. "Tomatoes, cucumbers, carrots, green beans, lettuce, peppers, potatoes, onions and several herbs."

"Wow. That's a great start."

"Oh, so you'd add to it."

"Of course I would. You probably need a dog, too."

"In the vegetable garden?"

"No, silly. A dog, in your life."

He coughed. "What? Why do I need a dog?"

"So you won't be alone. Dogs are great company. I like dogs."

"Then why don't you have one?"

"I have plenty. Erin brings Agatha with her to work every day, and sometimes Puddy tags along, too. Brenna and Finn have Murphy. There are days where three dogs are underfoot."

She'd smiled when she said that. Obviously, she loved her sisters' dogs. "And you love it."

"I do."

"Then why not get one of your own?"

"I . . . I don't know. Dad has really loved everyone's dogs and he and my mom have talked about getting one. That would be enough, I think. And I guess another reason is that I don't have my own place yet. When I'm living somewhere on my own, I'll definitely have a dog."

He put the salmon on the grill and made sure the heat was low enough, closed the lid, then picked up his beer and took a seat next to her. "What kind of dog?"

"Excuse me?"

"If you got a dog of your own. What type of dog would you pick?"

"I don't think I'd care. But it would have to be a rescue."

"Of course." He liked that she wasn't choosy, and that

she didn't want to go to a breeder, which wouldn't be the way he'd want to do it, either. Not that he was considering getting a dog or anything.

He got up and dashed inside to turn the heat down on the potatoes and take a look at the brussels sprouts before heading back outside to check on the salmon.

"How about you?" she asked. "What kind of dog do you like?"

He looked over at her. "The kind that comes fully housebroken."

She laughed. "Wouldn't that be nice. Though a lot of dogs from rescues are already house-trained."

"Is that right? You must be doing research."

"Maybe a little. There was this really cute dog I saw last week. She's probably already been adopted."

So she'd been doing more than a little research. "Show me."

"Really? Okay." She got out her phone and went straight to a link, pulled it up and handed the phone to him.

The dog was brown and black with one floppy ear and an adorable head tilt. Definitely cute, but Owen had no idea what breed the dog was.

"Her name is Bettie," Honor said. "She was abandoned by her former owners, who I hope suffer painful boils on their asses for the rest of their natural lives."

He busted out a laugh. "You're vicious."

"Whatever. They deserve it. Bettie's super friendly and sweet and housebroken and just needs someone to love her and give her a home."

He looked up from her phone. "Have you been to see her?"

"Maybe. She's the best dog, Owen."

"You should adopt her."

"I don't know. I just don't think I'm ready yet."

Or maybe she was scared that she was ready. He didn't know.

He handed the phone back to her. "She's a really cute dog. And from the looks of the page, she's still available."

She gave him a hopeful look. "You could adopt her. You have so much amazing space here. Bettie would love that."

"You want me to be your dog adoption proxy?"

"I would never ask you to do that."

"Except you just did."

"Okay, maybe. But she's a very good dog, Owen. And you need someone."

Yeah, he needed someone, all right. He just wasn't sure that someone was a dog.

Fortunately, dinner was almost ready so they brought the salmon inside, and he pulled the brussels sprouts out of the oven and put the cooked sweet potatoes in to broil while Honor grabbed him another beer. He got out plates and utensils and Honor set the table while he got the sweet potatoes out of the oven and brought them over.

"This all looks amazing," she said. "Thank you for cooking dinner for me."

"You're welcome. I hope you like it."

They dug in and ate. Owen was happy with how everything turned out.

"This is incredible food," she said in between bites. "The salmon is tender and full of flavor. These brussels sprouts are delicious, and I love sweet potatoes so much. And the best thing is the whole meal is healthy, too. You're doing an excellent job taking care of yourself."

"Thanks. I try. Though I do need a good greasy hamburger every now and then."

She gave him a smile. "Who doesn't? My downfall is cake. Any kind. I have a sweet tooth like nobody's business."

"I'll bet you enjoy doing wedding cake tastings with your clients."

She laughed. "I don't hate them, that's for sure. And, of course, at the weddings I have to taste the wedding cake to make sure our vendors are providing the absolute best to our clients."

"It's the least you can do."

"That's what makes me the best wedding planner in the state."

"And so modest."

She lifted her fork toward him. "That, too. Why don't you tell me about the attorney?"

"She's in Tulsa, so no one around here knows her, or knows of her. She seems confident and smart and I liked her. I think you will, too. When we have a Zoom call with her, we can discuss our options."

"Sounds good. Do you have questions you want to ask her? Like, anything specific? I brought my notebook so I can jot some things down; that way we'll be prepared."

"Oh. I guess timing of everything is my number one. Like, how long the annulment will take from start to finish."

She got up, grabbed a notebook out of her bag and came back, flipped it open and looked at a sheet she'd already written on. "That was on my list as well. What else?"

"I'm curious about the process. And if any of it is public."

She gave him a questioning look. "Public?"

"Yeah, you know, like if a petition for annulment has to be published in local newspapers or something. I mean, it's not like probate where someone could object or has a right to claim, but I just figured we could ask anyway, especially since we want to keep this low key."

"Oh, good question. I'll write that down."

"What about you?" he asked after he swallowed another bite. "What are your questions?"

"My main one was asking the difference between annulment and divorce. Of course I know the difference, but I'd just like her to walk us through each one."

He nodded. "Understood. It's good to be fully informed."

"Anything else?" she asked.

"Uh, I've got nothing right now, though I'm sure more questions will come up when we talk to her."

She took a bite and swallowed, then a sip of the water she'd poured herself. "Oh, I have another thing. I think we should find out what's on the record after the annulment. Can anyone look it up in court records, or is it like we were never married?"

"Hmm. Interesting question."

"I thought so, too."

They discussed a few other items while they ate, mostly minor details, and then she said, "Shoot me any other questions you think of, and I'll add them to the list."

"Great." He wanted to sound cheerful about their annulment, but for some reason he'd rather not discuss it at all.

And the reasons for that . . . well, he'd rather not think about that, either.

After dinner she helped him clean up. He did cook for himself as often as he could, though most nights he worked at the brew pub, so he'd make a sandwich or a salad to eat on his breaks. But when he was home he typically cooked healthy meals. Doing it alone sucked, but he'd gotten used to that. Having Honor here to eat with, and having her by his side doing dishes was . . . nice.

Really nice.

And also reminded him just how alone he'd been.

After they finished cleaning up, he asked Honor if she wanted a refill on her wine.

She shook her head. "I'll just take more water, thanks. Just one glass is my limit these days. At least until I know for sure if I'm pregnant or not."

"Oh, right." He might not be driving, but he'd had a few beers and that was more than enough for him for a night, so he fixed them both glasses of ice water and carried them into the living room. They took seats on the sofa and he turned on some soft music.

"If we were really married, where would we be right now?" she asked.

He leaned back on the sofa. "Probably on a beach somewhere."

She took a sip of her water and placed the glass on the coffee table, kicked off her shoes, then curled her legs behind her on the sofa. "I'd like to be on a beach right now. I could use a vacation."

"Want me to take you on a honeymoon?"

She tilted her head. "What would you do if I said yes?"

He shrugged. "Take some time off and take you someplace warm."

"Right. And how would we explain that?"

"I don't know. Would we have to explain it? And who would we have to explain it to?"

"Fair point. For you it's easier. For me, a little less so since I have family that's always in my personal business."

"You're an adult and they don't need to know all your business."

"That's true. Not easy, but true. So what tropical island should we honeymoon on?"

He liked playing these *what if* games with Honor. "Your choice."

She thought about it for a minute, then said, "I'm going to say no to Aruba since that's where you were going to go with Erin on your honeymoon."

"A good call. Though in the end neither of us went there, so it's still an option."

"Maybe. I've always wanted to go to Hawaii."

"Which is where Erin and Jason went on their honeymoon, so I'm going to say no on that one. I wouldn't want to copy her."

She rolled her eyes. "Fine. How about instead of a sandy beach we do Europe instead?"

"I could get into some German beer."

"And I would love to see England and France. All that amazing food and wine. And shopping."

He nodded. "Okay, we'll take a trip through Europe instead."

"Sounds ideal. If you're this agreeable about everything, we should have an easy marriage."

"Hey, I'm an easy kind of guy."

"Really. Does everyone know how easy you are?"

He laughed. "I didn't mean it that way."

"I don't know. I've seen firsthand how easy you can be after several shots."

"Oh, are your memories coming back?"

"Not really. Just the flashes I had after you kissed me that day."

"Maybe we should try that again and see if it sparks more memories."

"I'm game if you are."

She leaned toward him and his heart skipped a beat. He'd always known Honor to be fun and playful, but that was in a friendship kind of way. Not this way. Not hot and sexy and making him want to kiss her and touch her in ways that were becoming part of his everyday fantasies.

And for a fraction of a second, he thought of all the reasons they shouldn't get closer, why he shouldn't kiss her, why they shouldn't take this step.

All those reasons evaporated as soon as his lips touched hers and he pulled her closer so he could wrap his arms around her and feel her body touching his. She was warm, pliant, and she tasted like his wildest dreams. And when she reached up to slide her hand across his jaw, his body tensed as he realized how much he needed her to touch him.

She pulled back and searched his face. "You got tense. Are you all right?"

"More than. I like you touching me. Do more of that."

She straddled him and slid her hands over his shoulders, down his arms, and when she reached his skin he couldn't help but shudder.

"You're not cold," she said, smiling.

"Just the opposite."

"Kiss me some more, Owen. I really like the way you kiss."

She was so bold, so surprising in demanding what she wanted. He laid her on her back on the sofa and slid next to her, then teased her lips with his before going in for a deeper, much more satisfying kiss that made her grasp a handful of his shirt at his back. She'd wrapped a leg around his hip and arched against him, making him go hard with the need to feel all of her.

He was so ready to take this into the bedroom, to strip her naked so he could kiss her all over, to explore her body and make her moans turn into screams.

But then she palmed his chest and gave him a gentle push. He lifted.

"I can't," she said. "We shouldn't do this."

He sat up so she could, too. "What's wrong?"

She shook her head. "I'm . . . I don't know. Not ready, I guess. I don't know. I'm sorry."

"Hey." He took her hand. "You don't have anything to apologize for. If you don't want to do this, that's fine."

"It's not that I don't, I'm just . . . scared about how much I'm feeling so fast."

That, at least, made him feel really good. "If it makes you feel any better, it's the same for me, Honor. It's like a tornado sweeps over me every time I'm with you. And I'm just taken away without thinking."

Her lips curved. "I'm happy to hear that. But we should put the brakes on and take this slow, don't you think?"

"Yeah, for sure." Though right now his dick was

painfully hard and telling him that was the worst idea ever. "But I still want to see you."

"I want to see you, too. We'll just be better about keeping things more . . . friendly. No touching. No kissing. For now."

He grinned at her. "For now. Right. It'll be just like it was before we got married."

She got up. "Sure. That should be easy."

"Sure."

She went to the bathroom. He stood, taking their glasses into the kitchen, giving himself some time to get his riotous feelings under control.

She came into the kitchen. "Sorry about that."

"Hey, it's all good."

"I'm not trying to be a tease. It's just all these new feelings are confusing."

He wanted to put his arms around her, to hold her, but held back, so he slid his hands into the pockets of his jeans. "It's okay. You take whatever time you need to sort through your feelings."

"Thanks."

She walked around and picked up the bottle of wine on the counter and put it in the fridge, then studied his calendar there before turning to face him.

"You have an appointment with your oncologist on Monday?"

"Yeah."

"Is everything okay?"

He shrugged. "I hope so. It's a routine checkup. I get bloodwork run, then meet with my doc."

"Do you want me to go with you?"

He'd never had anyone go with him for his doctor

appointments. He'd had plenty of visitors sit with him during his treatments, but he'd always gone alone to meet with his oncologist. "It's not necessary."

"I'd like to go, unless you prefer to be alone."

It touched him that she cared. Probably more than he wanted to admit to himself. "You can come. I'd like it if you came."

She smiled. "Then I will." She looked at him for a bit, as if there was more she wanted to say. There was a hell of a lot more he wanted to say. And do.

"I should go," she said. "I have an early meeting tomorrow morning."

He walked her to her car and opened the door for her. She smiled up at him and all he wanted to do at that moment was pull her into his arms and kiss her. But they'd agreed.

"Thanks for tonight," she said. "For making me dinner. I had fun."

"Me, too."

"I'll . . . talk to you soon?"

"Yeah."

She hesitated, and he wondered if she was thinking what he'd been thinking. How easy it would be to fall into each other. He could tell by the way she lifted her arm, then let it drop, that, yeah, she wanted the same thing.

"Bye, Owen."

"See ya, Honor."

She got into her car and pulled down the drive. He waited until she disappeared around the corner before he went inside and closed the door.

Now that she was gone, the house seemed empty. It was funny how he'd become used to being single, and then Honor had come into his life and boom, like a sudden explosion, everything was changing. And now that he'd touched her and kissed her, he wanted more. He had a feeling Honor did, too. But if she wanted to keep it platonic for now, he'd do as she asked for as long as she wanted to play it that way.

But, no, this wasn't going to be easy.

CHAPTER

· · · · · ·

eight

SOME WEDDINGS WENT off without a single hitch to the proceedings. They were smooth and uneventful. Those were Honor's favorites.

Then there were the ones like today's, where it seemed like if something could go wrong, it would. One bridesmaid forgot her dress at the hotel, and she showed up late, which meant Honor had to send someone to go fetch the dress for her because said bridesmaid had also cried off all her makeup on the way to the vineyard after her boyfriend had broken up with her via text, causing Sarah, the bride-to-be, to have to console her. Which was so not the bride-to-be's job on her wedding day.

Fortunately, Mae stepped in to console the sobbing bridesmaid, and Honor pulled a now very angry Sarah away to calm her down before the bride-to-be left the venue to go have some words with the now ex-boyfriend.

And then the wrong flowers were delivered, which caused yet another meltdown, this time on Honor's part, as she had to call the florist and figure out where the flowers for the Bergman/Winterly wedding had gone. That took twenty minutes and several phone calls. In the middle of all that, the aforementioned sobbing bridesmaid had taken off. Like, left. According to Brenna, she was leaving to have a conversation with the ex-boyfriend.

Honor just stared, trying to absorb the latest disaster.

"What do you mean she left?"

"Apparently she told our bride that she just had to tell off her ex-boyfriend in person, and it couldn't wait another minute."

Erin gave an impressive eye roll. "You have got to be kidding me."

"I'm not," Brenna said. "Mae's in with Sarah right now trying to keep her from imploding."

"Okay, I'll deal with it. I don't know how, but I'll deal with it. Erin, I need you to call the florist again and make sure those flowers are on the way."

Erin nodded. "Got it."

"Brenna, I need you to—I don't know, make sure no other bombs go off."

Brenna gave her a severe look. "You got it. Absolutely no bombs."

She went to the bride's dressing room, put her hand on the knob and paused, taking a moment to breathe.

Just breathe, Honor. You've been through worse. You've got this.

After exhaling, she opened the door to find Sarah and Mae embracing.

"I don't know how I'll ever thank you for this," Sarah said, her eyes filling with tears.

"What's this about?" Honor asked. "And you can't cry, Sarah. Makeup, remember?"

"She's right." Sarah's mom dabbed at the corner of her eyes with a tissue. "No tears."

"Since Mae is the same height and roughly the same size as Lorelai, she's going to fill in for my missing bridesmaid for the ceremony."

Honor's stress level dropped at least fifty points. She cast a grateful look at Mae. "What a wonderful idea. Thank you, Mae."

Mae smiled. "It's no problem. I'm going to dash into hair and makeup, then get dressed." She stopped and squeezed Sarah's hand. "It's all going to be fine."

Sarah nodded. "Yes, it is."

After that, everything else ran smoothly. The flowers—the right ones this time—arrived, and Honor and her sisters finished nailing down every final detail. Mae came out in a bridesmaid dress that looked as if it had been altered just for her. They'd dodged a bullet there. It didn't hurt that she was gorgeous and curvy and her wild curls looked amazing pulled up, and with her warm brown eyes that just lit up a room, she more than made up for Sarah's now ex-friend's untimely disappearance.

"I don't know how we ever managed without her," Erin whispered as Mae made her way down the aisle during the ceremony.

"Right?" Brenna asked. "It's like she fits in perfectly."

Honor sighed in relief. "She's like the Mary Poppins of bridal. She just swoops in and saves the day."

Erin snickered. "I'm going to tell her you said that."

"Go ahead." Because it was the truth.

The rest of the wedding was perfect. Mae stood in for the first dance and tried to step out for photos, but Sarah wasn't having it, saying that without her one of the groomsmen—and one of her husband's very best friends from college—wouldn't have been able to stand up for him. And for that, she would always be memorable and needed to be in the pictures. As always, Mae was happy to participate.

At the end of the night, another happy couple had gotten married courtesy of Bellini Weddings. The crew came in to clean up, and Honor, her sisters and Mae sat in the Bellini house dining room to sip some champagne, though Honor wasn't drinking. Not that her sisters noticed, fortunately.

"Tonight was a wild one," Erin said.

Brenna took a sip of her wine, swirling the liquid around in her glass. "That's an understatement."

"I thought it was fun," Mae said. "Being a bridesmaid is always a kick. A bride? Not so much."

Honor kicked off her heels and wriggled her toes. "I'm exhausted."

"Maybe you just need more champagne," Mae suggested.

"Or a good night's sleep," Erin said.

She was way too wired for sleep. And, fortunately, the families had booked the venue only until ten p.m. so it wasn't too late.

"You were amazing today, Mae," Honor said. "Thank you for stepping in."

Mae beamed a smile. "It was easy, and I was lucky to fit into the dress. Plus, I've been a bridesmaid a time or two . . . or ten. I was happy to help out."

"We were all singing your praises earlier," Brenna said.

"You were?"

"Yes," Erin said. "I believe Honor even referred to you as the Mary Poppins of bridal. How you just show up and save the day."

"Really?" Mae's eyes widened. "The Mary Poppins of bridal. That is outstanding."

Honor was glad that Mae wasn't offended. "Hey, you're the bomb, Mae. The best kind. We wouldn't have made it through today without you. We're very glad you're part of our family."

"Aww. Thanks."

Brenna lifted her glass. "A toast to Mae."

"Who saved the day," Erin added.

"And look at us, rhyming away," Honor said.

Mae tilted her glass. "Hey. I came to play."

They all dissolved into laughter. After everyone else finished their champagne, Erin and Mae left and Brenna walked across the property to Finn's house, leaving Honor to put the glasses into the sink and head upstairs.

The house was so quiet with Mom and Dad gone. It was unnerving. She was used to the noise of the TV and people walking up and down the stairs, and someone was always talking. Now? Silence.

She undressed, washed her face and brushed her teeth, then climbed into bed and turned off the light, figuring she'd pass out pretty quickly after the stress of the day. But the stress hadn't quite let go of her yet and she couldn't wind down. She grabbed her phone to check the time.

Eleven p.m. She blew out a breath of frustration.

She was irritated that she was wide awake and thinking about . . . what was she thinking about?

You know what. And whom.

She'd put the brakes on with Owen. Told him platonic and friends only and all that. But maybe it was time to test the romantic waters and see where it went between them.

Sure, because you want to confuse the hell out of him, Honor.

No, she was just coming to grips with her own feelings, and said feelings had decided now would be a good time.

Satisfied with that answer and before she second-guessed herself, she sent a text to Owen, knowing he was working at the brewery tonight.

How's it going? You busy?

She figured he wouldn't text back until after he got off work, so she was surprised when she got a reply almost right away.

Not bad. How was the wedding?

She typed a reply. It was dramatic.

A few minutes later he replied with: That sounds like a story.

She laughed and replied with: A long one. Wanna come over after you get off work? I'm here alone.

This time it was ten long minutes until he responded.

It'll be after midnight. Will you still be up?

Her lips curved as she responded with: I'll be up.

He replied right away: See you then.

Her heart pounded.

Okay, Honor. Now you've done the thing. You invited Owen over.

She put the phone aside, turned on the light and got out of bed, pondering what she should wear. Right now, she had on a tank and her underwear. Some other clothes would be in order, probably. She went to her closet and nibbled on her bottom lip as she stared at her clothes rack, then realized she was being ridiculous.

She grabbed her pajama bottoms and slid into them, then headed downstairs to make something to eat, figuring Owen would be hungry when he got there.

After that she went back upstairs to brush her hair, staring into the mirror.

No makeup. Whatever. She wasn't putting any back on. Though she did add some lip gloss before she headed back downstairs and poured herself a glass of water, then decided what she really wanted was coffee, so she brewed herself a cup.

She turned a few lights on and wandered the house. After several sips, she felt a lot perkier. And excited about seeing Owen. Not hormonally excited, of course. Just . . . happy that he was coming over.

That was a start.

CHAPTER

......

nine

AFTER CLEANING UP and closing the pub, what Owen really wanted to do was go by his place to shower and change clothes. But it was already well past midnight and he didn't want to show up at Honor's house any later. He had a toothbrush and deodorant in the back room at the brew pub, so he at least managed to freshen up a little before he headed in her direction.

He had no idea what was going on with her or why she wanted him to stop by, but he was always happy to see her. Maybe she was lonely in that big house by herself since her parents were on vacation.

He pulled up in front of the house and got out, looking up at the oversized two-story ranch house, his lips quirking as he saw all the lights on inside.

Maybe she was afraid of the dark. Though as he walked up the steps, he remembered that time when they were all kids when he and Jason and Clay had camped out in the backyard with all three sisters, and Honor had been the one to insist they turn out the lantern in the tent so they could tell ghost stories in the pitch-black darkness.

He rang the doorbell and Honor opened the door.

"Hey, thanks for coming," she said as he stepped in. "I made coffee. And sandwiches. I thought you might be hungry and it's important that you eat. Are you hungry? You want some coffee? Maybe a beer or some iced tea?"

He stepped beside her as they made their way down the hall into the kitchen. "Just how many cups of coffee have you had?"

"A few. I wanted to make sure I stayed awake. Why?"

"Because you've definitely hit a caffeine high."

"Have I? Am I talking a lot? Do you want a sandwich? I made club sandwiches with bacon."

He tried not to laugh. "I'd love a sandwich. With some water, thanks."

"Great. Go have a seat in the dining room. I'll be right out."

He went into the dining room and sat at the table. She came out a few minutes later bearing two plates, which she laid down, then came back with two glasses of water.

"I took your advice and dumped the coffee when I saw that my hands were shaking. You're right about the caffeine. I don't know what I was thinking."

"The food will probably help. Come sit down next to me."

"Okay. You smell amazing, by the way."

He smiled at that and refused to attribute her comment to excess caffeine.

They dove into the food and Owen had to admit he was grateful Honor had made sandwiches. He was starving. He'd had a salad earlier in the evening, but that had been a while ago. The nice thick turkey and ham and bacon club, along with the sides of sliced carrots and apples, was perfect.

He was happy to see that Honor ate as well, though she only finished off half her sandwich and nibbled at her carrots and apples. But at least she got some food in her.

"This is really good. Thanks for making food for me."

"You're welcome. Thanks for coming over."

He took several swallows of his water and leaned back in his chair. "So why the invite? Were you lonely here in this big ole house?"

"No, not really. Okay, maybe. I guess after the big extravaganza of the wedding tonight, with all the people and all the craziness that went on, after everyone left and it was just me it felt, I don't know . . ."

"Too quiet?"

She nodded. "Yes. And I was wound up and couldn't sleep and I needed . . . you."

That was a direct hit, winding around his midsection like a hard punch. "All you ever have to do is ask and I'll be here for you, Honor."

"So I see. Thank you for that. I felt kind of bad, figuring you'd be tired when you got off work."

"I'm usually wound up from work, too. And it was hectic tonight. With it being spring and Friday night, we were crowded from open to close. I don't think I sat down once. I even ate my salad behind the bar."

"Aww. That's a long night. You probably need a back massage."

He let out a short laugh. "Yeah, I should probably have a masseuse on speed dial."

"I've been known to give excellent back massages. And foot massages. My sisters can attest to that."

"Is that right?"

"Yes. Do you trust me?"

"Absolutely."

"Okay. Come up to my bedroom and take off your shirt."

"Sure." That was an invitation he wasn't about to turn down. They took the dishes into the kitchen, rinsed them and put them in the dishwasher, and then he followed Honor upstairs to her bedroom.

"Shirt off," she said. "I'll be right back."

While she stepped out, he pulled his shirt off and laid it over the chair in the corner of her room, suddenly feeling weirdly naked, even though he still had his jeans and boots on. Since he was probably going to be lying on her bed, he decided to take his boots off. He was sitting on the edge of her bed slipping off his boots when she came back in.

"Hey, cowboy," she said. "I didn't say get naked."

He laughed. "Just taking my boots off since I figured I'd be on your bed."

"Oh. Okay."

He stood. "Besides. You've already seen me naked. Allegedly."

Her gaze traveled the length of him, then back up again. "Right." She cleared her throat and pulled the pillows off her bed, then threw the sheet she'd brought in over it. "Okay, face down."

He lay down on his stomach and turned his head to watch as she stepped into the bathroom. She looked hot as hell in her tank top and pink polka dot pajama bottoms, and when she got up and came toward him, he couldn't help but notice the outline of her nipples pressing against the white material of her tank top.

Dammit, he was trying to be good. It didn't help that Honor could tempt a saint. And he was no saint.

And then she climbed onto the bed and straddled him. "Is this okay?"

He wanted to groan, but he bit it back. "It's fine. Great."

"If I had a massage table I wouldn't have to do this, but it makes it easier to really lean into your back."

"Right. Sure. No problem." Except she was sitting on his ass, and he was conjuring up all kinds of scenarios where she'd lean her body against him, rubbing her tight nipples over his back.

Great. And now he was getting hard. Good thing he was facedown.

"I'm going to pour some oil on your back. It's unscented and vegan, so it shouldn't bother your skin."

"Go for it."

She did, and after the oil came her hands. Warm, soft, gently sliding between his shoulder blades and over the top of his back. He closed his eyes and focused on her movements, the way she seemed to find each tight muscle and ease the tension away.

There was something about her touch that he connected to. He'd had massages before. His oncologist had told him that it would be good therapy for him, to help him relax, so he'd tried it a few times. It had been nice, therapeutic even, but nothing like the way it felt to be touched by Honor.

Maybe it was because he was emotionally connected to her, that having her hands on him meant something to him.

"Feel good?" she asked.

"Really good."

"Are those muscles starting to loosen?"

Some of them, while others were rock hard and throbbing. "Yeah. Great."

It didn't help that she was moving against him—no, she was rocking against him, and all he could picture was him flipped over, both of them naked and his cock buried inside her while she made those same sweeping back-and-forth motions while her sweet hands swept all over his chest.

You're never going to be able to roll over with your current boner situation, dumbass.

Okay, fine. Instead, he thought about something a lot less pleasant. Hard to do with her hands on him, but he maneuvered his mental visuals into scrubbing toilets at the bar.

That did the trick.

"You're frowning. Am I hurting you?"

He popped his eyes open. She had leaned over to look at him.

"Not exactly."

"Then what's wrong?"

"You're touching me. My dick's hard. So I'm trying to think about other, less pleasant things."

"Really. Like what?"

"Cleaning toilets."

She laughed. "Gross. But I imagine that's effective."

"Like you wouldn't believe."

She continued to work her fingertips along his spine. "You know, tensing up like this is counterproductive to my efforts to relax you."

"I'm totally relaxed."

She swiped his back with a towel. "Are you, though? Maybe we should find other ways to relax your muscles."

He rolled over, holding on to her so she stayed where she was. Now she straddled his hips. "Got any ideas?"

He squeezed her hips, feeling her soft flesh through the thin material of her pajamas. "I could fill a book with the ideas I have."

She leaned forward, lengthening her body on top of his. "Let's start at chapter one, then."

Her hair had fallen forward, so he tucked it behind her ears. "I thought we were going to be hands off."

"Yeah, about that. I've been thinking that maybe we should give the whole 'hands on' thing a try."

"Oh, yeah? What made you decide that?"

"You're on my mind a lot, so as long as you're there, we might as well start up something and see where it goes. What do you think?"

He cupped his hand behind her neck and brought her face close to his. "I think I'm game if you are."

Their lips met, and with her body on his, it felt like he'd been thrown into a volcano, every part of him sizzling with heat. She moved against him, her tongue twining with his, her hands exploring, and that was all he could take. He grabbed hold of her and flipped her so she was on her back. Now he could grind against all those hot, soft parts of her, making her moan and squirm against him.

He lifted his head, staring down at her as he slid his hand underneath her tank top, gauging whether she would put a halt to it this time.

She didn't, so he continued his trek upward, enjoying the feel of her as he crept along her stomach toward her rib cage, pausing just underneath her breasts.

"You sure?" he asked, wanting to know for certain that this was where she wanted to go.

She nodded and propped one arm under her head. "Absolutely certain that I like where you're going."

His lips curved, so he cupped her breast, teasing the soft nipple until it hardened. He grasped the hem of her tank top and started to lift.

And then he heard the door close downstairs. Honor heard it, too.

"Dammit," she said, scrambling out from underneath him. "I'll be right back."

He grabbed her arm. "You will not. What if it's a burglar? I'll go down."

"No. It's probably Brenna."

He looked at his phone. "It's one thirty in the morning, Honor."

"So? She's probably up late and needs something from the fridge or pantry."

"I don't care who you think it is. I'm not letting you go down there alone."

She rolled her eyes. "Fine. But if it's Brenna, I'll deal with her."

"Okay."

He put his T-shirt on and slid into his boots, then crept down the stairs, hearing the noises coming from the kitchen. Honor was behind him.

"Burglars don't make sandwiches in the kitchen," she whispered. "They go for the TVs and laptops."

He still wanted to check it out, so he put his finger to his lips to keep her quiet, then walked stealthily down the hall. He saw a faint light and when he peeked around the corner, he found Brenna's fiancé, Finn, standing there.

Finn noticed them as well, making a sharp turn-around with a knife in his hand. He put it down as soon as he recognized Owen.

"Jesus Christ, you scared the hell out of me," Finn said. "I was hungry. We're out of lunchmeat, so I came over here to make a roast beef sandwich."

"Which is totally fine," Honor said. "I figured it was Brenna. Or you. No big deal."

Finn leaned against the kitchen counter and took a bite of his sandwich, chewing thoughtfully before asking Owen, "Having a sleepover?"

"No one was sleeping."

Finn snorted out a laugh.

"You cannot tell Brenna about this," Honor said.

"Ah, I don't keep secrets from her, Honor. You know that."

"Well, you're going to have to keep this one, Finn. I haven't talked to her about . . . and I haven't discussed this with Erin and . . . you see, some things happened and I just don't know how . . ."

"It's complicated, man," Owen said. "Can you keep a lid on it, just for a while?"

Finn shrugged, wrapped his sandwich in a paper towel and headed toward the back door. "Sure. You two have fun. Night."

He closed the door behind him. Honor's exhale was loud.

"You okay?" he asked.

She dragged her fingers through her hair. "Yes. Fine. No, I'm not fine."

"Hey, Finn promised he wouldn't say anything to Brenna. His word is gold."

"I know. It's just . . . like you said—complicated."

"Yeah."

She walked over to him and pressed herself against him. "I'm sorry that it has to be complicated."

He wrapped his arms around her. "That's okay. We'll figure it out together."

She stayed there like that, with him holding her, for a few minutes before pulling back. "Thanks for saying that."

He knew right then that they weren't going back upstairs, which was probably the right thing to do, even if it was frustrating. It seemed like every time they got together and primed and the engines started, something threw a wrench in and mucked things up.

Not everything was going to be perfect. But Honor was worth waiting for.

"I should go."

She tilted her head back. "I'm sorry."

"Nothing to be sorry about. I had a great massage. We'll continue the rest another time."

She walked him to the door. "I'll see you soon?"

"Yeah."

"Good night, Owen."

"Night, Honor."

He walked out and got in his truck, watching as she closed the door and turned out the porch light. He lingered as he watched the downstairs lights go out, then the ones upstairs, until the only light remaining was the one in her bedroom. That one stayed on, so he drove away, wondering what she was doing, what she was thinking about.

Hopefully, she was thinking about him, because he was definitely going to be thinking about her on the drive back home.

CHAPTER

......

ten

HONOR KNEW THAT appointments at the cancer center were probably routine for Owen.

But for her, this was new, and a whole lot of scary.

She'd met him at his house and they'd driven into the city together. Owen suggested that they go to breakfast after his appointment. She'd told him that sounded great, though she had no idea how he could be so cavalier about the whole thing. And maybe that was his way of dealing with what, to her, was a big damn deal.

It had only been two years since his diagnosis. She knew that to be considered officially cancer free, you had to hit the five-year mark. Which meant that every visit to the oncologist had to be nerve-racking.

You know you're here to support him, not the reverse, right?

Good reminder.

As they walked up to the building, she turned to him. "I did some research into the center, and your doctor," she said. "Quite impressive and very state-of-the-art in terms of treatment programs."

"Is that right?"

"You didn't research it?"

"Not really. My primary care physician recommended this place, so I came here."

"Owen. Seriously?"

"At the time I was kind of in a fog, trying to process the diagnosis. And I trust my doctor, so I figured he wasn't going to send me to a place that sucked."

She blew out a breath. "Well, obviously it turned out well. You're healthy."

"Hell yeah, I am. Fingers crossed it stays that way."

Honor knew it would take a lot more than crossing fingers to keep Owen in a healthy state.

He signed in at the front desk and was given an ID bracelet, then sent to the lab. Honor followed and waited outside the lab while he had his blood drawn, and then he led her to the coffee shop, which was actually quite substantial and fancy. There were coffees and teas and all kinds of baked goods. Honor definitely approved.

"It'll take a while for the lab work to process, and my doctor won't call me in until he gets the results. So we have time. What would you like?"

"An iced coffee sounds good. With cream, please."

Owen ordered their coffees, and once the barista fixed them, they took their drinks and sat outside in a beautiful courtyard filled with all kinds of stonework and incredible greenery. It was very zen.

"Do you ever get nervous?" she asked after she took a few sips of her exceptionally excellent iced coffee.

"About what? This?"

"Yes."

"No. There's no point in getting nervous about something I have no control over. I try to eat well. I exercise regularly. But the cancer that was inside me? I had zero control over that, so why get nervous about it? It's either gone, or it'll recur. In the meantime, I'm just going about my business, living my life."

She loved his healthy outlook. "It's a good philosophy. I know a lot of people who would be afraid to put one foot in front of the other for fear of making the wrong move."

He lifted a shoulder and took a long swallow of his coffee. "We only get one shot at this. Might as well live it up, right?"

"You mean take a few shots of tequila every now and then?"

He laughed. "Yeah. You never know who you'll wake up with the next the morning."

They finished up their coffee and then headed upstairs, where they sat in an oversized waiting area. There were a couple televisions and lots of very comfortable couches and chairs, and unfortunately, way too many people waiting to be called by their doctors.

That was the problem. Too many people fighting cancer, and Honor felt for every single one of them.

She hated this disease that took people of all ages without prejudice—only malice and intent to kill.

She blew out a breath.

"Are you nervous?" Owen asked.

"No, of course not. Just looking around and feeling . . ." She couldn't figure out the words.

"Yeah, it sucks to be a part of this club that no one wanted to join."

She reached over and took his hand in hers. He squeezed her fingers.

"Owen Stone?"

Honor looked up to see a small woman standing there with a clipboard.

"That's Corinne," Owen said, standing and pulling Honor up. "She's Dr. Pane's nurse. Come on."

She followed Owen while he chatted amiably with Corinne, asking about her three-year-old son. Corinne weighed Owen at the station, then walked them back into a private room where she took all his vitals and asked routine questions about medications.

She smiled at him and at Honor. "Dr. Pane will be in shortly."

"Thanks, Corinne."

The door closed and Honor looked around. She didn't know what she expected, but it was a typical doctor's exam room, with a wall desk, an exam table and a couple of chairs, along with a few innocuous pictures on the wall.

The door opened and Honor startled. A tall, thin man with a balding head and a white beard came in. He looked scary.

Until he smiled, and then he looked like bald Santa. "Hey, Owen."

"Hey, Dr. Pane."

"How's it going?" the doctor asked.

"Good. Dr. Pane, this is my wi—my friend, Honor."

Dr. Pane held out his hand. "Nice to meet you, Honor."

"You, too, Dr. Pane."

Owen had almost introduced her as his wife. How interesting.

"Okay, let's take a look at your test results," Dr. Pane said, sitting at the desk and pulling up information on the screen.

The doctor studied, while Honor held her breath.

"Everything is looking good, like it has been, Owen." He went over the results, most of which sounded like a foreign language to Honor. But if the doc said it was good, she believed him.

"Your CT scan was clear as well. I'm really encouraged by what I see."

Owen grinned. "That's great."

"We'll move your CT scans to every six months. I don't see any reason to scan you any more frequently than that unless you tell me you're having symptoms."

Owen blew out a breath. "That's great."

He got Owen up on the table to do a physical exam, listening to his heart and lungs and having a discussion about his general health. He asked him some questions about diet and exercise, and Owen answered truthfully.

"You're in great shape, Owen," Dr. Pane said. "Keep doing what you're doing, and stay healthy."

"That's definitely my intent."

"We'll see you in six months."

"Sounds good." They shook hands, Dr. Pane said goodbye to her, and then he left.

"Well," Honor said, standing. "That was so positive."

"Yeah, they've been that way lately. Makes me feel good. And hopeful."

It made her feel that way, too.

"Ready for breakfast now?" he asked as they walked out of the room and headed to the elevator.

"So ready." She finally had an appetite. And a new appreciation for cancer survivors.

And she was so very grateful that Owen was one of them.

CHAPTER
······
eleven

HONOR COUNTED THE days on her calendar. She had just finished up her period prior to going to Las Vegas. Of course she had no idea when she might have been ovulating since her periods were more screwed up than usual since she'd had the IUD removed, something her doctor had told her would probably reset now that the IUD was out. Still, the likelihood of her being pregnant was pretty low. Then again, she'd always had super irregular periods and who knew what was going on inside ovary-and-egg land? Those eggs could have been free floating, just waiting for some sperm to hit the target.

Which meant she'd just have to hold on for a while longer.

She blew out a breath and imagined what it would be like to have a baby with Owen. Maybe a boy with his dark hair and her green eyes. Or a little girl with her auburn hair and Owen's blue eyes. Either way, they'd make cute babies. Which would be awesome whenever—

or if ever—she was ready to settle down and have babies. And that whenever was not right now.

"Honor!"

She jerked straight up in her desk chair, dropping the pen she'd been holding. "What?"

Erin gave her a grumpy look. "What time is Alice due in this afternoon?"

"Oh. One thirty. And you didn't have to yell my name. I'm sitting right here."

"Are you? Because I said your name three times, and you were off in dreamland or something. Are you okay?"

She was definitely not okay. "I'm fine. I just have a long list of things to do before Alice gets here."

Erin nodded. "I can't believe her wedding is only two weeks away. And I have a lot to do since I'm in the wedding."

"Yes, you're on my list, too."

"I am? Do tell."

Grateful to have something else to think about besides herself, Honor flipped to the page on her list that featured her sister. "I need you to pick up your shoes before next Friday."

"Oh, right." Erin made a note in her phone. "I'll be right by the store when I take Agatha to the groomers on Thursday, so I'll grab them then. What else?"

"Since the florist is also in the same shopping center, would you mind popping in and double-checking the floral order for Alice and Clay's wedding? I spoke with them this week, but, you know . . ."

Erin was already typing on her phone. "We like to be thorough and make sure our vendors are on the ball. Got it. Anything else?"

"No, that's it. Hey, you look a little pale. Are you okay?"

Erin shifted to look outside the door to her office. "Where's Mae?"

"She's out meeting with a caterer."

Erin got up and closed the door before coming back to sit down. "I threw up this morning. And yesterday morning. Been having a few queasy moments. And my period is late by a week."

Honor's eyes widened. "Erin. Are you pregnant?"

She shrugged. "I might be."

"You haven't taken a test yet?"

"I've been busy."

"Have you told Jason?"

She shook her head. "Not until I know something for sure."

"We need to know something for sure. Brenna's out running errands right now. Call her and have her pick up a pregnancy test."

Erin frowned. "No. Why would she—okay, maybe."

"Erin, do it now."

"Fine." She rolled her eyes but pressed the button on her phone.

"What's up?" Brenna asked when she answered.

"Hey, are you still in town?"

"Yup. What do you need?"

"Could you grab me a couple of pregnancy tests?"

Dead silence. Erin looked at Honor, who just shrugged.

"Brenna," Erin said. "Are you still there?"

"Are you pregnant?"

"Well, I don't know. Hence, the pregnancy tests."

"I'll get them. And then I'll be right home. Do not move."

She clicked off and Erin laughed as she stood. "I'm moving. To my office. Don't tell Brenna."

Honor laughed, too, but her hands were shaking.

She wasn't going to think about her sister having a baby until they knew for sure. The possibility of it was so exciting, though.

Forty-five minutes later, Brenna flew through the front door, bag in hand.

"Where's Erin?" she asked, a wide-eyed look on her face.

At least Honor wasn't the only one feeling slightly panicked.

"In her office, I guess?"

Honor got up and followed Brenna. Erin was on the phone, so they both waited by the door until Erin finished her call. Brenna thrust the bag at her.

"You can just toss it on the chair."

"Oh, no," Brenna said. "I did not just break the speed limit for you to blow me off like that. Go take the test now."

"Now? Really?"

"Is there any reason you'd want to wait?" Honor asked.

Erin opened her mouth to speak, then closed it and shook her head.

"Good," Brenna said. "Go take a test."

Erin got up and grabbed the bag as she walked by. "Fine. I'll go pee on a stick."

She went down the hall to the downstairs bathroom.

"She told me her period was a week late," Honor said. "And she's thrown up the past couple of mornings."

"Huh. Does Jason know?"

"No. She said she didn't want to tell him until she was certain."

"Leave it to Erin to just ignore the obvious signs. I say she's pregnant."

"She has been stressed lately. It might just be stress."

Brenna shook her head. "Stress doesn't usually make you barf every morning."

Her sister had a definite point.

Erin came out a few minutes later and went back to her desk. "Okay, that's done."

"How long do you have to wait?"

"Oh, I already know the results."

Honor's brows lifted. "So fast?"

"And?" Brenna asked.

Erin inhaled a deep breath, then let it out. "I'm having a baby."

"Oh my God, Erin." Honor went over and pulled her sister out of the chair. "I'm so thrilled for you."

"Just like that," Brenna said, coming around to put her arms around Erin. "Like no big deal, she's having a baby."

They hugged like that, like they always had for their entire lives when something monumental happened, holding on to each other for a few minutes without saying a word. And then Erin looked at both of them. "I'm going to be a mom. Oh my God, Mom. She doesn't know. Should I call her? Should I wait until after she gets home from vacation? I don't want to spoil her fun with Dad. Wait. I should tell Jason first."

"I think you should sit down and take a breath before you do anything else," Honor said.

"You're right." Erin took a seat and then a deep drink from her glass of water.

Honor and Brenna grabbed seats in the chairs across from her desk.

"How do you feel about this?" Honor asked.

"A little surprised. A lot surprised. I went off birth control and we knew we were going to start trying. I just didn't think it would happen so fast. Like . . . really fast."

"Jason will be over the moon, won't he?" Honor asked.

Erin smiled. "He'll likely be impressed that his super sperm did the job so quickly."

"I'm calling BS on that. I think it was your super egg," Brenna said.

"Yeah," Honor said. "It's all you, Erin."

Erin crooked a smile. "I like being super. I'll tell him it was my amazing eggs."

Brenna nodded. "There you go."

Erin stood. "And there I go indeed. In fact, I think I'll go home early today, set up a surprise dinner and tell my husband the news. Then early tomorrow morning I'll call Mom and Dad."

"How exciting," Honor said. "Mom will be so thrilled."

"But first," Erin said, "we have our meeting with Alice. We will not be telling her—or anyone else—about this. I want to keep the knowledge circle small for a while."

"Of course," Honor said.

"I won't tell anyone," Brenna said. "Except Finn."

Erin lowered her head. "Brenna."

"But not until you tell Jason and Mom and Dad."

Erin nodded. "That's fair. But no one else."

Honor and Brenna both nodded, and then they all dispersed to their individual offices. Honor prepped her list for Alice's arrival, thinking about what would happen if she should turn up pregnant at the same time as her sister.

That would be a disaster. The last thing Honor needed was to show up Erin in any way, especially by having a baby with Erin's ex-fiancé. Talk about a catastrophe.

But she was almost certain she was not pregnant, so she likely wouldn't have to worry about it.

They were going forward with the annulment. And as soon as she got her period, this whole ridiculous accidental marriage would be like it had never existed.

So why did the idea of ending her marriage make her feel so . . . awful?

CHAPTER
······
twelve

OWEN DIDN'T KNOW exactly what had prompted him to do it.

Actually, he did know what the impetus had been— Honor. Except now he had this thing. A dog thing named Bettie, who turned out to be a mix of German shepherd and Labrador, a perfect dog for the ranch. She had tons of energy and loved running around barking at the chickens and the cattle and horses. From the first day she'd pranced through the backyard gate and looked around, he could see it on her face.

Yup. This place needs me to manage it. And she'd done it well.

She sure was cute, what with her head tilt and inquisitive expressions, and she was housebroken, too, which was a total plus. And she was a lot more well behaved than he'd expected. He'd had her a few days and they'd bonded. How could they not bond, with the way she looked at him as if to say, *Okay, bud, you got me and I need exercise and food and treats and toys and a place to sleep at night.* So he'd bought food and a dog bed and let Bettie pick out toys. She liked everything that was soft and squeaked. She also enjoyed cuddling— a lot. And she had a fine appreciation for attention and she didn't care much for being left alone, which meant he was forced to bring her to work with him. He couldn't very well leave her alone at the house, not when he'd just brought her home. After all, her last humans had abandoned her—assholes—and he wasn't about to do that to her again.

Owen found out the first night he'd brought her to the brewery that Bettie liked to play to an audience. The patrons at the Screaming Hawk had instantly fallen in love with her, which meant she wandered the bar like she owned the place, making her way around the tables and the outside patio. He worried at first that she'd wander off, but that girl knew a good thing when she had one.

He'd brought her every night since, though he was going to have to watch her pretzel intake. She liked going on morning runs with him, was great on the leash and seemed to enjoy everything he liked to do. At home, she was always wandering the gates and the chicken pens and chasing the horses, so she was definitely an active dog.

So far, so good.

He had the day off today, so he'd gotten up early to feed the horses, cattle and chickens. Then he fixed a broken fence post and cleaned out the chicken coop, all with Bettie's keen-eyed supervision. Then he'd run some errands, and now he had to mow the grass around the house.

Bettie did not have an appreciation for either the lawn

mower or the weed whacker. She found them to be evil things that needed to be killed, barking incessantly at them for about ten minutes, then had lain by the back door until Owen had to stop what he was doing to let her inside. Then she'd glared at the offending objects through the window until he'd finished. When he opened the door, he told her, "You might not like them, but you'll appreciate freshly mowed grass."

She did, running outside to roll around in it and bark at some bugs. Since she was having fun, he went in and took a shower. He put on his jeans and went to pour himself a glass of ice water. Bettie wanted inside, so he opened the door. She went over to her food bowl, licked around to see if something had magically appeared in it, and when she realized it was empty, she got a drink of water, grabbed one of her fluffy toys and followed him back to his bedroom. She climbed into her bed and went to sleep while he finished getting dressed.

He hadn't yet told Honor that he'd brought Bettie into his life. But since she was coming over later for their Zoom meeting with the attorney, she'd find out soon enough.

Still, he wanted her to come a little early so she could hang out with Bettie, so he texted her about helping him out with a project before their meeting.

She replied a few minutes later: Doing some redecorating?

His lips curved. He sent a text back. Sort of. How about staying for dinner, too?

She answered with: If you're cooking, I'm in. Also, will there be bread?

Owen looked down at Bettie, who was now awake

and staring up at him. "I think she's using me for my culinary skills."

Which didn't bother him at all, as long as he could entice her over to his place.

He replied: There will be bread.

After finishing up their text conversation, he went into the kitchen and looked in the fridge. There were chicken thighs he'd picked up at the store, along with some fresh broccoli. He checked the pantry to make sure he had quinoa, which he did. He'd also picked up some baguettes today, intending to have them with a salad for dinner tonight, so now there'd be bread for Honor. Now he had a plan, and it would be easy to put together. He did some advance prep with the food, then began cleaning up the house.

He wasn't exactly messy, but he did have a habit of leaving things out rather than putting them in their rightful place, especially since it was just him living here. Bettie followed him around, her favorite blue bear hanging out of her mouth.

"You also have a habit of just dropping things after you're done playing with them," he said to Bettie, who looked as if she didn't care at all.

He'd bought a basket for her things, so he tossed her toys in there. As Bettie watched him, she dropped the bear in there, too, so he took a minute to work with her on taking a toy out and then returning it to the basket before getting another. She was a smart dog who liked attention, so all the praise he gave her had an effect.

After that, he took Bettie for a walk around the property. Since she was a high-energy dog, he wanted to make sure she got a lot of exercise. When they got back he threw the ball around the backyard for her for a while. Then they came inside and both took long drinks of water. Bettie disappeared into his room, no doubt to curl up for a nap, which suited him just fine. Owen went to his desk to do some financials for the Screaming Eagle on his laptop, intending to incorporate some of what he'd learned at the conference in Las Vegas.

As he flipped through the paperwork he'd brought from the conference, he thought back to Las Vegas, to that moment he'd been at the front desk and Honor had texted him telling him she was there. He'd been surprised, and genuinely happy to see her. He was always fine traveling alone, but running into her had seemed like . . . he didn't know. Destiny, maybe?

And now they were married. At least temporarily. But there was something between them. Chemistry or an attraction or whatever you called it. Whatever it was, he wanted to explore it with her.

The doorbell rang. He'd been so engrossed in his thoughts he hadn't realized it had gotten so late.

He opened the door and smiled at the beautiful sight in front of him. Honor stood there cradling a bottle of wine. She wore a red-and-white polka dot dress and some cute shoes that made her legs look amazing. Then again, her legs always looked good.

"Come on in," he said, taking the bottle from her arms because he knew what was coming.

And what was coming was Bettie, bounding out of the bedroom and down the hall to greet Honor.

Her eyes widened as she looked from the dog to him. "You . . . you got Bettie?"

"I did."

She kicked off her heels and dropped to the floor,

wrapping her arms around the wriggling dog.
tie. I'm so happy to see you."

Bettie was obviously equally happy to see Honor, her tail flapping wildly while she made squeaky dog sounds. Honor made her own squeaky sounds, too.

He left the two of them in his entryway while he went into the kitchen and pulled the cork out of the wine bottle. In a minute or so, Honor came in, Bettie right at her ankles.

"I don't understand. Are you fostering her?"

"No. She's mine. Permanently."

"When did you bring her home?"

"About three days ago."

"And you didn't tell me?"

"I wanted her and me to get acquainted first. She's doing really well. She seems to be happy."

"Of course she is. She's a great dog, isn't she, Owen?"

"Yeah, she's pretty awesome."

"And I'm sure you're loving having the company."

He looked down at Bettie. He could swear the dog was grinning at him. "Twenty-four-seven."

Honor gave him a surprised look. "You took her to the Screaming Hawk with you?"

"She's not big on being left behind, so yeah. She's a hit with the customers."

"I'll just bet she is."

Owen poured wine into a glass for her.

"Thanks." She took a sip, staring at him the entire time, then set the glass on the island. "You did this for me."

"What?"

"Bettie. Bringing her home with you."

He lifted a shoulder. "Maybe."

She leaned into him, took his face between her hands. "Thank you."

She pressed her mouth to his. She tasted like mint, her lips soft and inviting. He couldn't resist diving in for a deeper kiss, folding his arms around her, feeling her body pressed against his.

But Bettie butted in between the two of them, whining.

They broke apart, laughing.

Owen sighed. "It's like having a kid."

Honor laughed and bent down to ruffle Bettie's fur. "She's so sweet."

"She likes attention. And being the center of it."

"I can see that. You just love being loved, don't you, Bettie?"

At least the dog was getting loved on, so that was something.

"I'll get set up for our call," he said. "You go play with Bettie."

She looked up at him. "Are you sure? I could help you."

He could tell that she didn't want to let go of the dog, so he said, "I've got this, and I know you've been missing her, so go ahead and spend some time with her."

"Okay, thanks."

And just like that, she was off, taking Bettie out back. He heard the dog barking and Honor laughing, which was kind of like the best music ever. They were both happy, and that was what mattered, so he got his laptop set up and cleared the table.

He figured Honor would hang out outside for a few minutes with Bettie, but it was ten minutes until their meeting and she hadn't come back inside yet. He went to the door and saw Honor sitting in one of the lounge chairs on the patio. Bettie was situated right next to her, her head on Honor's lap while Honor stroked her hand over the dog's head.

Honor was talking, but Owen couldn't hear what she was saying. He inched the door open just a crack.

"You're going to have an amazing life here, Bettie. Owen's a great guy. He has so much love to give and he's been alone for a while. He needs someone in his life and you're the perfect fit for him. I thought you and I were going to be together, but I think this is a good thing for both you and Owen. I can already tell he loves you, even if he hasn't admitted it yet."

She sat up straight. "Or maybe he has. Has he told you he loves you yet, girl? It doesn't take long to fall in love, you know. Sometimes when it's right, you just know."

He felt a twinge in his gut, or maybe it was more like a power-packed punch. He pulled the door all the way open. "Hey, you two, are you about done playing out here? Because it's time for our call."

Honor shifted around. "Oh, really? Wow, that was fast. Come on, Bettie, let's go inside."

They followed him in and Bettie padded over to her water bowl for a drink, while Honor went to the sink to wash her hands, then grabbed her glass of wine and took a seat at the table. The dog plopped down next to Honor's feet and went to sleep.

Honor blew out a breath. "I have to admit, I'm a little nervous."

"Me, too." He reached across the table and took her hand, squeezing it. "But it's all gonna be okay."

She nodded, and he typed in the information to connect them to the attorney's office.

A smiling brunette answered the call. "Hello, you must be Mr. and Mrs. Stone."

"We are. I'm Owen and this is my wife, Honor."

"It's nice to meet you. I'm Jessica Greene."

"Nice to meet you, Jessica," Honor said.

"Okay, why don't the two of you tell me what happened in Vegas and why you want an annulment."

Owen explained their situation while Jessica listened and took notes.

"Okay, so you both got bombed, and the next day, neither of you remembered what happened. All you know is that you ended up with a legal marriage license and wedding certificate."

"That about sums it up," Honor said.

"And you still have no memory of said event?" she asked.

"No," Owen said.

"Hmm. I don't know if either of you have the basis to prove grounds for an annulment, according to the laws of the State of Oklahoma. Yes, you got married in Nevada, but neither of you are legal residents there, so if you do file in Nevada, you'd have to appear in court there. Do you know where you want to file?"

She paused, waiting for them to answer.

"Hang on a sec while we discuss," Owen said, muting the sound on the laptop.

"What do you think?" Honor asked.

"I say we file here in Oklahoma."

Honor nodded. "Agree."

"Okay." He punched the button to unmute. "We'll file here in Oklahoma."

"Got it," Jessica said, pausing as she was obviously

making notes. "And neither of you committed fraud as far as I can tell, and that's really the only valid reason I could see that would fly. So the question is, do we waste our time going through annulment proceedings, only to have the judge deny the request, or do we go forward with a divorce?"

Honor looked over at Owen, who shrugged and asked, "What do you want to do?"

"I . . . don't know. I hadn't considered that we wouldn't be able to get the marriage annulled."

"It's all right for you to take some time and consider your options, then let me know how you want to proceed."

"Thanks, Jessica," Honor said.

"Yeah, we appreciate you being forthright with us. We'll let you know."

"Okay. Talk to you later."

She disconnected from the call.

Honor leaned back in the chair, her hand absently stroking the top of Bettie's head. "Well. That didn't go exactly how we planned, did it?"

"No. I thought getting an annulment would be simple. Guess it's not so simple after all."

She didn't say anything, but he finally did.

"I could say I coerced you into marrying me. That I got you drunk and forced you into it, and that you weren't aware of what was going on, so you didn't consent."

She cocked her head to the side. "Owen. I will not agree to that."

He shrugged. "It's not a big deal."

"You'd agree to say you committed fraud just so we could get an annulment?"

"If that's what you want."

"It is not what I want. And you shouldn't want it, either. We'll get a divorce."

"Are you sure?"

"Absolutely. Besides, divorcées are sexy. I'll be so much hotter now."

He laughed. "Okay, hot stuff. Divorce it is. I'll email Jessica and advise her to proceed with divorce paperwork."

"Fine."

"And now I'll get started on dinner."

"Even better."

Fortunately, dinner didn't take long to make and soon they were both sitting at the table.

"This looks amazing, Owen," Honor said as she looked down at the bowl. "Oh, and there's bread, too."

He grabbed his fork. "I was given my orders about the bread."

She took a forkful of the food. "I was only joking. Okay, mostly joking. I do like bread."

He shrugged. "Who doesn't?"

They ate and talked about work. He told her about his work week and she laughed, listening to him talk about Bettie's antics.

"You're so good with her," she said.

"She's having fun. We both are."

Then it was Honor's turn, and he enjoyed hearing about wedding stuff, mainly because it made Honor's eyes light up.

"Does it feel weird to be in a wedding at the vineyard next weekend?" she asked, pushing her now-empty bowl to the side.

"Clay and Alice's? No. After being a part of my ex-fiancé's wedding to her new husband, which was possibly the most awkward moment ever, anything after that is easy."

"I suppose that's true." She took a couple of sips of wine, leaned back in the chair, then looked at him. "Was that hard?"

"Was what hard?"

"Erin and Jason's wedding."

"No, not at all really. They belong together. Erin and I didn't. It's too bad that all that heartache had to happen—most of which I caused. I wish we had both seen that we weren't right for each other long before my diagnosis. But it all turned out for the best in the end, ya know?"

"I do know. And Erin is so happy and now she's—"

She went quiet and took another drink of wine.

"Now she's what?"

She smiled. "Now she and Jason have started a wonderful new life together. You know, they've got the house and the two dogs. They're both so happy."

"Yeah, they are. It's like the universe corrected itself and all that had to happen was for me to get cancer, have second thoughts about marrying Erin and fuck everything up first." He grimaced as soon as the words fell out of his mouth. "I didn't mean that."

She reached over and laid her hand over his. "I know you didn't. I also know everyone threw all their sympathy at Erin when it did happen, and no one seemed to be on your side."

"I didn't deserve for anyone to be on my side. If I'd just told Erin what was going on, and that I wasn't feeling the whole marriage thing, she wouldn't have had her heart broken. And everyone wouldn't have hated me."

"Not *everyone* hated you."

He laughed. "Yeah, they did. You did. Brenna did. Your parents did. Erin for sure did. All my friends sent me angry messages."

"Okay, so maybe people were upset. I was upset. But then we all found out the truth and everything changed. And by then Erin realized she was in love with Jason, and the two of you talked it out and realized you weren't in love with each other anymore."

He sighed. "Yeah, I guess."

She squeezed his hand. "You still feel guilty about it."

"Can't help it."

"You have to let it go, Owen. It's in the past, and they're happy together. It did all turn out right in the end."

In his head, he knew that. In his heart, he'd hurt someone he once loved. And that was unforgivable, because Owen hated hurting anyone.

He also hated that he'd brought a downer to this conversation. "Anyway, how was the food?"

She must have realized he needed a turn in topic, because she grinned. "My bowl is empty, this teriyaki sauce is the bomb and I want you to cook for me every night. You can make that happen, can't you?"

"Well, in case you've forgotten, I am your husband, so your wish is my command."

She let out a soft laugh. "Oh, I definitely haven't forgotten. And I can come up with some serious wishes."

"If you want me to manufacture a car, or make clothes for you, you're pretty much out of luck. But if those wishes have to do with making you food or . . . other things I'm really good at, I'm all yours."

She walked her fingers along his forearm, making his

muscles tense in a good way. "I'm very interested in those other things you're good at. Care to tell me about them?"

"I'm more of a show rather than tell kind of guy."

"Then show me, Owen."

He stood and pulled her out of the chair, threaded his fingers through her hair and kissed her, a slow, seductive kiss meant for exploration, to test her reaction, to make sure she was in.

Yeah, she was in. All in, because she rose up, wrapped her hand around his neck and pulled his head down to hers, made a moaning sound in the back of her throat that made his dick quiver, and if there hadn't been food on his table he'd have her laid out there right now like a feast.

Instead, he satisfied himself by teasing kisses down along her jaw, then her neck, feeling her body shiver in response. He took a nibble of her earlobe before continuing his trek down her throat to her collarbone, happy that her dress was low-cut so he had access to more of her skin.

She had a death grip on his arms and she reared back. "Owen."

He tilted back to look at her. "Yeah?"

"Bedroom. Now."

It was all he needed to hear. He scooped her up in his arms and carried her down the hall to his room, setting her on the edge of his bed. He looked down at her.

"You sure?"

She gave him a half smile, the kind that made his balls tighten.

"Pretty sure we've done this before. And, yes, I'm sure."

He wished he could remember that night. But either way, he wanted her. She was all he thought about when he lay in this bed at night, wanting to undress her, to feel the softness of her skin under his hands, to be able to explore her body and taste every inch of her.

And now she was here, and this time nothing and no one was going to interrupt them.

Bettie walked in and climbed into her dog bed, circled a few times, then laid her head on her paws and went to sleep.

Okay, then. Time to focus on Honor.

HONOR'S HEART WAS beating so fast, she was surprised Owen couldn't hear it. She'd been so disappointed the other night when they'd been interrupted at the house, and then she hadn't seen him for a few days and hadn't been able to tell him how much she'd missed being alone with him.

Now here she was, in his bedroom, and he was giving her a look that told her he had definite ideas. She liked that.

She was so ready for this. And they were technically married, so she had every right to use the husband merchandise as often as she wanted to for the duration of that marital relationship, right? So why miss out on a good thing? And from her still somewhat faint memories of that one night, said merchandise was extremely good.

"You're thinking," he said.

"Am I? I mean, yes, I am. How can you tell?"

"There's this line that appears between your brows when you're deep in thought."

"I have lines? You mean like wrinkles?" She quickly reached up and rubbed that spot above her nose to see if she could feel it.

He sat on the bed next to her. "No, not a wrinkle. Your face is perfect. Beautiful and perfect. Now tell me what you're thinking about."

"It might hurt your feelings."

"I can take it."

"I was thinking that we're married and you're my husband and via the unwritten rule in our marriage contract I should be allowed to use the merchandise."

He stared at her for a few seconds, then tilted his head back and started laughing.

"Yeah," he said. "You definitely should use me at your every convenience."

"Oh, good. Then you should get naked."

"As I said earlier, your wish is my command."

He pulled off his boots and socks, then stood and drew his shirt over his head and tossed it onto his dresser.

Honor soaked in every inch of his revealing skin. He undid his belt buckle, then drew the zipper of his jeans down before shoving them over his hips, leaving him in only his boxer briefs.

This had been the most enjoyable—and okay, only—striptease she'd ever experienced.

She motioned to his boxer briefs. "Okay, let's have those, too."

He shoved the briefs down, and wow, was he ever glorious. And packing. And he was hers, at least for the time being. She felt rather smug about that.

"Now you," he said, grasping her hands and pulling her to stand up. He turned her so her back was to him.

She looked at him over her shoulder. "Can't I just sit here and stare at your gorgeous naked body?"

"That hardly seems fair to me, and don't forget, I'm half of that marriage contract."

"True." She drew her hair to the side so he could access the zipper of her dress.

He pulled the zipper down, and she felt a delicious sense of anticipation. While he drew the dress from her shoulders and down her arms, he leaned in and pressed a kiss to the back of her neck, letting his tongue drift along the column of her spine. She gave a little shiver.

"Cold?" he whispered.

"Hot," she replied. "Tingly. Turned on. Want you."

She heard his deep inhale as he slid the dress off, holding on to her while she stepped out of it. He hung it on a hanger in his closet, then turned and gaped at her. She looked down and okay, she liked sexy underwear. Good to know he appreciated the flimsy pale pink silky bra and matching panties.

"Fuck me," he said, his voice coming out in a croaky whisper.

She shot him a wicked smile as she stepped up to him, tracing her fingertips over his well-developed chest. "That's my intention."

He swept his knuckles over the swell of one of her breasts, and when he tucked his fingers inside her bra to tease around her nipple, her breath caught, their gazes met, and she knew that the fire she felt whenever she was around him was because this man was incendiary.

He kissed her, and suddenly her bra had disappeared, and his hands were on her breasts, his thumbs sliding across her nipples, and every part of her trembled with the need to feel his hands and mouth all over her. She took his hand and slid it down over her rib cage, leading him where she wanted him to go.

He pulled his mouth from hers, his gaze hot, his eyes loaded with the same heat she felt deep inside.

He teased the rim of her panties, then slipped his hand inside, stoking the fire that burned there. "I know what you need," he said, his movements so sure, so right on the money that her legs began to buckle.

But he had her, holding on to her with his arm and leading her to the edge of the bed. He took a nipple into his mouth and sucked, and she arched upward, the sensation like being launched into space. She felt weightless, and every nerve ending was so tuned into Owen that she forgot everything else but his touch, his fingers never stopping those I-know-your-hot-spot movements as he brought her right to the peak, then over. She gasped and writhed against him as her orgasm hit, trembling through it until she finally landed back on terra firma.

She opened her eyes to find Owen staring down at her, his eyes still flaming hot.

"You have magical fingers," she said. "What else on you is touched by magic?"

She reached between them to wrap her fingers around his cock, learning the length and feel of him. He was hot, thick, and she wanted him inside her.

He grinned. "Let's find out."

He opened his nightstand drawer, pulled out a condom and slid it on, then rolled over to face her.

But instead of getting right to the action, he lifted her arm, pressed a kiss to the inside of her elbow and then up her arm, raining kisses along what seemed like every inch of her body—her collarbone, her breasts, her rib cage, teasing between her thighs but deliberately not

touching her sex, which by now was throbbing with
need again. He made his way down her legs, even kissing her feet. By the time he made his way up the other
side of her body, she was one giant ball of nerve endings, and between his kisses, licks and tiny bites across
her skin, she was panting and ready to explode.

He nudged her legs apart and slid ever so slowly inside her, his gaze firmly locked on hers. And then he
just . . . stilled, and she felt the pulsing, the feel of him
filling her, and the way he looked at her, and it was all
so . . . so . . .

Intense. She'd think it was like nothing she'd ever felt
before, but the thing was, she had felt it before. In those
bits and pieces of memory that kept flooding back from
their wedding night, she felt the punch of that same intensity, the slide of her leg over his, the incredible force
of feelings as he began to move. She felt like a volcano
before the explosion, all that boiling energy inside her
just waiting to erupt. And with every thrust, Owen was
the one to coax it out of her.

She was so in tune to his movements, to the way he
used his body to touch her in ways that made her sizzle.
She needed to tell him how good this was, how he made
her feel. But when she opened her mouth, the only thing
she could manage was "Yes."

But then he lifted, and ground against her, hitting
that sweet spot, and she supposed her "Yes" had been
enough, because that volcano inside her was just about
to erupt. She grabbed hold of his arms and squeezed,
raking her nails along his forearms. He grunted, whether
in pain or approval she didn't know. She didn't care. All
she knew was she was right there.

And then she climaxed, a burst of pleasure that

fanned out along every part of her. If light had shot out of her fingertips at that moment it wouldn't have surprised her, because she felt ethereal, as if she'd left her body at that moment.

Was that her voice? Was she yelling? She knew she was shuddering, but it was just so good, really so good, and it went on and on, and when he drove in deep and shuddered against her, taking her mouth in a soul-stealing kiss, her orgasm intensified, and it was one of the best experiences of her life.

She might not be breathing. She wasn't sure. All she did know was that she was supremely satisfied, and if this was the end, it was an exceptionally good one.

But then she felt Owen's breath on her neck. So warm. And then his lips teasing her throat before he rolled off her. She smiled.

Okay, she was alive. And definitely breathing.

"I thought I died," she said.

He lifted his head up, frowning at her. "What?"

"I think I had an out-of-body experience just now."

He propped his head on his elbow. "That good, huh?"

"As orgasms go, it was pretty good."

"If you thought you died, it had to be better than pretty good."

"Stupendous. Now I'm thirsty."

"Okay." He grinned, then got out of the bed and went into the bathroom. After he came out, she zipped out of the bed to use the bathroom, then came out and found him wearing his jeans. Mostly his jeans, anyway. They were half unzipped, the button undone. He was in front of the window, the setting sun casting him in shadow.

She took a deep breath and just . . . ogled appreciatively the utter sexiness of the man.

"What?" he asked.

"Oh, nothing. Just admiring your . . . everything."

He laughed. "Come on, we'll go get something to drink."

She didn't want to put her dress back on, so she grabbed a T-shirt out of his closet and put that on instead. It fit her like a dress, falling to her thighs.

Owen gave her a hot stare. "You look damn sexy in my shirt."

"It's soft. I might take it home with me." She didn't tell him that it smelled like him. That would be too much, right?

They went into the kitchen and Owen got out a couple of glasses.

"What would you like?" he asked.

"Water, please."

He filled the glasses with water. She took a couple of long swallows, sighing at the cool liquid relieving her parched throat.

That had been a workout. A sweet, delicious one.

Her phone buzzed on the kitchen island. She picked it up to check the message.

It wasn't one message, it was several, all from Brenna.

Hey, I'm at the house and you're not here. Where are you?

I called you and you didn't answer. Are you on a date?

Still no answer. Are you okay?

Honor. Where are you?

Damn. "I need to make a quick call."

Owen nodded. "Sure."

She got up and walked outside, then punched in Brenna's number. She answered right away.

"Where the hell are you?"

"I'm . . ." She thought for a second. "On a date."

"Oh. Obviously too occupied to answer your texts or calls."

"Sorry, I didn't have my phone with me."

She heard Brenna's low chuckle. "Good for you. I just got worried when you weren't here and you didn't answer."

"Everything's fine . . . Mom."

"Hey now, no need to go there. Finn was in the whiskey room working and I got bored, so I thought I'd come hang out with you. You're usually home and you weren't and I thought you were out shopping. And then you didn't answer."

Was she that boring and predictable? "Well, I'm obviously not home."

"Obviously. Is that chickens I hear?"

Dammit. "Of course not. Why would you hear chickens?"

"I don't know, Honor. You tell me. Where are you, anyway?"

"Outside. And maybe the neighbors have chickens. Though I haven't heard any."

"Sure. Whatever. Now that I know you haven't been kidnapped or murdered, I'm going back home. Talk to you later."

"Okay, bye. And, Brenna?"

"Yeah?"

"Thanks for looking after me."

Brenna laughed. "That's what we do. Later."

She hung up and tried to calm her rapidly beating heart. And then she heard them—the chickens. She should have thought about that before she walked outside. Now she'd have to come up with a reasonable explanation, because she knew that right this moment, Brenna was on the phone with Erin, giving her the lowdown of everything that had happened. By the time she saw her sisters tomorrow she'd need a plausible story, and said plausible story could not contain Owen's name.

Having secrets was a giant pain.

She went back inside.

"Everything okay?" he asked.

"Yes. Not really. Brenna went to the house looking for me and couldn't, and then got a little frantic trying to reach me."

"Uh-oh."

"Yeah."

"What did you tell her?"

"That I was on a date. Very nonspecific."

"Good."

She took a seat at the table next to him and grabbed her water, taking a sip. "For now. I'll get a thorough interrogation from both of them tomorrow."

Just the thought of it—of having to explain her marriage to Owen, how Erin might react—caused a deep pang in the pit of her stomach, obliterating all her warm after-sex glow.

Dammit.

He tilted his head to the side, studying her. "What's the plan?"

She shrugged. "I don't know. I don't plan to tell them

I was with you, that's for sure. I'll come up with something by then." She blew out a breath. "I'm not good at lying to people, especially my family."

He reached over and took her hand. "I don't want you to have to do that, either. I also don't want to stop seeing you."

Her heart squeezed at the same time that her nerve endings soared with panic at the thought of her sisters finding out what was going on between Owen and her. "I need a little space right now, Owen. To figure things out in my head."

He pulled his hand from hers. "You got it. Whatever you need."

"Thank you. And for the record, I don't want to stop seeing you, either. But this is complicated."

"It doesn't have to be. But you do what you need to do. I'll be here."

She went into his room and reluctantly pulled off his T-shirt, gathered up her things, paused for a minute and then folded his T-shirt, tucking it under her arm along with her purse. If Owen noticed, he didn't say anything. Instead, he walked her to the door. She turned to face him.

"Thank you for tonight."

He pulled her into his arms and kissed her. Bettie wriggled between them and her soft fur brushed Honor's legs.

This felt all too perfect, and she wished she could stay. But she couldn't. She pulled back, slid her fingers across his lips.

"Good night."

"See you later."

She bent down to give Bettie a hug and walked out to her car, got in and drove away, regret pulling at her with every mile.

Leaving didn't feel right. Something was going to have to give, and soon.

She didn't know what she was going to do, only that she felt more miserable every time she had to walk away from Owen.

CHAPTER
......
thirteen

I HOPE I don't throw up all over my bridesmaid dress today."

"I'm sure Alice hopes the same thing." Honor looked at Erin, who did, indeed, look a bit pale. At least it was an evening wedding, and Erin felt her best during the evening hours, so maybe there was hope.

"Did you tell Alice you were pregnant?" Brenna asked.

Erin shook her head. "Jason knows, of course. And I called Mom and Dad, who were in Dublin and said they were going to celebrate at a pub that night. Other than that, just you two know. I want to keep the circle of knowledge small since it's still early."

"Of course," Honor said. "Other than the nausea, how's it going?"

"I'm exhausted all the time, Jason said I'm moody as hell but he loves me, and my boobs hurt. Otherwise, it's awesome."

Honor had none of those symptoms, at least not yet.

Maybe that was a good sign that she wasn't pregnant. She mentally crossed her fingers.

Not that she didn't want kids. She did—maybe someday. But definitely not now. Getting pregnant from a drunken, accidental wedding night would not be her ideal baby-making scenario.

Though having a baby with Owen?

She inhaled and let it out slowly.

"Okay, you're stressed," Brenna said to her as they stood in what used to be Erin's bedroom. "What can we do to help today? Or at least what can I do, since Erin is in the wedding."

"Oh . . . nothing. I've actually got this one totally under control. Mae is at the barn overseeing the table setup and decorations, and Alice and the rest of the bridal party are due to arrive soon."

"Which means I need to get my collective self together," Erin said, gathering up her things. "Hair is done, makeup is done, I just need to get into my dress and hope it fits."

Erin slipped her robe off.

"Hey, you've got a tiny baby bump," Honor said, her heart doing little aunt-to-be flip-flops.

Erin turned sideways to look in the full-length mirror. "Yeah, there it is."

"How far along are you?" Brenna asked.

"I have no idea. Maybe eight weeks? Our first OB appointment is next week, so hopefully we'll get a clearer picture then. And an ultrasound pic to go with it."

Honor grinned. "How exciting."

"In the meantime, I have a belly to hide."

Fortunately, the bridesmaid dress was a simple floor-length chiffon that had ample room in the midsection and also flowed beautifully. If anyone had bumps or ridges, you could never tell.

The turquoise color looked stunning against Erin's skin and hair, as it would on all of Alice's bridesmaids.

After Brenna zipped her up, Erin turned to face the mirror.

"You're beautiful," Honor said.

Erin blinked back tears. "Did I also mention that I cry *all* the time? Hormones are so fun."

Brenna squeezed her. "Crying is only allowed by the bride today. And the parents."

Erin nodded, sniffed and lifted her chin. "Got it."

Erin waved her hand at Honor. "I'm good here. Go do your thing. Tell Alice I'll be right there."

"Okay." She dashed down the stairs and found the bride in the bridal suite. Alice Weatherford was a friend of the family and one of Erin's best friends. She was so happy that today Alice would be marrying Clay Henry, one of the sisters' longtime best friends. These two were the epitome of a couple who were meant to fall in love. She was so happy for them.

"How's everything going in here?" Honor asked.

"Perfectly," Alice said, looking serene and beautiful in her satin and tulle dress. Her lush brown hair had grown longer and was pulled up on the sides, leaving the rest slightly curled and flowing down her back. And her signature purple glasses matched the touch of lavender in her bouquet, plus she'd chosen purple shoes because she was just a little quirky, and that was why they all loved her so much.

"You look stunning, by the way."

"Oh, thank you. I feel kind of stunning. I'm not usu-ally this dressed up, or used to being the center of attention. Typically, my job is to get other people to fall in love. Who knew that would happen to me and in such a dramatic way?"

Honor walked over to smooth out the lines of Alice's dress. "You and Clay are perfect together. It was like . . . destiny or something."

Alice laughed. "In my matchmaking business, I don't believe in destiny. I used to not believe in chemistry, but we all know how that turned out for Clay and me."

"Yes, you couldn't fight that one, could you? And now it's your day." Honor checked her phone and saw the message from Brenna. "Are you ready to get married?"

Alice took in a deep breath and nodded. "I'm so ready."

Honor led her outside where her bridesmaids were all waiting, including Erin. Flowers were handed out and Honor got them all into position. Alice's dad was there and he held out his arm for her, and they were all set.

The music started playing and they all headed toward the arbor. Now all Honor had to do was make sure there were no glitches. She stood on the side, and that was when she caught sight of Owen standing next to the other groomsmen, looking tanned and smoking hot in his tux. He had a cowboy hat on, because of course this was a cowboy wedding with Clay being the groom.

Which only made Owen look even hotter.

Ugh. Girl, get it together.

She'd been so caught up with getting ready for this wedding she'd momentarily forgotten he was going to be here, and Brenna had been in charge of handling the groomsmen, so he hadn't been on her radar.

Until now. And now he was the only thing she could focus on, when her attention should be everywhere else.

She decided to move to a different angle where she wouldn't be ogling her husband, but then he directed his eyes on her and smiled, that sexy half smile of his that always got to her.

She couldn't help but smile back.

She was such a mess. She moved away and to the left of the arbor so she could watch the ceremony and the crowd, making sure the photographer was getting all the right shots, that the videographer was in place and that the skies stayed sunny—not that she had any control over that, but she could hope.

Vows were said, parents got teary-eyed and Alice and Clay had so much love on their faces that it filled the vineyard with joy. And when it was official and they kissed, applause rang out and despite this being a work event, Honor was near bursting with happiness for her friends.

After the ceremony, they led the attendees toward the barn for cocktails and appetizers while the wedding party stayed behind for photos. Brenna and Mae would supervise the crowd at the barn while Honor stayed behind to help out the photographer as needed.

Since the bride and groom were having their photos taken first, everyone else milled about. Honor made sure there was water and juice available since it was a warm day.

"What? No tequila?"

She turned to find Owen smiling down at her. "No tequila. I'm not sure I'm ever having tequila again."

He took a sip from his water. "Why? Does it make your clothes fall off?"

She let out a laughing cough at his quote from the song. "Among other things."

"You look beautiful tonight," he said. "I want to touch you. And kiss you."

Warmth curled around her. "Everyone thinks we're just friends, remember? The no-contact kind."

He laid a hand on one of the chairs. "Uh-huh. I've thought about you every day and every night since the last time we were together. I can't stop thinking about you, Honor. The way your eyes light up when you see something that interests you, and the way you lick your lips when you see food, the way your hair blows in the wind, like now . . ."

He swept her hair back behind her ear and she drew in a breath, his words and his touch evoking a chemical reaction she couldn't control.

"Oh, hey, Owen."

Honor swallowed hard as Erin came over.

Owen, on the other hand, was completely casual. "Hi, Erin. What's up?"

"Have you seen Jason?"

He hooked his thumb over his shoulder. "I think he went to the main house for something."

"Probably to check on Agatha and Puddy. We knew it was going to be a long night here and we didn't want to leave them at our house." She looked over at Owen. "I heard you got a dog. Jason said she's really cute. You'll have to bring her by so we can all see her."

"Thanks, I'll do that."

"I'm going to go find my husband."

"Don't linger too long, Erin," Honor said. "I think the photographer will be ready for bridal party photos soon."

She nodded and wandered off toward the house, and Honor turned back to Owen. "This is why we can't be around each other in public. Erin could have seen that."

"Seen what? Me fixing your hair? Seemed perfectly innocent to me. I think you worry too much."

"And I think you don't worry enough."

"I still plan to kiss you tonight. Sometime, somewhere. We'll sneak away."

She hated how much she wanted to do that. "Absolutely not."

"Okay. I'll let you make the call. Mrs. Stone." He winked and walked away from her.

Mrs. Stone. She was not—

Well, actually, she was Mrs. Stone. For a while longer, anyway. Which didn't mean he got to decide when and where he was going to kiss her.

And it absolutely was not going to be here, tonight, where family and friends could see them.

THERE WAS NOTHING better to Owen than hanging out with his best friends. That one of them had gotten married tonight was even better.

Time seemed to have flown by the past couple of years. And then at other times it seemed to have crawled, especially when he was undergoing his cancer treatments, and it felt like life was passing him by and he was missing everything.

But now as he stood back and watched everyone dancing, he realized that in the past year, two of his best friends had gotten married. And another was building a house with his forever love, and he knew they'd get married eventually, too.

Owen was supposed to be the first one to get married, but that obviously hadn't happened. Now Jason was married to Erin, and they were meant to be together.

And tonight Clay had married Alice, and as he watched his friend laughing as he twirled Alice around on the dance floor, he couldn't be happier for him.

His gaze tracked across the room and settled on Honor, who was having a conversation with Alice's parents, no doubt making sure they were comfortable and had what they needed since they lived out of state. That was typical for her, wanting to be sure that everyone was happy.

Owen had spent the past several hours watching Honor do her magic. She was excellent at her job, and she made it look effortless, when he knew it was anything but. She moved from table to table, occasionally stopping to give direction to Mae or talk to Brenna. Then she'd leave the room for a few minutes and come right back, a constant beauty in motion. He could watch her do this dance all night long.

"Got your eye on someone?"

He quickly shifted his attention to Jason. "Me? No. Just watching the dance floor."

"Yeah, it's like an old-style mosh pit out there." Jason got a fresh beer from the bartender.

"That's a good way to describe it. Speaking of the dance floor, why aren't you on it with Erin?"

"Oh. Uh, she wanted a break."

Unusual, since Erin was always the last one to want to leave the dance floor. "Can't keep up with your manic dance magic, huh?"

Jason smiled as he lifted the beer to his lips for a long pull, then said. "Yeah, that's me, man."

Clay came over and threw his arms around both of them. "I got married today. That's my wife over there."

Finn joined them. "He's had a little of my whiskey."

Owen laughed. "Hey, it's your wedding day. You're supposed to enjoy yourself."

"I am." Clay patted Owen's chest. "Life is short, got to live every second of it. Am I right?"

Truer words had never been spoken. "You are so right about that. I'm really happy for you and Alice."

"Thanks. I'm happy, too. Did I tell you she made me take a whole week off from the ranch to do the honeymoon thing?"

"Oh, she *made* you, huh?" Finn smirked. "I'm sure it's a real hardship to do a trip through all those pubs and castles in Scotland and Ireland."

"Not to mention all the great food you'll get to eat," Jason added. "I'm a little jealous of your itinerary."

"Okay, it won't suck. And we've both been working really hard, so we're looking forward to some relaxation time."

"Hey, husband." Alice came over and slid her head under Clay's arm. "You gentlemen wouldn't mind if I borrowed him for a few, would you?"

"He's all yours," Owen said.

"Forever and ever," Jason added.

Finn let out a chuckle as Clay and Alice walked off hand in hand.

"I would have said he'd be the last one to walk down the aisle," Jason said.

"Yeah?" Finn looked after their retreating forms, then over at Jason. "And I'd have said that would have been you."

Jason pointed at his own chest. "Me? Why?"

"Because you were always dating different women."

"Finn's right," Owen said. "For a while there you went through so many that I got confused over who was who. I was thinking you should put name tags on them."

"Well, fortunately for me, you fucked up and I got Erin."

Jason's eyes widened as soon as the words left his mouth. Finn just stared at both of them as if he expected them to come to blows.

But Owen laughed hard. "Lucky for you I'm such a jackass."

Then Jason laughed and slung his arm over Owen's shoulder. "Yeah, I'm damn lucky."

Finn blew out a breath and joined the group hug. "I think you're both jackasses."

Owen was the lucky one to have friends like this. Friends who were forgiving, friends who could see past major screwups, who were ride or die, like these guys.

He wouldn't have made it the past couple of years without them.

They eventually went their separate ways. Owen went to the bar to get a cold glass of ice water. As he stood there, his gaze hovered over the room. He didn't see Honor. Maybe she was taking a few minutes to sit and put her feet up. He wandered around and saw Brenna overseeing the caterers cleaning up the dinner area.

He made a leisurely stroll out of the barn and around the tree-lined walk, eventually ending up at the bridal room. The door was partially open, so he pushed it open fully and saw Honor in there. She was dressed in her peach-colored beaded cocktail dress, killer sparkly heels, but had added a tiara on her head. She had a broom in her hand and was sweeping the floor.

"Having your Cinderella moment?"

She lifted her head, then smiled at him. "Kind of Cinderella in reverse, don't you think?"

He closed the door, walked in and took the broom from her hand. "The crown fits, but definitely not the broom." He finished the task and swept everything into the trash can.

"Just tidying up." She pulled the tiara off her head and tucked it into the bag that sat on the tufted chair. "The bridesmaids had brought it for Alice this morning to let her know she was the princess of the day. I was just making sure it didn't get left behind."

"Is there anything you don't do?"

"What do you mean?"

He moved in close and pulled her against him. "I've watched you tonight. You monitored the wedding ceremony, chased down a wayward kid who ran amok in the vineyard, filled in for the bartender who had an emergency phone call, made sure the bride's parents felt comfortable and at home, danced with the bride's dad and now you're sweeping up the bridal room. Did you fix tonight's dinner, too?"

She laid her hands on his chest. "You know I don't cook."

"But you do everything else. You must be tired." He shifted his gaze down to her feet. "How do you walk all night in those heels?"

"Years of practice."

"You look beautiful. Sparkle suits you."

Her cheeks turned a lovely shade of peachy blush. "Thank you. This tux suits you. I couldn't tear my focus away from you when you were standing up there at the arbor. You know you're not supposed to outshine the groom."

"Trust me, I didn't."

She moved her hands up over his shoulders. "To me you did. You were all I saw."

His throat tightened. "Hey, remember what I said earlier?"

She gave him a slight tilt to her head. "No. What?"

He slid his hand along the side of her neck and leaned in, brushing his lips across hers, teasing and tasting, flicking his tongue against hers and enjoying the feel of her, the way she seemed to melt her body to his as if to say *Yes, I want this, too.*

He pulled slightly away. "That I was going to kiss you."

"Oh." Her voice had gone soft, breathy. "I do seem to recall that, but I'm still a little fuzzy. Can you help me out?"

"Yeah, I can do that." He went in deeper this time, settled there, taking them both on a journey of taste and exploration.

There was no denying that he enjoyed kissing Honor. Her lips were full and the way she moved her body when she was in his arms let him know she was more than into it. She ran her hands all over his chest and around his back, sliding lower until she grabbed his ass and squeezed. He was trying to take this slow and easy, but with Honor, there just wasn't a slow and easy. She went for it, and it was one of the things he liked best about her. When she was in, she was all in.

It was right then he got a flash of memory—a darkened hotel room, with just enough hazy light to see a naked Honor on top of him, her body moving in rhythm to his strokes. Her head was tilted back and her breasts thrust up and it was like the best dream a man could ever have.

Except it wasn't a dream. It was their drunken wedding night.

He wished he could remember all of it, because it must have been a really great night. Just holding Honor in his arms right now, listening to the sounds she made as they kissed and touched each other, told him everything he needed to know about the passion they felt for each other.

He'd had two nights with her, only one of which he could really remember. He wanted more.

He pulled his lips from hers and kissed her neck. "We should—"

The door handle jiggled. "Hey, is someone in there?"

Honor took a step back, licked her lips and answered Mae's question. "It's just me, Mae. I'm picking up in here."

"Oh, okay. Do you need some help?"

"No, I'm almost finished. But can you go check on Alice and see if she needs anything?"

"Sure. I'll take care of that right away."

Honor stood in front of him heaving in deep breaths. "I have to go."

He could tell from the look on her face that she was equal parts panicked and regretful. "Sure."

She grabbed the tote bag and brushed past him, then paused, reached out and took his hand. "Thanks for that . . . moment."

"Anytime."

She left the room and he took a few minutes before peeking his head out. No one was around, so he walked out and made his way back to the reception. He stopped at the bar and got a sparkling water, then went to grab a seat at the table, just in time for the cake cutting.

Good timing. After he ate, he got up and wandered outside.

"You're not fooling anyone, mate."

He turned to see Finn standing next to him.

"Fooling anyone about what?"

Finn motioned down the private walkway. "I saw you disappear down toward the bridal room. After Honor had gone down there a little while earlier."

"Oh. Anyone else see?"

Finn shrugged. "No idea. Why are you keeping it a secret?"

"Like I said. It's complicated."

Finn took a sip of whiskey from the flask in his pocket. "I don't know complicated, but I do know about secrets. And those tend to blow up in your face."

"You're the only one who knows." And even Finn didn't know everything. "I just need you to keep a lid on this one a while longer."

"Whatever you say, mate. But I don't think anyone would care if you were dating Honor."

Maybe. Then again, maybe not. Because he had a long history with the Bellinis. And sure, he'd been forgiven for his cataclysmic fuckup with Erin and welcomed back into the family fold.

But taking up with another Bellini sister? That might not go over well. And marrying her during a drunken night in Vegas?

Yeah, that would be a disaster.

So this secret would just have to continue to be kept.

CHAPTER

. . . . . .

fourteen

IT WAS SO great having Mom and Dad back home.

Honor had noticed a definite difference in them since their return, too. They had always been affectionate with each other, but now? Now they were downright nauseatingly romantic.

Dad would pop into Mom's office in the middle of the day, sit down in a chair, and they'd just . . . chat. For like ten, fifteen minutes, when normally Dad wouldn't set foot in the house unless lunch or dinner was served. He was always out in the vineyard or the warehouse or in the wine cellar.

And now Honor would occasionally see Mom in her hat wandering the vineyards alongside Dad, the two of them strolling and talking, hand in hand. Typically, Mom never left her desk, her head buried in numbers and schedules.

Honor stood at the window with her sisters watching her parents kissing among the grapes.

"What do you think's going on with those two?" Erin asked.

"I think they had a lot of really awesome sex on their vacation," Brenna said, offering up a smug smile.

"Ew, Brenna," Erin said.

"What? You can't tell the difference in them? They're gooey romantic since they got home. It's like they can't keep their hands off each other."

"I've definitely noticed," Honor said. "But it's more than just the touching and the kissing. It's a deliberate attempt to spend more time together. Maybe they realized they weren't doing enough of that."

"You know what," Erin said. "You're right. I guess that's a good lesson for all of us. Be more mindful of our partners and don't take time and attention for granted."

Brenna nodded. "You've got it pegged, Erin. And duly noted. I think I'll go make Finn a picnic lunch and we'll have our own alone time today."

"Aww, he'd appreciate that, Bren," Honor said.

"I agree," Erin said. "And I think I'll meet Jason after work tonight and take him to his favorite restaurant for dinner. Since I've been nauseated so much, we've been eating at home a lot. But now that I'm starting to come out of it, he could use a night out."

"This makes me so happy," Honor said. "Seeing you both—and Mom and Dad—so blissfully in love."

Erin laid her hand on Honor's shoulder. "Your time will come, honey. The right guy is out there for you."

"Erin's right," Brenna said. "Sometimes it happens when you least expect it."

"Right. I'm in no hurry."

If they only knew . . .

"We should set you up with someone," Erin said.

"Wait . . . what?"

Brenna sported a happy grin. "That's an excellent idea, Erin."

No. Terrible idea. "Thanks, but no. I'm pretty good at finding my own dates."

Brenna shot her a look. "Actually, you're fairly terrible at it. You always find these losers who treat you horribly."

"Hey, that's not—okay, it's not entirely true. Some of them were okay."

Erin rolled her eyes. "None of them were okay. Trust us, Honor. Brenna and I will put our heads together and find someone for you."

Honor could only force a smile that probably looked more like a grimace. She could only hope they'd get busy and forget about finding some random guy for her to date.

A few days later she'd totally forgotten about that conversation. On Thursday afternoon, Brenna texted her and told her a bunch of them were all meeting up at the Screaming Hawk that night for drinks and asked if she wanted to join them. Normally she'd say yes, but since that was Owen's craft brewery, she paused before answering.

She should say no. Then again, wouldn't her saying no ring a bell of suspicion? It wasn't like she had anything else going on. Besides, she'd be in a group and he'd be working. Easy enough for Owen and her to maintain a friendly distance without anyone noticing anything going on between them. She'd be on her best behavior and not touch him or smile at him or even glance his way. Or, at least she'd try.

She texted Brenna back and told her she'd be there.

Tuning out the whole idea of later, she took care of personal stuff during the day. Mom and Dad had some vague and noncommittal plans. Honor figured it was some kind of date, which was great for them. They'd gotten up early and left the house before breakfast. Louise and her husband, Marcus, had an appointment to go to, so they were gone as well, which meant Honor had the place to herself. She'd had breakfast outside, cleaned her room and done laundry and paid a few bills, and when she was finished with chores, she decided she'd do some personal pampering. She showered, then went and got a manicure and pedicure, and since her hair stylist had an available opening, she got a trim, which meant her hair was now freshly washed and blow-dried. By the time she got home she felt amazing. Now she just had to decide what to wear tonight.

No big deal. Just a group of friends along with her sisters hanging out at the brew pub. She opened her closet and stared at her clothes.

The day was already warm, and no doubt they'd want to hang out outside, so jeans were out, but a dress would be too fancy. She nibbled on her bottom lip as she tried to decide the best outfit to wear. Maybe capris would be good since it was getting warm out.

"Honor? You up there?"

She was relieved to hear Brenna's voice. "Yes. In my room. Come on up."

"Hey. Oh, heyyy. Your hair looks incredible."

"Thanks. Carly had an opening today so I got a trim. And I got a mani-pedi, too."

Brenna gave her a once-over. "Sweet. You're all set for tonight."

"Except I can't figure out what to wear. What are you wearing?"

"Oh. My navy and cream dress. But you should wear . . ." Brenna went into her closet and pulled out the powder-blue flowered sundress. "Wear this."

Honor wrinkled her nose. "Don't you think it's too fancy for the bar?"

"Not at all. Wear sandals or kicks with it. That'll totally tone it down."

"You have a point there. So who's coming tonight?"

"You, me and Finn, Erin and Jason, Mae, Clay and Alice and maybe some other people."

She stared at the dress, mentally trying to coordinate her outfit. "Okay."

"Great. Can I borrow your gold necklace? It goes with the outfit I'm wearing."

"Oh, sure. Go ahead."

Brenna went to Honor's dresser and opened up her jewelry box, fishing out the necklace. "Thanks. I need to go get ready. Do you want to ride with Finn and me?"

She thought about it, then shook her head. "Thanks, but no. I want to be able to leave when I want to, and there's no point in you two having to go before you're ready."

"Okay. We'll see you there."

After Brenna left, she did her makeup, added earrings and put on her dress, then examined herself in the mirror.

The dress fit her snugly in all the right places. She had to admit, it was a good choice—if she was going on a date, which she most certainly was not. Still, it was a pretty dress and she felt good in it, so why not?

She went downstairs and turned off all the lights, then grabbed her keys and her clutch and headed out the front door, sliding into her car.

On the way there she felt skitters of anticipation, and she knew they weren't because she'd get to hang out with her sisters or friends. It was because she was going to get to see Owen.

You have to stop thinking about him. He's not yours.

In her head she knew that. Her heart was thinking for itself. And that was the problem.

What if she did move forward with an actual relationship with Owen? What would that even look like? He was her sister's ex-fiancé. How would Erin react? She'd be upset, naturally, and right now upsetting Erin wasn't a good idea.

But how was she supposed to hide her growing attraction and feelings for Owen when they occupied the same space?

This was getting so complicated. She needed to calm down and remember that Owen was working tonight; he'd be busy, and she could focus on her family and friends. Keep it light and simple and no one would be the wiser.

Easy, right?

By the time she arrived at the Screaming Hawk, the parking lot was full. Good for Owen, great for his business. She parked in the back, happy she had decided to wear her white canvas slip-on shoes. Not only did they look cute with the dress, they also made it much easier to walk across the gravel parking lot.

The music was loud and so were all the voices inside as she opened the door. But the air conditioning felt cool and refreshing. She spotted Owen behind the bar dealing with a few customers, so she walked on by, hoping he wouldn't notice her.

No such luck. He might have been talking to other people, but his gaze tracked her as she walked past him. He waved, his smile warm and welcoming. She couldn't help but smile back in return, ignoring that little extra kick her heart gave her.

Bettie came bounding over, her tail flipping back and forth.

"Bettie," she said, crouching down to give her lots of pets. "I'm so happy to see you. Are you keeping Owen in line?"

It didn't seem that way because Bettie ran off to see to the other customers. It was easy to see that she was well loved here. Honor was so happy to see the dog living her best life, and she had Owen to thank for that.

She recognized the large group at one of the tables, so she headed that way. It looked like everyone had already arrived.

"Glad you could make it," Erin said. "Also, Jason ordered a few pizzas from the place next door. Owen said it was okay and I'm starving."

"Sounds good to me."

"Hey, you're here," Mae said. "This is my date, Raymond. Raymond, this is Honor Bellini."

She held out her hand. "Nice to meet you."

"You, too."

Raymond was incredibly handsome, with long black locs and beautiful dark skin. He was incredibly tall and muscular, filling out his T-shirt quite nicely.

There was another guy talking to Finn, though she didn't know him. Tall, good looking, wearing jeans and a long-sleeve button-down.

"Hot, isn't he?" Brenna asked.

"Yes, he's nice-looking. Friend of Finn's?"

"Sort of. Come with me and I'll introduce you."

Before she could say anything, Brenna had grabbed her by the hand and dragged her down to the other end of the table.

"Andrew, this is my sister Honor, that I've been telling you about. Honor, this is Andrew Williams. He's the co-owner of A Rose by Any Other."

The name sparked immediate recognition. "Oh, you work with Rose. Wait. Williams? Are you related?"

He smiled broadly. "She's my sister. Though she's the one with all the flowery talent. I'm just the numbers guy."

"I see. It's nice to meet you, Andrew." She shook his hand.

"What would you like to drink?" he asked.

"Oh. I'd love a Vanilla Black please."

"Great. I'll be right back."

"He seems awesome," Erin said as she came over.

"And you two look cute together," Brenna added.

She might have just arrived, but seeing everyone coupled up with the exception of Andrew and her, it didn't take Honor long to figure out that this was a setup. She glared at her sisters. "You didn't."

Erin slanted innocent eyes at her. "Didn't what?"

"Set me up on a blind date. Does he even know?"

"Of course he does," Brenna said. "I told him you weren't going out with anyone, and I thought meeting him tonight in a large group would be fun. And non-threatening."

She shifted her gaze over to the bar where Owen was pulling their beers. He chatted amiably with Andrew, but as soon as Andrew walked away, she could see the confusion on Owen's face. She gave Owen what could only be described as her best apologetic grimace.

"Here you go." Andrew handed the beer to her, then lifted his. "To what I hope is a good evening for both of us."

She clinked her glass with his, then silently wished for the floor to swallow her up so she could disappear.

CHAPTER
. . . . . .
fifteen

OWEN TRIED HIS best to pay attention to his patrons, but that was hard to do when his focus kept shifting to the table where Honor was chatting it up with a guy he didn't know. She smiled, though he couldn't say she was flirting. But she was friendly enough.

Dammit.

His wife. Was on a date. With some random dude. At his pub.

This was not okay. How dare the family do this to him?

The family doesn't know you two are married, jackass.

Fair point, but still, it stung. If they wanted to fix Honor up with someone, couldn't they see he was right here? Available. Decent enough to marry Erin, but not good enough for Honor?

Oh, the Erin you left at the altar? Great track record there, bud. I can't imagine why they wouldn't want you to hook up with another Bellini sister.

His annoyingly loud conscience was beginning to piss him off.

Even Bettie liked the guy, who gave her lots of pets whenever she came over to the table. When Bettie came back behind the bar, he slanted her a look.

"Traitor," he mumbled.

Bettie gave him a smile and a wag of her tail.

The only one sending him sympathetic looks right now was Finn.

"So, what do you think?"

He looked up to find Jason leaning against the bar.

"About what?"

"About Honor and Andrew."

"Oh, that's his name? I don't know anything about him."

"I'll take another pale ale, by the way. He co-owns a floral shop with his sister, who does flowers for some of the vineyard's weddings. Brenna and Erin hooked him up with Honor."

"Ah. Well, isn't that awesome." Owen slid him the pint.

Jason took the beer, then gave Owen a look. "Something we should know about Andrew?"

"No, nothing. I don't know him. I'm sure he's great."

Jason took a sip, still studying Owen, then asked, "Something you wanna tell me?"

"Nope." You'd think after all the years of playing poker with these guys he'd have a better face by now. Fortunately, the door opened. "Hey, look, your pizzas are here."

"Oh, great. Thanks for letting us have pizza."

Jason's attention now occupied elsewhere, thankfully, he grabbed the pizzas and took them to the table.

And Owen could get back to work and hopefully focus on his job and not on how close Honor and Andrew were sitting together.

At least it was busy here and he got slammed with serving customers, so he spent the next hour serving up beers with no time to stare a hole into the back of Andrew's head. He had Virginia step behind the bar while he walked out to the warehouse to grab a keg of lager.

He was in the far part of the warehouse when he heard breathing. He stilled, then slowly turned, exhaling when he saw Honor behind him.

"What are you doing out here?"

"I came to explain. I didn't know there was going to be a setup here tonight. I was stunned."

That made him feel marginally better. "That's never fun."

"No. Andrew is nice, but it's not like I can tell him in front of everyone that I can't go out with him because I'm currently married."

He wished she'd tell him exactly that. "Yeah, I understand."

"I just wanted you to know that I didn't plan this. I would never do this in front of you."

She looked so upset that he knew he was going to have to defuse this. "Oh, so you're dating behind my back?" He raised his eyebrows.

She cocked her head to the side. "Owen, you know me better than that."

"I do. I'm sorry. I can tell you're uncomfortable. Just relax and go with it. I'm fine."

"But are you? You looked . . . mad."

Mad? Nah, he wasn't angry. He just wanted Andrew

to conveniently fall down a hole and disappear forever. "Not gonna lie, I'm a little jealous."

That got a smile out of her. She moved closer. "Are you?"

"Yeah. I don't like seeing some strange guy sitting so close to my wife."

She laughed. "I'll make sure he backs off. And honestly? Nothing is going to happen."

"You don't like him?"

"Actually, I do. He's a really nice guy. But he's not you." She looked out through the doorway, then back at him, lifted up on her toes, grabbed his face and planted a hot, lingering kiss on his mouth. She pulled back, licked her lips and walked away, leaving him staring after her, dumbfounded.

He'd wanted that kiss to last longer, but he knew she'd already been away from the table for a while. And he had to get back to work, too.

But he's not you.

Okay, it was gonna take him a minute to digest what she'd said. He wasn't one to linger on words, but those words had meant something to him.

Deciding to get his head back into work and out of . . . his own head, he guessed, he hefted the keg and carried it back into the brewery, relieving Virginia so she could go back to doing her job. After he got things settled behind the bar, he took a quick glance over to the table, noticing that Honor was now seated at the other end of the table talking to Mae and her date, while Andrew was huddled up with Jason and Finn. It stayed that way for a long time, too, and while Honor and Andrew got together and talked throughout the night, there was no more close huddling between the two of them, but rather more group conversations. She always had either one of her sisters or one of the guys next to her whenever she was talking to Andrew.

Had she done that on purpose? Based on the looks she occasionally threw his way, he'd say yes.

He couldn't help but feel smugly happy about that.

CHAPTER

. . . . . .

sixteen

"WAS HE MEAN to you?"

"I didn't see him put his hands on you the whole night, so it couldn't have been that."

"He seemed really nice, but then again, I was focused on my date so I didn't notice much."

Honor faced her sisters and Mae—along with her mother, who hadn't been with them the other night but still listened with an interested expression on her face. She wished they could focus on their meeting instead of putting all their attention on her so she'd be forced to lie to everyone again.

"Andrew was very nice," she said, then shrugged. "There just wasn't a connection between us."

"Bullshit," Brenna said. "Andrew is a catch, and he could have chemistry with a rock."

"I agree," Erin said, studying her intently. "He's smart, successful, good-looking and funny. So what's the deal, Honor?"

She shifted her gaze to her mother, who she hoped

was back to studying the agenda for today's meeting. Instead, her mother continued to look at her.

"I don't know. We hit it off more as friends. There wasn't a spark."

Brenna opened her mouth to speak, then shut it.

Erin started to say something, but Mom raised her hand.

"I think that's enough critiquing of Honor's dating life, don't you think? We all have a busy day ahead, so let's get on with the meeting."

She sent a grateful smile to her mother, and they got through the agenda in record time without another mention of Andrew. After the meeting, Honor gathered up her laptop and notebook and started toward her office.

"Honor," her mom said. "A minute, please?"

"Sure." She followed her mother to her office, where her mom closed the door and motioned for her to sit in one of the cushioned chairs.

Mom sat across from her.

"What's going on?" Mom asked.

"I don't know what you mean."

"Typically you're eager to date new men. I wasn't there so I can't speak to this Andrew guy, but it seems as if he didn't have much in the way of flaws, so why the sudden reluctance?"

She wished she could spill everything to her mother, tell her all about Vegas. And then explain to her how much fun she'd been having with Owen lately, how close they had been getting. She wondered how her mom would react to that news.

Probably not great, all things considered. She'd be concerned, maybe even angry with Owen. And that she couldn't allow.

She swept her fingertip along her brow, trying to find the right words to extricate herself from this conversation. "Oh, well, you know how it is, Mom. Sometimes you're in the mood to date, and sometimes you're not."

"What you're saying is you're not in the mood?"

She could tell from the look on her mother's face that she wasn't buying it. "Not really. We're deep into spring, we have a lot of weddings coming up and I'm incredibly busy right now. I mean, I'm just buried with work and planning. Who has time for men? I know I don't."

Mom studied her for a few seconds longer. "Okay, as long as everything is all right with you."

She resisted letting out a giant sigh of relief. Instead, she stood. "Everything is fine. Except my to-do list right now, so I've gotta go. Thanks for checking in on me, Mom." She bent over, kissed her mother on the cheek and made her escape back to her own office. She closed the door, took a seat at her desk and then sighed.

She couldn't remember ever feeling so under the microscope with her family. Had it always been like this, or was it a recent development? Either way, she felt exposed, and this wasn't a good time for that kind of scrutiny.

She opened her planner and looked at the dates. She wished she knew when to expect her period, that way she could confirm a pregnancy or not. But oh, no, she was irregular on that front. Didn't that just figure?

But she should have a period soon. She had to. She didn't feel any pregnancy symptoms, which made her feel optimistic. The sooner this was all over with and they could dissolve their marriage would be for the better, right?

So why didn't she feel happier?

Her phone buzzed with a message. She picked it up, her heartbeat kicking a little higher when she saw that the message was from Owen.

We have a Zoom call with our divorce attorney tonight. Is my place okay? Bettie misses you.

Her lips quirked.

She typed a response: That sounds great. What time?

He replied: How about five thirty? After the call I'll throw something together for us to eat, too.

Of course he would. Only she doubted whatever food he served would be thrown together. Owen knew how to cook a meal. Her stomach already growled at the thought.

She sent back another text: Sounds good. See you then.

Bettie's really looking forward to seeing you.

She sighed as she stared at her phone, realizing she felt warm and tingly all over.

There was a knock at her door. She dropped the phone like it was on fire as she looked up and saw Mae's smiling face.

Pull it together, Honor.

She motioned for Mae to come in.

"Something—or maybe someone—put a smile on your face," Mae said as she placed a pile of books and her laptop down on the table in her office. "What's up?"

"Oh, definitely not a someone. Just a confirmation of a floral order."

"Really? Which wedding? I'll mark it off the list."

Crap. She stumbled over her mushy thoughts. "The Hanverson/Daley wedding."

"Oh, good."

Honor was lucky she'd gotten that call from the florist this morning so she didn't have to make up a bald-faced lie. Then again, she was getting good at lying, wasn't she?

"Who knew a flower order would put such a dreamy look on your face?" Mae said as she took a seat at the table.

Honor joined her. "Well, you know me. Weddings just do it for me."

"They are sweetly romantic, aren't they? Unless they're mine, in which case, ugh, no thank you."

Honor laughed. "You have such a good attitude about not marrying that bastard who cheated on you."

Mae grinned. "Thank you so much for referring to him that way. And hey, the way I look at it is—better to find out he was a cheating piece of shit before I married him rather than after, right?"

"That is so true. But still, he broke your heart."

She shrugged. "I got over him. And now look at me—I'm content and doing what I love. And making all these brides happy, too."

Honor wasn't sure she could be that accepting—or want to be involved in the whole wedding thing if the same thing had happened to her. But that was Mae's personality. She always took the high road, always turned the worst into the best. That was one of the things Honor loved about her friend, and why she wanted her at Bellini Weddings. Not to mention her crazy talents for everything bridal. Honor hoped that one day the right guy would come along for Mae, because no one deserved it more than she did.

The two of them ripped right through the upcoming weekend's activities, and, armed with her to-do list, Mae headed out. Honor dug into her own priorities, keeping her mind occupied and off Owen. Fortunately, she had a lot to do, including two off-site meetings with vendors. By the time she got back home it was four o'clock. She needed to jot down notes from her meetings and update her calendar, and that finished off her workday. She shut off the light in her office, closed the door, then passed her mother in the hall.

"How did the meetings go?"

"Oh, great, Mom. I'll send you an email about them in the morning."

Her mother nodded. "I'll see you at dinner, then?"

"Uh, no. I made some last-minute plans with friends, so I'm going out tonight."

"Okay. Have fun." Her mother walked off and thankfully didn't ask any further questions.

Honor went upstairs, took a fast shower and then, since today was on the overly warm side, decided on shorts and a sleeveless cotton shirt. She brushed out her hair, put on some light makeup and slid into her tennis shoes. She made it to Owen's with about five minutes to spare, then realized she'd forgotten to grab a bottle of wine on her way out the door.

Dammit. That was what she got for being in such a hurry. Now she felt naked and like a terrible guest. But she was still going to ring the doorbell.

She waited. And waited.

Hmm. No answer.

Okay, fine. Figuring Owen was likely out back, she went around the side of the house and opened the gate, making her way to the backyard. She didn't see him, so she slipped inside and laid her purse on the table, then went back out. She caught sight of Bettie slipping around the barn and figured she was following Owen, so she headed that way.

Following the sound of barking, she found Bettie at the fence giving rather loud advice to the three cows in the pasture while Owen handled the feed. Honor went up to greet Bettie, who turned her attention on her with wiggles and licks.

"It's good to see you, too. I've missed you so much. I see you're helping Owen with his chores."

"'Helping' is a matter open to discussion," Owen said as he closed the gate and came up to her. "Hi."

"Hi yourself." She looked him over, admiring the way sweat made his T-shirt stick to all that incredible lean muscle. He was covered in dirt and hay and she'd never seen him look sexier. Or, frankly, smell better. What was it about sweat and dirt on this man that hit her libido so hard? She was around good-looking men who worked outside at the vineyard and got sweaty, and they had never hit her hot buttons. But right now she wanted to lick Owen's neck, push him down on the filthy ground, strip his clothes off and climb on top of him while she—

Well, that fantasy went places in a hurry. Fortunately, a swift breeze brought her back to reality, because she found herself walking in step with Owen as he made his way back toward the house.

"You look pretty. I'd like to pull you against me and kiss you." He looked down at himself. "But then you'd be dirty and sweaty."

And there went that fantasy again, blooming into colorful life. "Nothing wrong with a little dirt and sweat."

"If you'd been out here working the cattle and horses with me, I might consider it." He opened the door and waited for her to go inside. "But since you look nice and clean, I'll pass on my dirty thoughts."

She pivoted. "You had dirty thoughts?"

He was headed down the hall, but stopped. "Where you're concerned, Honor? Every day. I'm gonna take a quick shower. I'll be right back. There's wine in the fridge. Help yourself."

She stared after him until he disappeared, then let out a sigh and uncorked the Red Moss Vineyards bottle of pinot grigio she found in the fridge, pouring herself a small glass. Since there was still a small chance she was pregnant, she was allowing herself a maximum of one glass of wine a day, which, according to what she'd read online, was perfectly healthy for pregnant women.

She wandered over to the bay window and stared for a few minutes, then pulled up a seat at the table and looked down at Bettie, who had curled herself in a ball on the cool kitchen tile and had gone to sleep.

"I could be naked in the shower with him right now," she said to Bettie. "So why didn't I follow him? Then again, he didn't invite me, either." She took a couple sips of wine and pondered.

"But he did make that comment about having dirty thoughts about me. Maybe that had been the invitation. And I was just too obtuse to follow through." She took another few sips of the wine and thought about her next move.

She could go down the hall to his bedroom and slip into the shower with him right now.

She stewed and thought, stewed and thought some more.

Besides, they'd already had sex. It wasn't like something happening between them was some kind of surprise or anything. It wouldn't be their first time together. Or even their second.

So again, Honor—why are you hesitating?

She replied to herself by taking two more swallows of wine.

"You're being ridiculous, you know. He wants you naked."

"If by 'he' you mean me, then the answer is always yes."

She pushed back from the table and stood abruptly, nearly spilling her glass of wine as she turned to find Owen leaning against the wall.

"I was . . . talking to myself."

He pushed off the wall. "Obviously. About being naked." He grabbed a beer from the fridge and twisted the top off, tossing it in the trash on his way toward her. "Were you thinking about joining me in the shower?"

"I—I was going to—then I thought—well, that was the problem, actually. Too much thinking."

He swept his thumb across her bottom lip. "Next time don't think. Go with instinct. I would have liked you to join me."

See? Overthinking never got her anywhere. "I'll make a note of that."

He brushed his lips across hers, and she leaned into the kiss, wanting, needing it to go on longer. She'd missed his touch, the taste of him. Just breathing him in and feeling his tongue sweep across hers was like taking in much-needed oxygen. When he pulled back, he smiled at her.

"Ready for the call?"

She nodded. "Absolutely."

He typed the information in and Jessica's smiling face popped up.

"Hello, you two. It's nice to see you."

"Nice to see you as well, Jessica," Honor said.

"You know, for two people getting a divorce, you sure show up in the same room a lot."

Owen laughed. "We're friends. Just accidentally married ones."

"Right. Anyway, I have the paperwork complete. I can send it over for you both to sign. Since there are no assets to haggle over and no children, it's likely we can have you divorced within about ten days."

Honor's stomach tumbled. "Oh, about that. Is there any way we can put a temporary hold on filing that paperwork?"

"Of course. May I ask why?"

"Well, there's a possibility I could be pregnant, and I need to wait until my period shows up to be certain."

Jessica seemed not at all shocked by the revelation. "Not a problem. I'll hold the paperwork and you let me know when you're ready for me to file it. All it'll require is your signatures and then I'll date it and send it off. After that, as far as finalization, everything will go smoothly. Or, if you don't want it filed at all, let me know that, too."

"Awesome," Owen said. "Thanks, Jessica."

They signed off, then turned to face each other.

"How long before you know for sure?" Owen asked.

She shrugged. "A couple more weeks, maybe? My periods are anything but consistent, but I should know within two to three weeks for sure. Maybe."

He laughed. "I'm in no hurry, Honor. I'm not going anywhere. In the meantime, I don't know about you, but I'm hungry. How about I fix us some dinner?"

She was relieved he wasn't in a hurry for the divorce. She was also interested in something other than food, but the logical side of her realized she probably needed to eat. "Sure, that sounds good."

He got stuff out of the refrigerator and it all looked amazing. He'd obviously marinated some chicken ka-bobs along with veggies, and then he put rice in the cooker, and now her stomach took notice.

"Anything I can do to help?" she asked.

He cocked his head to the side. "You want to help me cook?"

"Not particularly. I was just being polite."

He laughed. "Come on. You can keep me company outside while I put these on the grill."

"Sounds like a plan." She had finished her wine, so she rinsed her glass and followed him out to the patio, where he got the grill ready and laid the kabobs on.

As he worked, she looked out over his property. It was beautiful out here. Green and lush, with so much space she could walk forever. It was one of the things she loved the most about living on the Bellini property, and probably why she had never moved out. Living in some cramped apartment would make her feel claustro-phobic. Having wide open spaces was home to her.

This felt like home, and as she got up and wandered outside the fenced area of the yard, Bettie followed. She inhaled the pungent smell of hay and horses and cattle, listening to the sounds of mooing cows and watching as the horses nudged each other in their pasture.

She could lose a lot of time out here. But she also

realized that despite its small size, Owen had a lot of responsibility, on top of being the owner of a craft brewery.

She made her way back to the yard and closed the gate behind her.

He looked up and smiled. "Hey, you're just in time. The rice is finished and so are these. You ready to eat?"

"Sure."

"You want to eat inside or outside?"

She looked around. "Let's eat outside. The weather is so perfect tonight."

"Okay."

They went inside and got plates together, and Owen put the rice in a covered bowl. He also pulled out a fruit salad from the fridge. They carried everything outside and set it on the table. Owen went back inside and came out with a couple of glasses of iced tea.

"I don't know about you," he said as he took a seat. "But I'm so hungry."

"Me, too."

They dug in, and the chicken and veggies tasted amazing. So did everything else.

"This is so good, Owen," she said. "Thank you for inviting me over."

"Oh, I didn't," he said, sliding chicken and veggies off a skewer. "It was all Bettie's idea."

She laughed. "Right, I forgot." She looked down at the dog, who was curled up under the table. "Thanks for inviting me, Bettie."

"Bettie's thinking of having a big barbecue for Memorial Day, inviting a bunch of people over. What do you think?"

"I think it's a fantastic idea. Do you need help organizing?"

"Always. Bettie likes to think she has everything handled, but just between you and me, she's all paws and could use a good assistant."

She took a sip of her iced tea, then set the glass down and smiled at him. "I'll be more than happy to be Bettie's helper."

"Okay. She doesn't have fingers so I'll have to act as go-between and text and call you."

"I can suffer through that." She scooped up some rice on her fork. "This rice is amazing. What do you do to it?"

"It's a secret. Can't have you stealing my recipe, can I?"

"Oh, right. Like I'm going to take up cooking."

"Good point. Lemon and gin, and I add almonds."

"No kidding. There's gin in here?"

"First, I never joke about food. Second, just a little splash."

"Huh. You're very good with the food thing. And I consider myself kind of an expert. At eating it."

He laughed. "Then I accept the compliment."

They finished the meal and cleaned up, put away the leftovers and washed dishes. Or, rather, she pushed him out of the kitchen while she rinsed and washed, and he went outside to clean off the grill.

Once she was finished in the kitchen, she stepped outside. Owen was just covering the grill. He turned and smiled at her.

"Before the sun goes down, I thought we might take a walk."

"That sounds perfect."

He reached into one of the cabinets on the patio and pulled out some bug spray. It was light and unscented, which she appreciated.

"Can't have the mosquitoes biting on you," he said, then stepped behind her and crouched down to spray the back of her legs.

"No, I definitely don't want to be bitten." Not by mosquitoes anyway.

They headed out beyond the yard with Bettie on their heels. The dog stayed right next to them as they strolled past where the cattle grazed in the pasture. Their gentle mooing was a balm to Honor's normally frenzied, to-do-list-filled brain, allowing her mind to settle as they slowly made their way toward the other side of the road where the horses nuzzled in the grass.

It was so serene here, the orange glow of the setting sun shifting below a bank of clouds, casting a breathtaking purple glow to the horizon. She was so lucky to be able to view that kind of vista. It brought a peace to her soul that she desperately needed. She imagined that was one of the things that appealed to Owen, too.

"I'm so glad you bought this place," she said. "It fits you."

He looked over at her. "Yeah? How so?"

"You always liked open spaces. That's why you were always hanging out at our place when we were kids—it sure wasn't because you liked us girls."

He laughed. "I did like it there a lot. If you remember my house, it didn't have the biggest backyard, and yours was extra large—like endless."

"Yes, it's the best. So when you and Erin got engaged and leased the condo, I just couldn't see the two of you there. I mean, I could see her there, because it was small and efficient, and that suits Erin's sensibilities. But definitely not yours."

"She thought it would be a jumping-off point."

"And you agreed."

He shrugged. "I guess I went along. It didn't seem like a big deal at the time, and I wasn't planning on it being long term."

"But did the two of you ever discuss what would be long term? Did she know you wanted all this acreage?"

"We talked about it. She didn't want cows or horses or a lot of land, that's for sure. It's one of the many things we didn't have in common that we both ignored, hoping it would somehow work itself out."

She cocked her head to the side. "Right. And how did that end up?"

He chuckled. "Yeah, well, everything worked out, didn't it? She's happily married to Jason, the two of them have an amazing house and a couple of great dogs and a decent-sized backyard. Kinda perfect, right?"

For her sister, yes. She had ended up with the right guy after all.

"What about you, though, Owen? Are you happy?"

He slipped his hand in hers. "Right now? I'm walking down the road with the most beautiful woman I've ever known, on land that I own, with my dog by my side. I don't know what could make me any happier."

Her breath caught and it took her a minute to unscramble her thoughts. "Do you always say the right thing?"

"Hey, you know me. I can fuck things up more than anyone. Ask your sister."

She squeezed his arm. "You've got to let that go.

Shove it in the past, where it belongs. She's happy now. And you're happy, too. Time to move on."

"You're right, I guess. But a part of me will always feel like shit for the way I hurt her. It's hard to let go of that."

She wrapped her hands around his arm and leaned against him as they walked. "It's because you care so much. People who care have a difficult time hurting someone. If you were a heartless bastard it would be easy to walk away from what happened and not think twice about it."

"If I weren't a heartless bastard, I wouldn't have done it in the first place."

Honor had no idea that Owen was still dwelling so hard on what he'd done to her sister. And sure, at the time, it had been awful and Erin had been heartbroken and really angry. But once they'd found out his reasons for calling off the wedding and pulling his disappearing act, everyone understood, Erin most of all. Not that they'd agreed it had been the right way to go about it, but no one had stood in his shoes with a cancer diagnosis, either. So how could they judge his actions in the moment? She felt for him, for the ache he'd been carrying.

"It still hurts you, doesn't it? The breakup."

He stilled. "With Erin? No. The pain I caused her and you and your family? Yeah, that hurts. We all used to be so close."

"And we're all close again. No one holds a grudge against you, Owen. You have to know that. To the Bellinis, you're still family and always will be."

"Right. Until they find out I got you drunk and married you in Vegas."

She stopped in the middle of the road and turned to

face him. "Excuse me. But I don't recall you forcing those shots of tequila on me. In fact, if I recall, I was the one who started it."

"I'm still a little fuzzy about that part. I'm pretty sure I suggested the first shot."

"And then I egged us both on to continue."

"So, you got me drunk and took advantage of me."

She rolled her eyes. "I don't think either of us got taken advantage of."

Now his eyes twinkled when he smiled. "Ohhh, now what you're saying is we were secretly hot for each other all along and we couldn't hold back once we got a little alcohol in us."

She leaned forward and tipped her finger down the center of his chest, lingering at his abs. "I don't know, Owen. Just how long have you been hot for me?"

He bridged that short distance between them and tugged her against him. "I can't answer that question on the grounds that it might incriminate me. But I can say that I'm extremely hot for you right now."

They were wading into some dangerous waters. Looking into his eyes, she realized she'd had a profound crush on Owen for a very long time, something she'd never admitted to anyone—including herself—until now. Once he'd decided that her sister had been the one for him, that crush had crumpled and died like a thirsty, unwatered flower. So this grand tease he was doing with her right now had her riled up and turned on in the worst—or maybe the best—kind of way.

It felt good to be wanted. Chosen. Showered with attention.

Loved.

Whoa. No one had said *love*. They were married, but

there was no love in this equation. Love was scary and no one had talked about love.

She needed to keep all of those deeper feelings bundled up and locked inside. She had no idea what was going to happen after the divorce. Maybe they'd just walk away from each other and it'd be the end.

And that'd be okay, because that was the kind of relationship she was used to having.

Fun and done.

That was all they were doing here, and she needed to keep reminding herself of that.

THE MIX OF emotions across Honor's face was a combination of curiosity, desire and confusion. Owen didn't know what to make of it. He also didn't know whether right now, when he was holding her in his arms, was the right time to ask her what was going on in her head. Because she was warm and soft and all he wanted to do was kiss her, and having a deep-dive conversation about her thoughts seemed like a giant mood killer. Probably the right thing to do, but also—mood killer.

Deciding to table that question until later, he cupped the side of her neck and kissed her, and all the angst and doubt fell away. Honor always made the rest of the world disappear, so that it was just the two of them and the way her body felt against his, the sweet taste of her, her lemony scent, all combining to ease away any tension he might feel.

Now all he wanted was to touch her, dive in further and slide his tongue alongside hers, soak in the sounds she made and the soft sensation of her hands gliding up along his arms.

Thunder rumbled, low and menacing, and the flash of lightning off to the east was bright enough to make him pull back from Honor. The wind started to pick up, swirling dust around. Bettie barked and danced around them, sounding out a warning.

"Storm's coming," he said. "We should head back to the house."

She nodded, and they made quick paces toward the yard. By the time they reached the gate, the first drops had started to fall. When they made it to the covered patio, the skies opened, and a deluge of rain came down.

They got inside and Bettie went to her water bowl, got a long drink, then settled on the kitchen floor and passed right out, ignoring the rumbling maelstrom going on outside. Owen fixed them glasses of iced tea and carried one over to where Honor stood looking out the window.

She took a long swallow from the glass, then said, "Great storm."

He watched the skies light up with each crack of lightning while the thunder rolled loud and long. "Yeah, it's pretty impressive. Rain's coming down hard. You might be stuck here."

She turned and tilted her head back, looking up at him, a half smile on her face. "Oh, that would be a shame, wouldn't it? Having to stay here with you all night."

He saw the invitation, felt the vibe between them. It rocked him hard to feel that intimacy. He took the glass from her and laid it on the table next to his, then pulled her into his arms. "Don't worry, I'll take care of you."

She dug her nails into his chest. "I don't doubt it for a second."

His mouth came down on hers and suddenly it was like the storm moved inside the house. They both took and gave as shirts and shoes came off and he could touch her skin, lick her neck, and her hands roamed his body freely, causing his desire to rise just as the storm rose in intensity outside. As pieces of clothing were tossed to the floor, they made their way to the bedroom, never once losing contact with each other, with their mouths fused together as if neither one of them wanted to ever let go.

They were nearly naked by the time they fell onto the bed. Honor still wore her panties and he had one sock still on, which he shoved off with the other foot. He made quick work of her underwear so he could palm her sex. He felt the heat of her as he began to stroke her gently, easing her into a frenzied state as his movements became more focused on her clit. He needed to taste her, so he spread her legs and put his mouth on her, breathing her in, taking a long, slow lick. Her skin was hot, she was wet and she writhed against him, saying words that made no sense, but sounded so damn sexy all the same. She tasted like fire and salty cinnamon, and he'd never wanted a woman more than this one.

He took her right where he wanted her to go—up and over as she rocked against him, letting go with a loud cry. She was beautiful in climax, her body shaking all over as she came.

He was doing a little shaking of his own, and more than a little breathless as he felt her movements. He licked her gently, kissed her thighs and the top of her sex, then climbed up next to her. She rolled over and slid her fingers into his hair and put her lips to his. They didn't say anything to each other as he rolled the condom on. She lifted her leg over his hip and he slid inside her, feeling that connection he'd experienced with her since the beginning. It had always been perfect with Honor, that sense that they belonged together. They just . . . fit.

He grasped her hip and rolled into her, watching her eyes widen, feeling her clutch his shoulders as they moved in unison.

As the storm continued to pound the windows, Owen fought back the one spiraling out of control within him. Touching her, tasting her, had just about done him in. He was close, but he wanted Honor to get there first. And when he felt her tighten around his cock, he gritted his teeth and gave her what she needed. Only when she climaxed did he let go, pulling her against him and grinding against her, holding on to her like he never wanted to let her go.

Because in this moment, he didn't.

Maybe he never wanted to.

He felt the beat of her heart against his chest, fast at first, then regaining normal rhythm. He took a short trip to the bathroom and came back, pulling her right back into his arms.

The storm outside was still heavy. "This could go on all night," he said.

Honor tilted her head back to look at him. "Well, aren't you confident."

He laughed. "I meant the storm."

"Oh. And here I thought you were making some hefty promises."

He bent and pressed a soft kiss to her lips, teasing his

tongue with hers before pulling back. "Hey, I can definitely go all night."

"I'm game if you are."

He slid his hand over her breasts, teasing his fingers down her belly, ready to explore every inch of her that he'd missed the first time. "Game on."

CHAPTER

......

seventeen

I THINK WE'RE going to have a get-together at our house on Sunday to tell everyone about the baby, since there's no wedding scheduled."

Honor looked up at Erin, who was leaning against the doorway. "Really? How exciting. Who are you inviting?"

"The families, of course. And a few friends. Mae, because oh my God it's been so hard not to say anything to her. Jason wants to invite people from work because he keeps stumbling over not telling anyone there. And then let's see, Clay and Alice."

"I know it's been really difficult not to tell Alice."

"You have no idea. Fortunately, she's in and out of town all the time so she hasn't seen my issues with nausea, which are mostly over now, thankfully. Oh, and I definitely want to invite Owen. He'll come, don't you think?"

She felt the flutter in her stomach at the mention of Owen's name. "Of course he will."

"Anyway, we'll have drinks and cook up some food, and then make the big announcement."

"I'm so excited for you, Erin. For you and Jason."

"We're pretty excited, too. You should have seen Jason's eyes light up when he saw the little peanut on the ultrasound. It seriously just looked like a peanut, but he got all teary eyed when he heard the heartbeat."

Honor could feel that love. "Aww. That's so sweet. And the pic of the little peanut is quite adorable."

"True. I can't wait to frame it, which is why it's time for the announcement. Doc says baby looks good and I'm further along than I thought, so we're good to go."

Honor was ecstatically happy for her sister. "I can't wait for the party."

"What party?" Brenna asked as she poked her head in the door.

"At my house on Sunday. We're going to do the pregnancy announcement then."

"Oh. Cool. I assume Finn and I are invited."

Erin nodded. "You assume correctly."

Brenna grinned. "I do love a party."

After they all dispersed to their respective offices, Honor texted Owen to give him a heads-up about the invite. He texted back shortly after.

You're going to be there, right?

She replied with: Of course.

It didn't take him long to send his response: Then I'll be there, too.

She smiled, and there was that warm feeling, the one

that felt as if someone had just covered her with her favorite blanket.

Ridiculous. But there it was, and she wasn't about to try to decipher what it meant.

They were slammed on Friday and Saturday with weddings, so she hadn't had a moment to even breathe. She was exhausted. But by Sunday she was filled with renewed energy, knowing that she was going to get to see Owen. She spent at least an hour showering and shaving and primping, ignoring the fact that this wasn't a big event she should even be fussing over. But she wanted to feel good, so she went with it. She chose a cute sundress since it was hot as Hades today, along with her white sandals. Then she made some sangria, both alcoholic and nonalcoholic since Erin had told her she'd been craving it and she'd decided not to drink alcohol right now. And since one of the veterinarians that Jason worked with was also pregnant right now, as was another vet's wife, it would make perfect sense to have a nonalcoholic sangria, so no one would be suspicious. Perfection.

Once she had packed everything up and put it in her car, she headed over to Erin's house. By the time she arrived, there were already several cars parked in their oversized driveway, and more than a few on the street. She recognized Owen's truck right away—not that she was looking for it specifically or anything.

She was surprised to see him walk out of Jason's open garage. He looked amazing in his shorts and a white T-shirt that clung to his chest. She took a deep breath as she admired his tanned skin and muscles.

"Saw you pull in," he said as he made his way to where she'd parked. "Need any help?"

"Actually, I do," she said as she popped the lid on the trunk, then grabbed her bag from the front seat. "Can you get the cooler back there?"

"Yup." He hefted the cooler with both hands as she followed him into the garage and through the door to the house.

It was nice and cool inside. Erin was in the kitchen looking gorgeous with her hair flowing around her shoulders. She wore a full-length sleeveless maxi dress and sandals. She could swear her sister glowed. Maybe that was what pregnancy did to a person. If it was, then Honor was not pregnant because all she felt was the oppressive heat of impending summer. She was definitely not glowing. Just sweating.

"Where do you want this?" Owen asked.

"On the counter would be great." She smiled at him. "Thanks for bringing it in."

"Hey, no problem." He looked around at the crowd of women in the kitchen. "I'll . . . talk to you later."

She nodded, wishing they could have some alone time, but it wasn't going to happen right now. After he walked out the back door, she went to her sister and hugged her.

"You look breezy and stunning."

Erin grinned. "Thank you. And you look hot as hell, and I don't mean the sweaty kind of hot. I mean, damn, girl. Did you bring a date or something?"

"No. Just me. And thanks."

"You do look amazing," Brenna said as she made her way into the kitchen. "Both of you, actually. You look so fancy. And here I am just in shorts and a tank top."

Honor surveyed her sister, who wore a pair of navy shorts that highlighted her incredible legs. The shorts were complemented by a silky beige sleeveless top. She'd pulled her hair up into a high ponytail and wore her slip-on tennis shoes. Her trademark bracelets were her only jewelry, which was all she needed, since her sister was absolutely beautiful. "You are gorgeous."

Brenna smiled. "I'll take it."

"I think all three of you are beautiful," Alice said as she came over and put her arms around Erin. "And that maxi dress is to die for."

"Thank you. I bought it on our honeymoon, and it's so hot today I just knew it was the perfect day for it. It's loose and comfortable and I'll be able to wear it all through my—"

She stopped, then smiled at Alice. "All through the summer."

Alice nodded. "It is a perfect summer dress. Excuse me, I'm going to go fix something to drink."

Alice wandered off and Erin exhaled. "I'll be happy once I get to make the announcement, so I don't have to keep stumbling over my sentences. Or sucking in my stomach."

"At least you wore the right dress today," Brenna said.

Honor nodded. "Yes, no one can see your bump. When do you plan to announce?"

"As soon as everyone gets here. That way I can relax and enjoy the party. Jason says I've been jittery and cranky the entire week."

Brenna cocked her head. "And have you?"

Erin shrugged. "Probably. I'm not good at keeping secrets."

Honor knew all about the secret thing. The three sisters had always shared everything—all their secrets.

And Honor was keeping a big one from her sisters. Her stomach ached just thinking about it. She wished she could tell them, but the repercussions could be devastating. So despite not wanting to keep her relationship with Owen and their marriage from Brenna and Erin, it was for the best.

And soon enough their marriage would be over, and no one would ever have to know.

That made her stomach hurt even worse. She rubbed her hand across her middle.

"Honor, are you feeling all right?" Brenna asked, a look of concern on her face.

Erin had that same look, and Honor realized she'd been rubbing her stomach. She snatched her hand away.

"Oh, uh, yes, I'm fine. Just hungry. I didn't eat much today and I can already smell whatever Jason's grilling out there."

"Well, come have some snacks." Erin dragged her over to the table where there was an amazing spread of food. A beautiful woman Honor recognized as one of the docs from Jason's practice hovered over the table, her plate loaded with vegetables and some kind of dip. She was very obviously pregnant.

"Oh, hey, Erin. I swear, I can't stop eating this veggie dip. It's amazing."

"Honor, Brenna, do you know Maggie Whitehall? She's a veterinarian at Jason's practice."

"Of course." Honor held out her hand. "We met at Jason and Erin's wedding. It's nice to see you again."

"You, too. Hi, Brenna."

"Hi, Maggie. How's your husband?"

"He's great, thanks. No doubt trying to help Jason at

the grill. I was just telling Francine here that I'm more interested in the food."

"Francine is married to Mike Randall, another vet that works with Jason."

They all made introductions and then Honor put a couple of snacks on her plate. After that, a few other women wandered in and everyone chatted about everything from kids to husbands to fashion.

"Oh," Honor said. "That reminds me. I have sangria in the cooler. Both alcoholic and non. Let me get it out."

Erin went over to help her and soon they were filling glasses with ice and handing them out. Erin grabbed one of the nonalcoholic ones and took a sip.

"Mmm, this is delicious and just what I was craving. Thank you for making these."

Honor made herself a drink of the nonalcoholic variety. "You're welcome."

"Hey, it turned out so well," Brenna said. "We should start making these every night."

Honor thought about all the fruit she'd sliced to make these batches. "Sure. You come over and slice the fruit. I'll pour the wine."

"Oh, you're funny. But since I run the vineyard, how about I choose the wines, and you slice the fruits?"

She pursed her lips and glared at her sister. "You think I can't choose wine? Who just said she loved the sangria? Oh, wait, it was you."

Brenna started to object, then said, "Fine. We'll switch off."

Mae arrived and everyone hugged her.

"Did you come by yourself today?" Brenna asked.

"Yes. Just me."

"Where's the hot guy from our get-together at the Screaming Hawk?" Erin asked.

"Oh, he was just a one-off. Nice, but I don't get involved. And I wanted to free-wheel it today. Just drinks and barbecue with friends, ya know?"

"Do I ever," Honor said, grinning. She wandered off, making her way to the back door where all the guys and some of the women were talking outside. She searched the crowd, immediately spotting Owen talking with Clay and Finn and some guy she didn't recognize. She heaved in a deep breath and sighed.

"Gorgeous, isn't he?"

Her eyes widened as she turned to Erin. "Who?"

"Dave Asher, the new veterinarian they just hired over at Jason's clinic. He's awesome, Honor. Very nice, has two dogs, a house of his own and he's single. Want an intro?"

Oh, hell no. She'd already gone through the fix-up. "You know, I don't think I do. What I do want is a refill on my sangria. How about you?"

Erin looked over her shoulder to Brenna, and she could see the confusion on her sister's face. "No, I'm good, thanks."

She hurried away and poured herself another drink. By then, her sisters were occupied in conversation with Mae and others, so she hightailed it out to the backyard, immediately slammed by heat and humidity. But at least she was away from the fix-her-up sisters.

Where had all these good-looking, available guys been when she'd actually been single? Not that she hadn't dated, because she had. But she'd admittedly picked some not-so-great guys. Now that she was married—okay, technically married—she was suddenly bombarded by very attractive, successful men.

Men she wasn't the least bit interested in. How could she be, when she was married to such a smart, sexy man like Owen?

You do realize you don't get to keep him, right?

She shrugged, as if that motion could get rid of the voice in her head reminding her of the reality she'd just as soon ignore. Instead, she moved around, saying hello to people she knew, taking sips of her drink, engaging in conversations while she gradually made her way toward Owen. Unfortunately, her sisters were also outside now, and Owen was standing with a group that also included Dave, the handsome new vet.

She was about to turn and head in the opposite direction when Brenna grabbed her arm.

"Dave, this is our sister, Honor. Honor, this is Dave Asher."

Shit. She smiled and shook his hand. "Nice to meet you, Dave."

"You, too, Honor." He looked over at Erin. "Wow, what an amazingly beautiful group of sisters. And you all work together?"

"Yes," Erin said. "You'll have to stop by the winery sometime."

Brenna nodded. "That's right. We give tours and our wines are incredible. We have several kinds here today if you want to try some."

"I love wine, I'll definitely do that." He turned to Honor. "What do you do at the winery?"

"I'm the wedding planner and coordinator."

"Oh, yeah? That must keep you busy."

"Very."

"What are you drinking?"

"Sangria. I made some, it's in the house."

"Really? I think I'm going to start out with some of the infamous Red Moss Vineyards wine Jason and Erin have been telling me about. Recommendations?"

"You can't go wrong with any of them, honestly."

"Okay, great. I'll be right back."

"Sure." He had a gorgeous smile, perfect white teeth and incredibly thick dark blond hair. As she watched him walk away, she noticed his muscular build. He was her exact type, and still, she felt . . . nothing.

"Another potential boyfriend?"

She whirled around to see Owen standing behind her. "Another potential fix-up by my sisters."

He rolled his eyes. "Relentless, aren't they?"

She was relieved that he wasn't upset with her, and that he didn't think she was hitting on Dave. "Like you would not believe. I don't know what it is with them lately. They've never tried to fix me up before."

He had maneuvered her out of the sun and toward the shady part of the backyard. "Yeah, but you were typically always dating someone before. Now you're not. They probably think you're lonely."

"That might be it." She sipped her drink. "Maybe I should tell them you need a fix-up."

He looked around, then teased his fingertips along her arm, making chill bumps pop out on her skin despite the heat. "Yeah? You think I need a fix-up?"

"I absolutely do not. I was just joking. Do not give my sisters ideas."

He laughed. "So, you don't want your sisters parading a bunch of gorgeous eligible women in front of me?"

The thought of it made her physically ill. And mightily irritated. "I do not. You are a married man, Owen."

"That's true. Which is why I don't want your sisters fixing my wife up with a different guy every week."

His wife. The words curled around her stomach and traveled upward, settling somewhere in the vicinity of that soft, marshmallowy place in her heart. She reached out and was about to touch him when Jason's voice rang out.

"Okay, so, since everyone's here, I need you all to come inside for a minute."

Owen frowned. "I wonder what this is about?"

She knew, but she couldn't ruin the surprise. "I guess we'll find out."

They followed the crowd into the house and Honor was relieved by the cold blast of the air conditioning.

"Gather round, y'all," Jason said from the living room. "Take a seat if you can find one. Erin and I have something to say."

Jason looked over at Erin, who smiled and said, "First, thank you all for coming. I hope you're enjoying the snacks and drinks. We've wanted to do this for a while now and we're so glad you're all here. Especially since we have some exciting news to share."

You could hear a pin drop, it had gotten so quiet.

Erin looked to Jason, who grinned, then turned to everyone. "We're pregnant!"

"Actually, *I'm* pregnant," Erin said. "He is not."

The whole room erupted in laughter, cheers and applause, and then the couple was surrounded by hugs and kisses.

"Wow," Owen said. "Did you know?"

"I did. But I was sworn to secrecy."

"Can't believe you didn't even tell your husband." He winked at her, then went to join the throng of people congratulating the couple.

Honor stayed back until most everyone had gotten their hugs in, and then she went to hug both Erin and Jason. "You know how happy I am to be an aunt. And so excited about this baby."

Jason couldn't keep the smile off his face. "Thanks. We're just happy Erin and the baby are both healthy, and now we don't have to keep the secret anymore."

"Yeah, man, keeping secrets is hard," Finn said, slinging his arm around Honor's shoulders. "Isn't it?"

Her face flamed hot, but she smiled at Erin and Jason. "I'm sure it was so hard not to scream this thrilling news out to everyone. But now they know and we can all celebrate tonight."

"Speaking of that," Jason said, "I'd better get back to the grill."

Finn kissed her cheek, winked at her and followed Jason out the door.

Owen gave her an apologetic look and went with them.

Erin blew out a breath. "Well. Now that's over with. I need some water and then we'll get the plates and everything else ready. Jason said the chicken and ribs are almost done."

Erin wasn't the only one exhaling. Finn's remark about secrets got to her. At least he was the only one who knew. At least she hoped he was the only one.

He had to be. If he'd told Brenna about it, Brenna would have said something. She'd have more than said something. There likely would have been lectures and yelling. So, no, he hadn't told Brenna. He was probably keeping their secret out of some sort of man code or something.

Whatever. As long as no one found out, they'd be fine.

Just fine.

In the meantime, she was going to enjoy celebrating tonight with her sisters, and not think about anything else. And maybe later she could figure out how to carve out some alone time with Owen.

CHAPTER
. . . . . .
eighteen

IT HAD BEEN awesome getting to hang out with his buds, but what Owen really wanted was some time with Honor. Time he was unlikely to get. He'd barely gotten to talk to her today, since practically everyone they knew was at the party.

So, basically, this whole day had sucked. Okay, maybe it hadn't been entirely bad. There'd been beer and barbecue, and that part had been good. And he'd enjoyed the company of his friends. But he had to watch Honor—from afar—and not touch her, or smell her sweet scent, or kiss her. That part definitely sucked.

He'd thought that maybe somehow he could find a way to steal some time with her, but between hanging with the guys and Honor being surrounded by her friends and sisters, it was like there'd been a wall separating them. If they'd been an official couple, it would have been easy enough to walk over there, put his arm around her and steal a kiss or two, just like the other couples had done.

But no. He'd had to act as if they were just friends and nothing more. He was getting kind of tired of this act, because they were more than just friends. They were married, dammit. He just wanted to be with her.

The party started to break up around eleven and everyone began to head out. He caught sight of Honor packing up her things. She saw him and sent him a regretful look, so he knew she missed him, too.

He said his goodbyes to Jason and Erin, congratulated them again on their good news, then left. But instead of heading back home, he hung out on a side road and waited the appropriate amount of time for Honor to make it home. It was late and maybe he should just go home. But then again, he wasn't one to sit on his feelings, so he sent her a text.

I need to see you.

She replied right away: I want to see you, too. Where?

He thought about it. It was a thirty-minute drive to his place, and it was late. Her place was out of the question since her parents were there. But he had an idea. He sent her the location.

It took her a few minutes to answer, and then she texted back with: I'll be there in ten minutes.

"Oh, yeah," he whispered to himself. Adrenaline pumping, he put his truck in gear and headed out. It didn't take him long to get to the parking area by the lake.

It was a moonless night, which made it an even better night to meet someone in the dark.

He thought about that and laughed out loud. That sounded nefarious, like he was up to no good, when in fact it was more the hot-deeds-in-the-dark scenario that he had in mind.

He saw headlights coming down the road and tensed, hoping no one else was coming. Or, even worse, what if a cop was patrolling the area. Not that he was doing anything wrong. This area didn't close at a certain time so he knew they'd be okay, but it would be nice to not be questioned as to what he was doing there.

Fortunately, Honor's car pulled up alongside his and he exhaled. She got out and climbed into his truck, giving him a spectacular glimpse of her amazing legs. She tossed a bag into the back, closed the door and turned, smiling at him. "What, no movie?"

He laughed. "Damn. I didn't think of that. Let's go—"

She grabbed his hand. "Not a chance. I've waited hours to get my hands on you."

In what he considered one hell of a gymnastic move, she vaulted over the center console and settled herself on his lap, then winced.

"Your steering wheel is hitting my ass."

He reached down and slid the seat all the way back, giving her—and him—more room.

"Mmm," she said, leaning against him. "That's much better."

It sure as hell was. He smoothed his hands over her ribs, grasping her hips. "You feel good—right here."

"I'll feel a lot better once your dick is inside me."

He cocked a brow. "Ma'am. Do you have wicked intentions?"

"Not at all. My only intent is to use my husband for sex. Have you got a problem with that?"

He was already hard and throbbing. "No complaints."

"Good. I brought condoms."

"Multiple? Are we camping out in the truck tonight?"

She shrugged. "Maybe."

"Good thing I have a full tank of gas."

She kissed him, and it was a long session of hot lips and tangling tongues. She tasted sweet, and her movements were urgent as her hands roamed over him and her body undulated against him. The feel of her on top of him made him wish they were somewhere stretched out and naked, so he could put his hands—and his mouth—all over her.

But they'd make do with what they had. And having her on top of him like this? No complaints.

He slid his hands under her dress, surprised but also pleased to discover she'd left her underwear at home. The feel of her soft skin nearly undid him. He swept his fingers across her sex. She arched and moaned, shifting her body backward, giving him access.

"Yeah," he said, lifting her dress over her hips so he could see her. "I know what you need."

He shifted his focus to her face as he slid one, then two fingers inside her, pumping gently in and out of her as he used his thumb to circle her clit. He felt her tighten around his fingers as she rode his hand. Watching her writhe against him was the hottest damn thing he'd ever seen. She was unabashedly beautiful in the way she owned her pleasure, and when she came, she tilted her head back and let out the sweetest sounds.

He could watch her come apart like that all night long.

Except now his balls were throbbing and his dick was painfully hard. He ached to be inside her.

"Condoms are in the bag I threw in the back," she said, her voice a little low and breathless and a lot sexy.

He lifted and pulled one out of the back pocket of his shorts. "I've got it covered."

She let out a short laugh. "What you're saying is you *will* have it covered."

He grinned. She shifted down to his thighs, then shoved his shorts and briefs down his legs before he got the condom on in record time.

"In a hurry?" she asked.

"You could say that."

"Then let's not waste any time." She sank down over his cock, and she was hot and tight, squeezing around his dick. He had to count to ten to keep from exploding right then.

And then he let her lead. He grasped her hips and held on as she rocked against him, settling them both into a rhythm. She was like a wild Valkyrie, riding him across the black night, her hair tossed back as she undulated back and forth, seemingly oblivious to everything but her own pleasure.

"Damn." He watched her ride him, one hand on his chest, the other planted on the ceiling of the truck. Seeing her rise and then sink onto him nearly undid him.

He pulled her close and drew the straps of her dress down, taking a nipple into his mouth to suck, and was rewarded with her low moans. She dug her nails into his shoulders and ground against him, and he arched up into her, feeling her convulse around his cock.

She shifted and took his mouth in a blistering kiss when she came, her entire body quivering against him. That was all it took to make him let go. He erupted in violent spasms, wrapping his arm around her to hold her close while he shuddered through waves of hot pleasure.

Finally, he settled enough to smooth his hands over

Honor's back, to feel the softness of her hair brushing against his cheek, to notice that her whole body had gone lax. It felt good to just hold her like this.

"We've got a problem," she said, lifting her head to look down at him.

"Yeah? What's that?"

"I've gotta pee."

He laughed. "There's a restroom a short walk down the path. I'll take you."

"Okay." She climbed off him and moved to the other seat while he pulled up his shorts, figuring he could dispose of the condom in the men's restroom. They got out of his truck and he grabbed her hand.

"Thanks for showing up," he said.

"Thanks for the amazing orgasms."

He laughed. "Happy to give you one—or two—or more of those anytime."

Her lips curved. "I'm happy to receive them. Multiple ones are the best."

He liked that she was so open about her sexuality, and her enjoyment of it.

They made it to the restrooms and took care of business. A few minutes later he stepped out, waiting for Honor. It had gotten cooler and was getting cloudy. This was the time of year they got a lot of rain, so it wouldn't surprise him to see a storm pop up.

She walked out of the restroom and looked up at the sky. "Smells like rain. Do you need to get home?"

"Probably."

"Too bad. I could have gone a couple more rounds."

He took in a deep breath and let it out. "Now you're just teasing me." He pulled her close. "You could come home with me."

"I could, couldn't I? Then again, I don't think anyone knows I even left the house." She chewed her bottom lip. "And then where would I say I was?"

"You do know you're an adult and don't have to explain your whereabouts to anyone, right?"

She slanted a look at him. "You've met my family, yes? If I don't show up, they'll have me declared a missing person before dawn and the National Guard will be out looking for me. If I text and say I'm spending the night with a friend, Mom will have the entire family assembled at the table for breakfast and a full interrogation."

Not having that kind of family, Owen didn't understand them being in Honor's business. But having grown up around the Bellinis, he knew it all came from a place of love. And, okay, they could be a little overly nosy, too. He'd gone through that when he'd first started dating Erin, but he'd adjusted.

Until he'd blown everything up and hurt Erin. Then it had taken a while for him to earn his way back into the family's good graces. He couldn't imagine how they would feel if they ever found out he was married to Honor.

"You're right," he said as they made their way back to their vehicles. "But I still don't like that we can't tell anyone we're seeing each other."

"I don't like it, either. Maybe when this is all over— this whole being-married thing, we can figure something out. I just want to get past this possible pregnancy and accidental-marriage thing first, you know?"

"Yeah." He understood where she was coming from. There was still so much up in the air. But what he did know was that he didn't want to walk away from Honor.

Thunder rumbled in the distance. He knew their time together was coming to an end, and he hated it.

She moved into him, threading her arms around his neck and tilting her head back. "In the meantime, it's kind of hot to have these secret meetings, isn't it?"

He smiled down at her. "I have zero complaints about tonight."

"Me, either. Now kiss me before it pours down on us."

He kissed her. Whenever he kissed Honor, it could never be simple or fast. It was slow, and hot, and he ended up pushing her against the door of his truck so he could press his body against hers. She made all kinds of sounds and tangled her fingers in his hair and he swore to God if he could have one wish right now, it would be to take her home so she could sleep in his bed tonight. Though he knew there would be no sleeping.

But that wouldn't be fair to Honor, because she was the one who'd have to answer all of her family's questions, so he stepped back, took her hand and walked her over to her car.

"You press me up against my car and kiss me like that again, we're going to camp out here for the night and I'm going to use your dick until you can't walk."

His balls quivered at the thought. "Tempting. But you're going home. And so am I. And we'll both suffer."

She wrinkled her nose. "Fine. Not my preferred option, but of course you're right."

He grabbed her tote bag from the back seat of his truck and handed it over to her. "What's in here anyway?"

"Condoms. Hand sanitizer. A towel. Some water. Chips. M&Ms."

He nodded. "A most excellent sex bag."

"I try to be prepared."

"Well, hang on to it for, you know, next time."

"I'll do that."

He leaned in and brushed his lips across hers, very lightly and briefly this time. "See you soon."

She tipped her fingertips across his lips. "I hope so."

She slid into her car and he watched her back up and drive away before he climbed into his truck. He blew out one long, frustrated breath, then headed for home.

CHAPTER
......
nineteen

Honor was knee-deep in satin, lace and tulle as she did her best to calm a very stressed-out bride who needed some last-minute alteration, which she was happy to provide. Not the first time she'd had to dive under a wedding dress and repair a hem, but still, it made for an incredibly busy day. She was always prepared for a hectic wedding, except that the entire week had been this way. She'd had meetings with prospective wedding couples the past four days, along with a rehearsal dinner at the barn Friday afternoon, followed by a small wedding last night and now a big event tonight.

She'd be so happy once this weekend was over.

At least she had tomorrow off. It was Memorial Day weekend and she'd promised Owen she'd help him plan the party at his ranch. So after the wedding tonight she was going to have to drag out her planner and make sure everything on her to-do list for tomorrow was set.

As she helped Abigail, the bride-to-be, calm her pre-wedding jitters with some slow and deep breaths, Honor also took some calming breaths herself.

She left Abigail in the very capable hands of Mae and the mother of the bride, then dashed out to the barn to ensure that the decorations were all in order. They were, thanks to Erin. Brenna had the wine covered, of course, and was barking out orders left and right if something wasn't absolutely perfect. Everything was under control, so Honor hurried over to the vineyard. The flowers on the arbor looked spectacular. All the chairs had been arranged just as the bride and groom wanted. Catering had just arrived, so she directed them where to set up. She was about to make her way back to the bride when she spotted Owen's truck parked in front of the house. Her heart skipped a beat and she thought about heading over there, but she didn't have time. The wedding was set to start in fifteen minutes and the last thing she needed was to hike up Abigail's stress level all over again, so despite her curiosity, she made her way over to the bridal room.

Fortunately, the wedding ceremony was perfect, Abigail and Jeff were all smiles and love, and Honor could finally exhale because the bride and groom were happy. After the ceremony, the guests made their way to the barn for refreshments. The wedding party was having pictures taken by the awesome photographer, whom Mae was overseeing, so Honor took a minute to dash to the house for some much-needed air conditioning and a quick glass of something cool to drink.

She ran into Owen in the kitchen, downing a glass of lemonade. Louise wasn't in there, and neither were her parents.

"What are you doing here?" she asked, simultaneously filling her own glass with lemonade and copious amounts of ice.

"I went fishing this morning and caught a lot of trout, so I thought your mom and dad might like some."

"Oh. Well, that was nice." She took two large swallows of the sweetly tart lemonade, which didn't help at all to cool her down—not when she stood in the same room as Owen.

He inched over to where she stood. "Why? Did you think I came by to see you?"

"Did you?"

He shrugged. "Maybe. But not really. I knew you'd be busy. But I thought I might catch a glimpse. You look pretty today."

Warmth curled around her lower belly. "Thank you. You look hot and sweaty."

He grinned. "Yeah, I need a shower. I smell like fish. Otherwise I'd kiss you."

She reared back, then peeked around the doorway before giving him a warning look. "You would not. My parents are here. Somewhere."

He laughed. "You gotta live a little, Honor. Take a few chances."

He leaned in and, okay, what harm would a short kiss do? She so wanted to kiss him.

"Oh, hey, Owen. I didn't know you were here."

Honor almost dropped her glass of lemonade. She moved a few feet away from Owen.

"Hey, what's up, Brenna?" Honor asked, turning toward her sister. "Is there a problem?"

Brenna frowned at Honor. "No. I'm just here to do exactly what you're doing."

"What? I'm not doing anything. Just having some

lemonade. Owen brought over some trout. He went fishing today."

Brenna went to the fridge and grabbed the lemonade while continuing to stare at Honor. "Uh, okay. Why are you being weird?"

"I'm not being weird. I should go."

Brenna shrugged and turned her attention to Owen. "Trout, huh? That sounds great. Are you saving some for the party tomorrow?"

"Yeah. I've got quite a bit. Gonna put it in the smoker."

"Sounds amazing. I've got an arugula salad recipe that would go really well with that."

She left Brenna and Owen talking, shooting Owen a quick, apologetic smile before sliding out the back door.

Her heart beat like the wings of wild butterflies as she made her way to the barn. Why was it that every time she saw Owen, she was either utterly panicked or completely turned on, and no matter which situation she found herself in, she was completely unable to focus her brain cells?

She was going to have to figure out how to maintain her cool while keeping this secret, or before long she was going to self-combust.

And maybe it was more than the secret that was making her brain cells go haywire. It was seeing Owen, talking to Owen, touching Owen. When she wasn't with him, she wanted to be. And when she was with him it made her so happy.

What do we call that, Honor? Is that love?

She shook her head and picked up her pace, refusing to even consider the possibility.

Today she had a bridal party to attend to, and she intended to focus all her attention on her job. Tomorrow, she'd worry about how to handle her growing feelings.

CHAPTER

······

twenty

OWEN WAS TYPICALLY a chill kind of guy. He didn't worry about the minutiae of things like whether he had enough cups for beer. He ran a craft brewery. Of course he had enough cups for the beer.

Honor, on the other hand, had made a checklist, because that was her thing, and if it made her happy to do that, he wasn't going to get in her way.

"Okay, we've got tables, chairs, cups, plates and utensils. People are bringing side dishes. We've also got plenty to drink with wine, beer, water and pop, along with iced tea, both sweet and unsweet, and lemonade."

He watched as she focused on the list like this was some important event instead of a casual backyard get-together. Which was why he'd asked her to help, since he'd likely have forgotten something important.

She looked up from her list. "Did you remember to get the vegan stuff?"

He nodded. "Meatless burgers will be offered for our vegetarian and vegan friends."

She smiled and put a checkmark on her list. "Awesome."

He watched as Bettie stood at attention at Honor's side, as if she, too, was prepared with her own list. Said list probably included digging more holes in the backyard, something Owen had spent all of yesterday filling in.

"I also made a couple of vegan side dishes," he said.

"You did? When did you have time for that?"

He slid his arm around her. "They weren't hard. And we'll have a few salads here as well, but some salad dressings aren't vegan, and I want to cater to everyone."

She reached up and smoothed her hand across his jaw. "It's nice that you think of others."

"I try." She smelled like lemons, making him want to lick her neck. He leaned in and—

"Oh." She moved toward the door to survey the backyard. "We should put those umbrellas over the tables to shield people who don't want to be in the sun."

Damn. Thwarted by the to-do list. "I'm on it."

"Good. You do that and I'm going to call Brenna. I forgot something at home that I need her to bring."

"Okay." He went outside and took care of the umbrellas over the round tables, then made sure to walk the yard and check for Bettie's handiwork. So far so good. It was warm today, but he'd gotten lucky and the weather had cooled down some overnight, so it wasn't unbearable. He hoped it was going to be a great day, since this was his first party at the ranch.

Once he finished setting up, he went inside, dashed into the bedroom to change into a nonsweaty pair of shorts and a white tee, and then came back out to see that Jason and Erin had arrived, along with Honor's parents, Maureen and Johnny.

"Nice place," Johnny said. "How are your ponies?"

It was a known fact that Johnny Bellini was a lover of horses. "They love the land. You'll have to check out the corral and the barn while you're here."

Johnny nodded. "Si. You know I will."

Owen saw some people arriving through the gate. "I see we have some other guests. Excuse me."

"Go ahead," Honor said. "I'll take care of things in here."

"Thanks." He liked knowing Honor was there, handling everything, acting as his unofficial partner today. He wondered if anyone would notice that.

He wasn't too worried about it.

He just had to convince Honor that it was time to let other people see them together.

OKAY, FOOD WAS cooking, snacks were on the tables and wow, what a crowd had gathered. Honor was impressed. Her entire family was there, and many of their friends, too. Several of the people Owen worked with at the brewery were here as well. It was one hell of a party.

Bettie was ecstatic since Owen had told everyone that their pets were invited. Which meant it was a free-for-all of dogs. Murphy, Homer, Puddy and Agatha were all bounding outside the backyard with Bettie, who was currently demonstrating how to bark at the cattle.

The cattle had gathered at the fence, seemingly bemused by so many dogs.

"Do you think they're unhappy?" Honor asked as Owen came over to stand next to her.

"Nah. They're curious."

"Hey, you two," Mae said as she walked outside,

hand in hand with yet another new guy Honor had never met before. "This is my friend Jameson. Jameson, this is Honor Bellini and Owen Stone, who owns this awesome ranch."

Jameson, tall and muscular, was utterly gorgeous and had the most amazing smile. "Nice to meet you both. Thanks for the invite."

Owen shook his hand. "Great to meet you, too. Any friend of Mae's is a friend of ours. What do you do, Jameson?"

"I'm a personal trainer. How about you?"

"I own the Screaming Hawk craft brewery."

"Oh, cool. I just moved here about a month ago and haven't been there yet. I'm a big fan of craft beers."

"I have a couple of kegs here. You wanna try some?"

"Love to." Jameson turned to Mae. "I'll be right back."

Mae smiled at him. "I'll be around."

Honor caught sight of the quick smile Owen sent her way before he disappeared outside.

"Well," Honor said, turning to Mae. "He's hot. And seems very nice."

She shrugged. "He's definitely hot. But he's just a date. And yes, he's nice. But I'm not looking for a relationship. Right now, I'm enjoying making my way through the alphabet of available men."

Honor laughed. "It's a very attractive alphabet."

"Indeed it is," Mae said with a satisfied sigh. "How about you? Did you bring someone with you today?"

"Oh, uh, no. I've been so busy I kind of forgot."

Mae tilted her head down and pinned Honor with a look. "You forgot. About men."

Excuses on the fly never worked. "That wasn't exactly what I meant. It's been busy, what with wedding season being so hectic, and then I helped Owen plan this event today. It's like nonstop events. Who has time to find a guy, am I right?"

"Uh-huh. You've also turned down every guy your sisters have tried to set you up with. And from what I saw, they were a couple of fine-looking specimens."

"Okay, fine. I'm just not . . . in the mood."

Mae snorted. "In the mood for what, exactly? A nice dinner? A movie? Some conversation? Blow-your-mind sex?"

Dammit. Mae was too smart. "Maybe my priorities are a little out of whack. I'll work on it."

"Funny you should say that, because I know this amazing guy. He works with Jameson at the gym, and girl, he is incredible. Super nice and respectful, broke off with his last girlfriend about six months ago, so he's over her, you know what I mean? He's dated a little here and there, but he's not burning up the sheets or anything. He really wants to settle down and find some stability."

Oh, crap. Now what was she supposed to say?

"Let me think about it."

"What's there to think about? Oh, other than the fact that you're already burning up the sheets with Owen so you're not interested in any other guys."

She momentarily lost the ability to form words. And maybe breathe. Okay, Honor, think. Deny. "What? How . . . I mean, *pfft*, of course not. What would make you think that?"

Mae rolled her eyes. "Anyone who pays attention can see what's going on with the two of you, especially when you're in a room together. It's . . . sparky."

"Sparky?"

"Yeah . . . like someone lit a fire in the room. Very hot, Honor."

She had no idea. "Has anyone else said anything? Noticed it?"

"No one's said anything to me. And I haven't said a word to anyone else, so don't worry about it."

Maybe Mae was the only one who'd noticed it. She thought they'd been careful—they *had* been careful.

"So . . . are you gonna tell me what's going on?"

She took a deep breath and blew it out. "It's complicated."

"Why? Because of Erin?"

"Yeah." Among other reasons.

Mae waved her hand back and forth. "Ancient history, don't you think? She's happy and she's moved on."

Honor would like to think so. But there was also the huge issue of having accidentally gotten married. At least Mae didn't know about that. "Maybe. I don't know. We're just keeping it under wraps, for now."

"Up to you. I won't say anything. But wouldn't it be easier if you just told people?"

"Yes. Maybe. I'll think about it."

Mae put her arm around Honor's shoulders. "Honey, relationships aren't supposed to be this hard. You like him, right?"

It was getting to be much more than like, and that was what scared her. "Yes."

"Then talk to him, and work it out so you can be free to just be a couple, if that's what you both want."

"I'll do that. Thanks, Mae."

"Hey, I want all my friends to be happy."

They made their way outside where everyone was hanging out. They'd gotten so lucky to end up with a beautiful day. It wasn't too hot, and there was a nice breeze and even partial cloud cover, with no rain in sight. She'd so wanted this day to go well for Owen, who seemed relaxed and happy and in his element. Then again, this was what he did for a living. He loved being around people, hanging out, serving beer and talking. Right now he stood at the grill, flipping chicken and drinking a beer while simultaneously having conversations as people walked by.

He was good with people. There was never a lag in conversation no matter who he was talking to. It was something Honor was adept with as well, considering her own line of work.

It also helped that she genuinely liked people and found all their unique personalities utterly fascinating. Even a difficult bride or a pesky mother-in-law didn't ruffle her feathers. She knew tensions were high on a wedding day, and it was her job to make people relax. A smile and a little reassurance often went a long way.

She imagined Owen often got an earful at the pub, listening to people vent about work or relationships. He was probably good at listening to them. He always listened to her.

He glanced her way while he refilled his beer, smiling at her in that particular way that always set her heart fluttering.

What would it feel like to be able to walk over to him, lean against him and brush her lips to his? To be that comfortable and not have to worry about what her family and friends might think or who might be hurt?

Maybe she and Owen needed to have a discussion about that, because right now all she wanted to do was be near him. She inhaled a deep breath of fresh air, wishing it were his scent against her nose. Though the barbecue smelled good, too. She'd wager if she slipped her nose into his neck right now, he'd retain some of that smoky scent as well.

Now she really needed to get closer to him. And why couldn't she do that? After all, even Erin had wandered over to talk to him. If she could, Honor could as well. She stopped and talked with Clay and Alice, along with her parents, then casually drifted over to the grills where Owen was chatting with Finn and Brenna.

"How's it going over here?" she asked.

"Pretty good," Owen said, giving her what she thought was his best friends-only smile. "The chicken and ribs are nearly ready, and the trout has been in the smoker all day, so it's done."

"My stomach is gnawing with hunger. Everything smells so good," Brenna said. "I've already had enough snacks, so I'm resisting diving in for more."

"It does smell delicious." She leaned in toward the grill, but more in the general direction of Owen. "Yes, it's intoxicating."

But she was looking at Owen when she said it, and this time his smile was hot and directed at her. Which didn't help her feelings of longing at all.

But Brenna and Finn had wandered off, which meant they could at least have a semiprivate conversation.

"I need to touch you," she said. "Maybe kiss you."

"Same. How about while everyone's eating, we sneak away and find some alone time?"

"That sounds like a great idea."

"What sounds like a great idea?"

She looked up to find her mother standing there.

"Honor offered to mix up some barbecue sauce,"

Owen said. "She mentioned something about trying out a new recipe."

Her mother's brows shot up. "Honor. Has a recipe for sauce. That she's going to make."

"Sure I do," Honor said, hoping like hell she could Google something amazing that was also simple.

"Okay." Her mother shook her head and wandered off.

Honor punched Owen in the arm.

"Ow." He rubbed his arm. "What was that for?"

"You know I don't cook."

"Don't stress about it. I made sauce last night. It's in the container on the top shelf in the fridge."

"You'd allow me to take credit for your homemade sauce?"

He laughed. "Of course I would."

"I'd kiss you right now if there weren't thirty people around us."

"I can wait a while for that kiss. But not too long."

A couple of the guys wandered over, and her mother was giving her a curious look, so she went inside and hid in the kitchen for what she figured was a respectable amount of time to have made up some barbecue sauce. Then she wiped down the counter and turned on the water in the sink, washed her hands. Just in time, too, because Mom, Erin and Brenna walked in.

"Don't tell me we missed it," Erin said.

Honor wiped her hands on the towel, then turned around. "Missed what?"

"Mom said you were cooking." Brenna frowned. "I said you bought sauce at the store and you'd dump the jars in the container."

"Oh, ye of little faith. It's homemade sauce and it's in the fridge. And, yes, you missed it."

"So when did you start cooking?" Mom asked. "Because you've never even stepped foot in the kitchen before, unless it's to taste something Louise was making."

"I've been dabbling here and there. When you and Louise were on vacation. I figured that was a good time to start." She couldn't believe how good she was getting at lying. Not exactly a virtuous undertaking on her part. She could only hope no one asked her to actually cook anything. Then they'd know she was full of shit.

"Okay, then," Mom said. "Let's taste it."

She lifted her chin. "It's not ready yet. It has to sit for a while for the flavors to . . . meld together."

"Makes sense," her mom said. "I'm looking forward to it."

Fortunately, Owen came in and waved at them. "The meat's ready, so we're about to start serving. I could use some help with the sides if you don't mind."

She was relieved that all talk of barbecue sauce was shut down. They got the side dishes and toted them outside to the two tables, along with condiments, including the barbecue sauce she had not made.

After that, people lined up and started filling their plates. Honor stepped aside, murmured to her sister that she was going inside to grab some ice and lemonade, and made a mad dash for Owen's bedroom.

She walked into the bathroom and washed her hands, looked in the mirror and finger-combed her hair. She heard the door open and close and she stepped out of the bathroom. The first thing she did was walk up to him and press her face into his neck.

Mmm. Smoky, just as she'd imagined. She tilted her head back. "You smell good."

He put his hands on her hips. "You feel good. Bet you taste good, too."

Then his mouth was on hers, and it fired up all the hot passion she'd been trying so hard to contain. He walked her backward until her knees hit the bed, and they both fell onto the mattress, his body on top of hers. Desire coiled within her and she reached up to slide her fingers in his hair, moaning when he raised his leg, his thigh rubbing against her sex.

The door opened and she heard Erin's voice.

"Honor, are you in—"

Owen rolled off her and bolted upright. She sat up on the edge of the bed, pushing her dress down.

Erin stared at them. "What the hell is going on here?"

Oh, crap.

CHAPTER

······

twenty-one

OWEN'S FIRST REACTION was to step in front of Honor, to shield her from her sister, who had a look of shock on her face.

"Erin, I can explain," Owen said.

Then Honor slipped in front of him. "No, let me explain."

But Erin held up her hand. "Just . . . don't."

She closed the door, leaving the two of them alone.

He turned to Honor, who looked pale and upset. "Are you okay?"

"No, I'm not okay. She's probably off telling my family right now. And then everyone here will know."

Shit. "I'll go handle this."

"Handle it in what way? What exactly are you going to say?"

"I don't know." He dragged his fingers through his hair. "I'll figure it out."

"No. We'll figure it out. We got into this together, we'll explain it together."

He nodded. "That works."

She started for the door, but he grabbed her hand. "Honor. It's going to be all right."

"Is it?"

"Yeah." He pulled her against him and held her. Her body was tense. He understood why. He was the reason for a lot of the angry responses they were likely about to get. He would try his best to take the brunt of it so Honor wouldn't have to.

"We should go," she said.

"Okay." He didn't want to let go of her.

But he did, and she walked out. He took a second to catch his breath, then he stepped outside.

It was Jason that waved him over to the table. "Hey, Owen. This trout is amazing. And, okay, the sausage is, too."

"He didn't mention the chicken only because he hasn't dug into it yet," Finn added.

"Yeah," Clay said. "But as you can see, we've all piled onto our plates. Good food, man."

"Thanks. I'm glad you like it."

No questions or accusations about Honor. No one staring at him like he'd just committed the crime of the century. He looked across the tables at Honor, who was sitting with Mae and Brenna. She shrugged and sent him a questioning look.

He searched the crowd and spotted Erin sitting at a table with a few of his friends from the brewery. She was calmly eating, chatting and most definitely not making eye contact with him or with Honor.

Huh. He wasn't about to question her reaction. Not right now, anyway. He grabbed a plate and put some food on it, found himself a place to sit and eyed Erin warily while he shoved food into his mouth, all the while feeling like there was a ticking time bomb in his yard, just waiting to go off.

HONOR CHEWED NUMBLY, not even tasting the food that she was certain was absolutely delicious.

"It's great, isn't it?" her mom asked. "There was so much food to choose from I couldn't put it all on the plate."

"Yes, it's so good."

"And yet you're moving it all around on the plate like they're puzzle pieces. What's wrong?"

She laid her fork down and smiled at her mom. "I nibbled at everything beforehand, so now I'm full. And nothing's wrong."

"Really. Did you have a fight with Erin, Honor? Because she's sporting the same grumpy face that you are."

She glanced across the yard to where Erin sat. She did not look happy and was on her phone, typing. Honor hoped it wasn't a family group text announcing that she'd caught Honor in bed with Owen.

Her face flamed just thinking about it. Though why should she feel guilty when she hadn't done anything wrong?

Other than lying to her family for weeks.

Okay, there was that.

Her phone pinged. Her mom's phone pinged, too. Honor felt faint.

She picked up her phone, and, sure enough, it was the family group text, and the text was from Erin. Honor was surprised she'd even been included.

Need to talk to all of you after the party. It's
important. How about we meet at our house?

She started seeing replies from Dad, Mom, Brenna
and Finn.

"You're coming, aren't you?" Mom asked.

Not knowing how to answer, Honor stood. "I'll be
right back."

She knew it was rude to walk away from her mother,
but she was at a loss for words, and a little bit panicked.

She needed to talk to Owen.

She found him inside putting away some of the leftovers. She grabbed his arm and dragged him down the
hall. "We need to talk."

They ended up in the guest bathroom.

She locked the door and immediately realized it was
a tight squeeze. "Okay, this won't arouse suspicion or
anything," he said.

"Fine. Not the best idea, but this won't take long.
Erin sent out a family text for all of us to meet at her
house after the party."

"So you think since she didn't say anything here,
she's going to make a family announcement about us at
her house? That doesn't sound like Erin."

Honor shrugged. "What else could it be about?"

He leaned against the wall. "I don't know. Anything?
Maybe she bought a new rug for the living room and
wants to show it off."

She cocked her head to the side. "Owen, really. This
is serious."

"Fine. So what do you suggest?"

"I don't know." She chewed on her bottom lip, hoping

for some magical solution to this dilemma. "I suppose I could tell Mom."

"Or we could tell people we're together."

Which was what she'd been thinking about as well. But right now she was filled with regret and guilt, and announcing her marriage to Owen? Talk about worst timing ever.

"I don't know, Owen. I think telling everyone we're married right as Erin found us together could really hurt her."

"I've got a better idea. Come with me." He took her hand and left the bathroom.

She tried to tug her hand away, but he had a firm grip and wouldn't let go. And with every step they took toward the backyard, her panic rose higher and higher.

They stepped outside.

"Hey, everyone. I have something to say."

The crowd was loud; Owen, however, was louder, so everyone quieted and turned their attention on him. And on her. And the fact that they were holding hands.

"Honor and I are dating. And there's dessert in the kitchen, so help yourselves. I've already tried the chocolate mint cupcakes and they're awesome."

She was going to die of mortification right there on Owen's back porch.

CHAPTER

······

twenty-two

OKAY, SO EVERYONE stared at them—for about ten seconds. Then people got up and headed toward the kitchen. After all, dessert was way more important than Owen's dating life. Though Finn stopped to pat him on the back and mumble, "I sure hope you know what you're doin', bro."

He had no idea what he was doing. He was just trying his best to protect Honor from the onslaught of family drama.

A few people stopped to congratulate them. Honor was great about it, accepting the hugs. No one questioned them or asked for any details. And her family steered clear, her parents and sisters huddled up together at a table.

Jason and Clay came over, though. Jason hugged Honor, then held out his hand to Owen. "I'm shocked. You and Honor, huh?"

Owen shrugged. "It just . . . happened. Kind of suddenly."

"Hey, if you two are happy, then I'm happy. Have fun with each other."

Owen grinned. "We are."

"Thanks, Jason," Honor said.

"I like that you're keeping it in the core group," Clay said. "I was getting kind of tired of vetting those losers you've been dating, Honor."

She shot Clay a look. "Hey."

Clay laughed. "Just kidding. Mostly. Not really. They were bad, honey."

"Don't you have some dessert to get to?"

"Now that you mention it . . ."

They wandered off, leaving Honor and Owen alone.

She turned to face him. "I can't believe you did that. You didn't even talk to me first."

"We did discuss it. You said you didn't want to tell everyone we were married."

She cocked her head to the side. "So you decided—on your own, by the way—to tell everyone we were dating. Which we aren't. Not really, anyway."

"Well, I guess we can now."

He could tell from the irritated look on her face that maybe they should have talked this out a bit more. But he'd had enough of the two of them hiding in the shadows. "And this big meeting at Erin's later. You knew that was going to be about you and me. I figured announcing it before Erin had the chance to drop a bomb on everyone was the smartest thing to do."

She gave him a pained look, then said, "I guess you're right, but now my family's all staring at us."

He took her hand. "Then let's go answer any questions they have."

She tugged on his hand to stop him and he turned to

reassure her. "Look, I know it's complicated, Honor. We'll figure it out. One step at a time, right?"

She nodded. "Right. Dating. Just dating."

"Yeah, right."

He just wanted her to be okay. Married or not, she was his to protect, and he planned to do that no matter what, even if it meant protecting her from her own family. Though he doubted it would come to that. Surely, they couldn't be upset about the two of them dating, could they?

They made their way to the table, where everyone suddenly went silent.

Owen slid into a seat. Honor stood.

"Honor, sit down," her mother said, so she took the seat next to Owen.

"How long have you two been seeing each other?" her father asked, his attention focused solely on Owen.

"Not long. About a month."

"And why didn't you tell us?" Maureen asked, her focus on Honor.

"Because if we were just going to go out once or twice, I didn't want it to be a whole third-degree thing, like it is right now."

"Obviously it's more than that, though, isn't it? I mean, a month is a long time for you, Honor."

"Thanks for that, Brenna," Honor said, shooting her sister a scathing look.

"I didn't mean it that way. I only meant that with your dating record and all . . ."

"I get what you meant."

"It's the truth, though," Erin added. "Most of your relationships burn out after a week or two."

Tension rolled off Honor in waves. He could feel it,

and could see the way her shoulders rose toward her neck. He wanted to reach out and rub away the stress he knew she was feeling.

"Well, this time is different. Owen and I are—"

Everyone looked at her and for a second there, Owen thought that maybe she'd tell them about Vegas.

"You're what?" Erin asked, her voice tight.

She finally gave a nonchalant shrug. "We're having a good time together, and I wanted to keep that to myself for a while."

Erin stood. "I can't believe this. I can't believe you're going out with him. Of all the guys, Honor."

Honor laid her hands on the table and leaned toward the opposite side. "Why should it matter who I date?"

Owen knew why it mattered. Because it was him.

"Normally it wouldn't," Erin said. "But you know why this matters."

Now Jason stood. "Wait a minute. Why *does* this matter, Erin?"

Erin flipped her attention to her husband. "Because . . . because . . . it just does. You know what happened with Owen and me."

"Yeah. But it's over now and I thought that was all behind us."

"Well, maybe it's not."

Shit. Owen's stomach sank. "Erin, do we need to talk about this?"

"You and I do not need to talk about anything. How dare you date my sister?"

Now Maureen stood. "That's enough, Erin. You can sit down."

"I'm not sitting down. I'm leaving."

She walked away, storming through the yard and into the house.

"I'm really sorry," Jason said, giving them both a sympathetic grimace before going after Erin.

"Well, this was a hell of a day," Brenna said. She walked over to Honor and folded her into her arms. "I'm here for you, no matter what."

Finn patted him on the back.

"Let's go get some dessert," Brenna said. "Family arguments make me hungry."

Finn snickered and they walked away.

Honor's parents got up next. Johnny left without saying anything, which pained Owen more than he could say. Losing his relationship with Johnny after he and Erin had broken up had been one of his greatest hurts. It had taken a lot for them to make amends, and he'd felt such relief when things had gotten back to normal. Now it felt like they were back to square one.

"We'll figure it all out," Maureen said. "I just wish you had said something to me, Honor."

And then they left.

Owen couldn't have fucked this up more if he'd planned it. And now Honor looked miserable and unhappy and completely broken.

He shifted in his chair to face her. "I'm sorry."

"It was bound to happen. There was no way to tell them that wasn't going to upset someone."

"I get Erin being upset," he said. "Though I don't know why she's so angry."

"Me, either. I'll talk to her."

"No, I will. I'm the one who broke her heart. It should be me."

Honor shook her head. "Honestly, I think a little distance is probably the best right now."

He didn't like the direction this conversation was going. "Distance from . . . the family?"

"No, you and me. I need some time to think, Owen. To process all of this and come up with a plan."

"Which we should do together, don't you think?"

She shook her head. "I just need some space. This was a lot. My family is really shaken up right now, and I'm responsible for it."

He reached for her hand. "You didn't do this alone. We did it together. So we'll figure out a solution together."

She went silent for a minute, and he gave her that time to wind through her thoughts. Finally, she lifted her head and he saw tears shimmering in her eyes. He hated that he'd put them there.

"Just give me a few days, okay?"

He'd never deny her what she needed. "Sure."

But he worried that the more time they spent apart, the more she might realize she was better off without him.

And it would also give the family more time to convince her of the same thing.

Maybe they should have continued to keep their relationship a secret, because he might have just screwed up the best thing that ever happened to him.

CHAPTER

······

twenty-three

Meetings for the past week had been tense. Honor had never felt more uncomfortable at work—which was also home. The family had clearly taken sides in the Honor-versus-Erin battle, and every day that passed made Honor more upset.

Erin had been quiet and sullen, and while Honor had done her best to understand her reasons for it, she wished they could talk things through. But she couldn't ask her sister any questions, because she and Erin were barely on speaking terms. Erin only broke her frosty silence when it was absolutely necessary to discuss something work-related. Now, as they all sat at the dining room table, no one said a word. There was a lot of shuffling of papers and typing on laptops and phones. Normally, they'd all be catching up and talking over each other. Instead, there was just painful silence.

It was brutal.

At first Mae, who always attended the meetings, had

tried making small talk, but no one took the bait. Then even the always-cheerful Mae had fallen into the same routine of uncomfortable silence.

Mom cleared her throat. "Erin, would you like to start the meeting?"

Erin looked up from her laptop, a flat expression on her face. "Fine. Honor, the budget for the Xavier/Latham wedding isn't finalized yet."

Honor went to her spreadsheet and pulled up the wedding details. "We're still waiting on a quote for floral and cake. I should have cake in by next week. One of our grooms, Max, is undecided about which floral setup he wants. He's changed his mind about their choice, and he and our other groom, Brandon, would like to peruse other floral options. We're meeting with Florals by Beth on Thursday, who I think would be a great fit for their wedding."

Erin was making notes in her laptop. "We're just about to hit the five-month mark on their wedding date. We should be finalizing all sections."

"I've got it covered."

Erin made another note. "I'll follow up in a week on that wedding. Next up is the Barnett/Green wedding. They're late paying their deposit. It was due two weeks ago. I assume you'll contact them about it? You told me in last week's meeting you were going to discuss it with them when you met with them to go over invitations."

Honor had extensive notes that she kept for every meeting, so she pulled them up. "And then you said to forget it, you'd contact them before more time passed."

Erin perused her laptop. "Hmm. I don't recall having that discussion and it's not in my notes. You must be mistaken."

"Well, I was in that meeting and you did say that, Erin," Brenna said. "It's in my notes, too."

Honor resisted a smile, while Erin flat-out looked irritated.

And poor Mae just sat back, made notes and stayed quiet. She'd known the family for years, but Honor was sure that Mae was wildly uncomfortable to be sitting in the middle of this war zone.

"Maybe you just forgot to add that notation, Erin," their mother said. "You know how our meetings go. There are always so many details flying back and forth."

"Hmmm. Maybe." Erin frowned at her laptop, clearly flummoxed.

"Anyway," Mom said, waving her hand. "I can follow up on that item. I need to have a discussion with them about another financial matter anyway."

Honor looked to her mother. "What detail is that, Mom?"

"Oh, nothing for you to concern yourself with."

"Actually, every wedding detail is something I concern myself with."

"Not this one, Honor." Her mother shot her a "Mom" look, the one she had been giving the girls for as long as Honor could remember, the one that said the subject was no longer open to discussion.

"Okayyy," Honor said.

Erin slanted a smug smile in her direction, making Honor want to throw her shoe at her sister. Erin was getting on her last nerve today.

The rest of the meeting flowed without incident, thankfully, because ten a.m. was a little too early for a large glass of wine. When they finished, everyone headed to their respective offices.

Mae stepped into Honor's office and closed the door. "Well. That was intense."

"You could say that." Honor laid her things down and took a long swallow of her now-cold coffee, grimacing at the harsh flavor. She pushed the offending cup to the side.

"Do you want me to get you something cold to drink?" Mae asked.

"No, thanks. I'll go get something in a minute."

Mae slid into the chair in front of Honor's desk. "I don't get it. Shouldn't Erin be past all this by now? Maybe she could have been a little miffed that you didn't tell her you were dating her ex-fiancé. I get that part. But it's been a week. She should have yelled at you, the two of you could've talked it out, and then done, right? I didn't grow up with any siblings, but I know your dynamic and everything. Isn't that what you all do?"

"Typically, yes. But she won't talk to me. I've tried." She'd tried a lot, and at every attempt, Erin slammed the door in her face—sometimes literally. "It's like she's deliberately dragging this whole thing out to cause even more drama. I know she's pregnant and hormones may be at play, so I've tried to be sensitive and back off, but . . ."

"But you're irritated."

"Yes." At least Mae understood.

The door opened and Honor held her breath, part of her hoping it was Erin, the other part of her not ready for some type of confrontation.

Fortunately, it was Brenna. "Oh, hi, Mae. Am I interrupting?"

Honor shook her head. "No. Come on in."

Brenna shut the door and took a seat in the chair next to Mae. "So. Are we talking shit about Erin?"

Honor lifted her chin. "We are so not."

Mae looked over at Brenna. "We are."

"Dammit, Mae."

Mae winced. "Sorry."

"Hey, I'm happy to join in. She came at you hard during the meeting today and it was totally unnecessary. What bug crawled up her ass about Owen, anyway?"

"I don't know."

"I get that she's upset you didn't tell everyone you were dating Owen. But why does she even care if you're seeing him? I thought we were all friends now?"

"We are. We were. I've tried talking to her, Bren, and she won't let me."

Brenna raised her hands in the air. "Then I don't get it. How are you supposed to fix it if you don't know what you're supposed to fix?"

She'd never been happier to have her sister in her corner. "That's it, exactly. I don't know what I'm supposed to do. And it's extremely annoying."

Just then, Erin walked past her office, spotted them all in there and opened the door. "Oh, and I suppose this is about me."

"Why?" Brenna asked. "Are you feeling vibes of guilt over your pissy behavior in the meeting?"

Erin glared at Brenna. "Butt out. This isn't about you."

Honor stood. "Erin. Let's go talk somewhere. Just the two of us."

"I don't have anything to say to you. You had your chance to talk to me and you didn't, so we're done."

Honor's stomach sank. She walked around her desk. "If we could just—"

Erin raised her hand. "We just can't. And I'd really appreciate it if you all would stop talking about me behind my back, because it's pissing me off."

She stormed off, but Honor followed. So did Brenna.

"Maybe we wouldn't have to talk about you behind your back if you'd let Honor have a conversation with you."

Erin stopped in her tracks and pivoted. "Did you not hear the part where I said this is none of your business?"

"I heard you just fine. But I also have to put up with your attitude at work, and with you being shitty to our sister, so I'm voicing my opinion."

Honor had always been the peacemaker between Erin and Brenna, and always hated it when they fought. Now they were fighting about her, which was even worse. "Please stop, both of you. Erin, if we could just talk—"

"I told you, we have nothing to talk about."

"Yes, we do." She deliberately kept her voice low and calm, hoping it would defuse this escalating situation.

But Erin came toward her. "You know what I want? I want you to leave me alone. Unless it's business related, don't speak to me."

Honor could only take so much. "Now you're being childish, and we're not children. If we could just sit down and have an adult conversation, I'm sure we could—"

"I said no!"

Erin had yelled that last sentence. Mom came out of her office.

"What's going on?"

"Ask them," Erin said, turning around and hooking her thumb over her shoulder. "They're the ones ganging up on me. I'm going to your room to lie down for a bit. I've got a headache."

Mom gave Erin a worried look. "Okay, honey. You do that."

After Erin left, Mom gave them both a harsh stare. "Does someone want to tell me what happened?"

"Yeah," Brenna said. "Erin's being overly dramatic and picking fights with Honor."

"I just asked to have a conversation with her," Honor said.

"And she obviously doesn't want to talk to you right now, Honor," Mom said, "so you need to give her some space. I don't know why you keep pushing her."

"If we could just talk things out—'"

Her mother raised a hand. "You caused this. Now you need to let it settle. I'm going to go see if Erin needs anything. Go back to work, both of you."

Mom went upstairs and Brenna turned to Honor.

"Well, it's easy to tell whose side Mom is taking on this," Brenna said.

Unfortunately, yes. Not having her mother's support or understanding was crushing, weighing her down like a mountain of guilt.

She wished she could talk to Owen about it, but he was part of that guilt mountain. She hadn't spoken to him since the barbecue. He'd texted and called, but she'd told him things weren't great at the house and she just needed some space.

What she really needed right now was Owen. Her period still hadn't arrived and that only added to her anxiety.

What if she really was pregnant? She wasn't experiencing any pregnancy symptoms or anything. Physically, other than being constantly stressed out, she felt fine. But that didn't really mean anything, did it?

She'd even taken a pregnancy test and it had been

negative. And in her heart of hearts, she knew she wasn't pregnant. It had to be stress. Right?

What if, on top of the family knowing she'd been seeing Owen, she did end up pregnant and then had to tell them they were married? She couldn't begin to imagine how that would go. Erin might actually implode when she found out.

Honor was so frustrated, and she needed an outlet.

She turned to Brenna. "Would you like to go have a drink after work tonight?"

"Hell yeah. Actually, Finn and I were planning to try this new seafood place in the city. We could go have drinks, then he could meet us there later for dinner."

"Sounds like an ideal plan. We'll invite Mae, too."

"Perfect. Send me a text and let me know what time."

"Will do."

She headed back to her office, feeling marginally better knowing she'd at least get out of the house tonight. Clearing her head and hanging out with Brenna and Mae could be exactly what she needed.

CHAPTER

......

twenty-four

MIDWEEK NIGHTS AT the Screaming Hawk tended to be slower than weekend nights, giving Owen time to catch up on brewing and marketing plans. His bartender and servers had things well in hand, which meant he could hide out in his office, doing some planning for the summer months.

He hoped to branch out with some fun summer beers. He'd already tried a few new samples, with good success. The watermelon wheat had been a big hit and the lemonale was going strong. Anything that would bring in the crowds on a hot summer weekend was good for business.

His phone buzzed. He frowned, seeing Brenna's name come up on the screen. He swiped to answer.

"Hey, Brenna."

"Your girlfriend is mega upset and is annoyingly talking about you nonstop. I think she misses you and things have been shitty at work. She's on emotional overload and drowning herself in chips, dip and sadness. It's annoying. Can you help?"

His heart did a leap. He'd tried his best to give Honor the space she needed, so hearing that she missed him made his heart squeeze just a bit. Okay, more than a bit. "Where are you?"

"At that new seafood place a few miles from your brewery. You know which one I'm talking about?"

"I do."

"Are you working tonight?"

"Yeah."

"Can you break loose and come rescue me? Finn's due here shortly and I don't want to have to drive Honor home and ruin our date night. Mae was supposed to come with us, but she ended up making other plans so I'm Honor's driver now. Plus, I think if Honor doesn't see you soon, she's going to start crying, and nobody wants that."

He grinned. "I can get away. I'll be there soon."

"Saving my life here, Owen. I owe you one."

He hung up, realizing how excited he was to see Honor. Even an upset Honor. He went to tell Aaron that he was going to be leaving for the night. Aaron had it covered, so he got in his truck and drove to the restaurant, parked and went inside.

He'd heard about this place and had been hoping to bring Honor here for dinner. It had a nice ambience, was well lit and the food was supposed to be great. He saw Brenna sitting at a table. Honor had her back turned to him, but he'd recognize her beautiful hair anywhere. He made his way over.

"And I was nice about it. I haven't even seen Owen. It's been a whole week, Brenna."

"So you've told me," Brenna said, lifting her glass of wine for a long swallow. She spotted Owen and offered up a grateful smile. "Oh, look who's here."

"Hey," Owen said as he made his way to the table.

He caught Honor just as she stood, her bottom lip wobbling. "You're here. Oh, you're here. I've missed you."

She flung her arms around him and he wrapped his around her.

He nuzzled her neck. "I missed you, too."

She pulled back. "I have so much to tell you. Do you want a drink? We should get a table. Is Finn here yet? Did he come with you? I've been having a great talk with Brenna and she's had lots of wine. I had one glass."

Brenna rolled her eyes. "And apparently you didn't eat enough today, because that one glass has gone to your head. What you need is some food."

"How about we go to my place? I'll fix us something to eat. We'll talk."

"Ohhhkay, let's do that. Oh, wait. I don't want to leave Brenna."

Brenna smiled. "I'm fine. Finn already texted that he's on his way."

"You sure?"

"Absolutely positive. I'll just wait here for him. Alone. In the blissful quiet."

"I need to pee." She looked at Owen. "Wait for me?"

"Absolutely."

She left to go to the bathroom.

"She's not even drunk, she barely finished her tiny glass of wine," Brenna said. "But she's an emotional wreck. I think she's been trying to hold all of it inside for too long, and the dam finally broke."

"I'm sorry. That's on me."

Brenna frowned. "What's on you? This whole thing? Bullshit. This whole mess is on Erin, who won't talk to

Honor, and then Honor gets upset and in her head and . . ." Brenna waved her hand back and forth.

He couldn't imagine what Honor had been through. He wished she had texted or called him so he could have at least been a sounding board for her the past week.

"Okay, I'm ready," Honor said, leaning against Owen.

"Don't forget to eat something," Brenna said.

Honor smiled. "I love you, Bren."

"Love you, too, Honor. Thank you, Owen." She lifted her glass toward him.

"No problem. See you later."

He looked down at Honor. "You ready?"

She laid her head on his shoulder. "So ready. We have so much to talk about."

He walked her out to his truck, his arm around her. God, he'd missed her scent, the feel of her body against his.

"You hungry?" he asked.

"Yes. I'll help you make us some food when we get to your place."

He resisted laughing. "Sure you will."

By the time he pulled up in front of the house she was out cold, her mouth open, tiny snores coming out. How could she look so adorable like that?

Man, you've got it bad for this woman.

He shook his head, got out and went over to the passenger side and gently nudged her.

"Honor, we're here."

She resisted, so he tried again.

"Hey, babe, wake up."

"Uh-uh. Tired."

He scooped her up and carried her inside the garage, bending a little to reach the door knob. He was glad he hadn't brought Bettie to the brewery with him tonight so he wouldn't have to go back to pick her up. She met him at the door, tail wagging excitedly as she saw Honor in his arms.

The dog followed him into the bedroom. He didn't bother to turn on the light, just laid Honor on the bed, pulled the covers down, got her shoes off and drew the sheet over her. She rolled over and that was it.

He figured any conversation they might have was going to have to wait. Maybe she'd take a nap and wake up in a couple hours, so he let Bettie outside, made himself a sandwich and went to the backyard. He sat on the porch and watched the dog sniff the ground while he ate.

After he finished, he cleaned his plate, then went back into the bedroom to check on Honor. Somehow, she'd gotten out of her dress and removed her bra. She was curled over on her side, the covers pulled up to her chin.

He figured that was it for her for tonight. Bettie went to her dog bed and curled up as well.

Okay, fine. He might as well go back to work.

He left a note for Honor next to her purse just in case she woke up, but he had a feeling that wasn't going to happen.

She must be physically and emotionally exhausted. He really wanted to talk to her, to ferret out what was happening. But he figured she needed sleep more than anything right now.

He got into his truck and headed back to the brewery.

At least he got to see her. And later tonight, he'd get to sleep next to her.

That, at least, was something.

CHAPTER

· · · · · ·

twenty-five

HONOR'S HAND WAS wet. She opened her eyes and found Bettie's cute face looking at her.

"Oh, hi, Bettie. Was that you licking my hand?" She scratched behind Bettie's ears and was rewarded with more hand kisses.

She rolled over and sat up, once again in unfamiliar surroundings. Not that Owen's place was unfamiliar, but how did she end up here?

Think, Honor, think. Then it all came rushing back to her in mortifying detail. She'd had a glass of wine with Brenna, and no food, which was never a good combo. And all she'd done was talk about Owen. She could imagine her sister had tired of that and had called Owen to rescue her. Of course he had, which was now why she was mostly naked in his bed. And she didn't remember any fun sex last night, either.

At least she wouldn't find herself unexpectedly married—again. She dragged her fingers through her wildly out-of-control hair, utterly embarrassed to have been put in this position yet again.

Her purse was on the dresser—*thank you, Owen*. She slid out of bed and went into the bathroom to freshen up as best she could. She got dressed, finger-brushed her teeth and dug into her purse for her hairbrush.

She needed to get a grip. She was stressed and out of control, and this couldn't happen again.

She walked out of the bathroom, the smell of coffee—and was that bacon?—perking her up considerably. Bettie had already taken off, so Honor walked down the hall toward the incredible scents.

Owen was in the kitchen wearing shorts and a sleeveless shirt, standing in front of the stove. He looked up at her and smiled. "You're alive."

"Barely." She walked over to the coffeepot and fixed herself a cup, the smell of it intoxicating to her senses. After her first couple of sips, she decided she might live after all.

He lifted the bacon out of the pan and placed it on a plate. "Eggs?"

"Definitely."

She took a few more swallows of coffee, then felt competent enough to get plates and utensils out, as well as pour some juice into glasses. By then the eggs were done, so she was ready to eat.

Owen pulled some cantaloupe from the fridge and a tray of biscuits out of the oven.

"What time did you get up, anyway?"

He shrugged as he started scooping food onto their plates. "I don't know. Five thirty or so? I had to feed the animals."

He was an amazing man. Who knew what time he'd gotten to bed last night. She took her plate and followed him to the table. "You're a caring soul, Owen. And thanks for coming to my rescue last night."

He lifted the fork to his lips, then smiled at her. "You're my wife. I'll always be there for you."

She laughed. "Right. Anyway, I was kind of a mess. Sorry you had to deal with that."

"Actually, you fell asleep in the truck and I put you to bed. You were hardly a mess. Though before you conked out you did say we had a lot to talk about."

"Did I? I suppose I did." She ate and pondered, wondering how much she should tell him. The bacon was good and definitely helped to clear her muddled mind. "Things are kind of tense at the house."

"I figured since I haven't heard from you. Tell me about it."

"Erin and I are fighting. Well, not exactly fighting. She won't talk to me. Mom has taken her side, Dad is neutral, Brenna is on my side and, as you can imagine, it's like a cold war whenever we're all together."

He winced. "I'm sorry you're having to deal with that. I don't know why she won't sit down with you and tell you what's bugging her about all of this. It sure as hell isn't because she has mad love for me."

"No, I'm sure it isn't that, but she won't talk to me about it. I've asked her countless times and she keeps shutting me out."

He took a swallow of juice, then set the glass down. "Then stop trying."

"What?"

"You've done your part, Honor. You've tried to make

peace and she's not opening the door. So stop letting her kick you around. Go back to living your life. She'll come around eventually."

Somehow Honor didn't think it would be that simple.

"I don't know." She put some jelly on her biscuit and took a bite. "These are tasty."

"Thanks. We should go out. In public."

She lifted her head and looked at him. "What?"

"Everyone knows we're dating. So . . . let's date. Go to a restaurant and have a meal. Or go to a concert, or a movie. I'm tired of hiding like we're criminals, Honor. I want to go out with you."

She hadn't thought about how awful she'd been to Owen, making him hide out, sneaking around with him because they'd been holding this secret.

Now the secret was out—and half her family was pissed about it. And what had she done? She'd distanced herself from Owen and made herself miserable. Had it made any difference in her relationship with Erin or with her mother? Not at all.

"Yes, we should go out. We should do . . . couply things."

He laughed and leaned back in his chair. "Couply things?"

"Yeah. You know. Go have coffee together and play mini golf and go to the lake and do all those things you said, too."

"Okay, then. We'll date."

She held up her hand. "I still would prefer we not mention the married thing."

He shrugged and munched on a slice of bacon. "And why would we? That's our secret."

"Thanks."

"So what are you doing Sunday?"

She thought about it for a few seconds, mentally going through her calendar. "I'm free, actually."

"Great. We'll go out and do something."

"Sounds fun. In the meantime, I need to go. I have a meeting with a client at ten."

"It's only eight, Honor."

"I know. But I need a shower."

"I'll drive you home."

"Thanks."

She helped him clean up, though he insisted he'd take care of washing pans and such after he got back home. She felt kind of guilty about that and reminded herself to learn to cook so that someday soon she could make him a meal.

He pulled to the end of the Bellini property and stopped. "Want me to drop you here so no one sees us together? I mean, I know it's a half-mile walk, but you can take it in those heels, right?"

"Oh, you're funny. I think I can handle the walk of shame to my front door. Besides, Brenna has likely told everyone by now that you picked me up last night."

He shook his head. "I do not understand female dynamics."

"Don't even try."

He pulled up in front of the house.

"Thanks again for the rescue," she said, leaning over to brush her lips across his. "I'm sorry I couldn't linger for . . . after-breakfast dessert."

"Dessert, huh? You're going to have to bring that dessert with you when I see you on Sunday."

She swept her hand across his jaw, slanting him a wickedly hot smile. "Guaranteed."

She got out of the truck and waved as he pulled away, then sighed and walked inside, only to find her mother standing there, arms crossed, reminding her of that time she was seventeen and had showed up an hour after curfew.

"Morning," she said, bypassing her mom and heading for the stairs.

"Where do you think you're going?" Mom asked.

"Upstairs to take a shower."

"No, you're not. We need to talk."

Honor paused on the stairs. "About?"

"What were you doing with Owen last night?"

It was like she was a teenager again. "Mom, we're dating. I think that's been made clear."

"And it upsets your sister. You should think about what you're doing, Honor. This isn't a game."

"No, it's not a game, Mom. It's my life. It affects me. And I'd really appreciate it if you could see my side of things and not just Erin's."

Before she said anything else she might regret, she went upstairs.

She undressed, got into the shower and let her tears fall. She could handle a fight with her sister. It wasn't the first time and wouldn't be the last time it happened.

But not having the understanding and compassion from her mother? That broke her heart.

Why didn't her family support her? Why couldn't Erin talk to her?

Why was this so hard?

She finished showering and dried off, then put a cold washcloth on her face so she wouldn't look blotchy or like she had just cried. The last thing she needed was for Erin to have a tactical advantage during a meeting. She was going to be strong about this, weather it out and at some point, Erin would get tired of freezing her out.

Until then, she was going to go on dates with Owen. And her sister could just suck it.

CHAPTER
. . . . . .

twenty-six

IT WAS ALWAYS good to have a friend drop by, especially one who had insight into the goings-on of the family drama. Owen was lucky that Jason was a veterinarian who dealt with large and small animals. When Jason came by to vaccinate and deworm Owen's cattle, he offered him a sandwich and a cold drink after. They sat outside on the patio.

"Cattle are in good shape," Jason said. "They're all healthy and show no signs of infection or disease. You're doing a great job with them."

"Thanks. How's business?"

"Busy. Adding the new vet has helped take some of the load off, though."

"How's Erin feeling?"

"She's good. Thanks for asking."

"Are you hoping for a boy or a girl?"

Jason laughed. "Man, I don't care either way. You know how people say that, but they really want one or the other? I'm being honest when I say I don't care. I just want Erin healthy and the baby, too. I'll be ecstatic when that kid shows up, no matter what it is."

"Gender's an old way of thinking anyway. The kid will tell you what they are."

Jason lifted his glass and clinked it against Owen's. "Amen to that."

They finished eating and Jason walked over to check out the horses.

"Has Erin talked to you about this thing between Honor and her?"

He looked up at Owen. "I tried to talk to her about it twice and she shut me down cold. Cold and angry. I don't know what all that is about, but she's pissed about something."

"Maybe it's about me and not Honor at all."

Jason considered it. "Maybe it is."

"Do you think I should try talking to her?"

"In the state she's in right now? I wouldn't attempt it. You could lose a body part."

Owen smiled. "Good advice."

They finished with the horses and started walking back toward the house, Bettie staying between them because of course she always had to be in the middle of everything.

"Give Erin some time to cool down and get used to the idea of you and Honor together. I get her surprise at you and Honor dating. After all, she was engaged to marry you at one point, and now you're dating her sister. But I've tried to think of a hundred different reasons why she's so pissed off—all without bringing pregnancy hormones into it. Frankly, I can't figure it out. But there's something bugging her and until she's ready to talk about it, everyone just needs to give her some space."

Owen nodded. "You know her better than anyone, so you got it."

"Thanks. And thanks for lunch."

"Thanks for stopping by."

"Hey, you're still getting billed for the vet services."

Owen laughed. "True that. But I appreciate the free advice anyway."

Jason grasped his shoulder. "That's what friends are for, bro."

After Jason left, he thought about what his friend had said. He'd been thinking a lot about Honor—and about Erin—and what he could do to help that situation.

But Jason was right. Getting in the middle of that argument would be the worst thing he could do. If Erin was angry with him, then eventually she'd let him know why. Having been in a relationship with Erin and grown up with her, he knew she could stew for only so long before she exploded.

In the meantime, he had his own life to take care of, and a woman he was falling in love with. It was time for the two of them to start stepping out and having some fun.

Everything else could stay on the sidelines.

For now.

CHAPTER

· · · · · ·

twenty-seven

HONOR HAD SURREPTITIOUSLY stared at her watch the entire day yesterday, counting down the hours until her date with Owen.

Fortunately, they'd had a big wedding yesterday with two hundred fifty guests, which had kept her mind occupied. And she and Erin had both been so busy, neither of them had time to fuss at each other. The one thing both of them excelled at was putting the bride and groom above any personal differences. So no one in the wedding party was even aware there was animosity between them. They might be fighting with each other, but to the bride and groom? They were organized and in sync with the wedding party's every need.

A Bellini never let a client down.

Now that that was over with, this morning she got up early, having gotten a list from Owen of what she'd need for the day. They were going out. In public. Where people could see them. She realized it was something she had done all the time with other guys she'd dated, but she had yet to do it with Owen. She wasn't sure whether to be excited or terrified.

They'd talked about where to go. Or, rather, he'd asked her if there was something in particular she wanted to do. She'd hesitated and hemmed and hawed until he'd told her he'd take care of it. Poor Owen. He probably thought she didn't even want to do this, which so wasn't true at all. It was more like her abject fear of running into her sister or her parents that made her utterly terrified about this date. She made a mental note to be fun today.

Hence, her list, which included a swimsuit and towel and things that went along with what Owen had called "boating and beach things." Okay, she was totally down for that since it was hot and sunny and perfect weather for a day at the lake.

She'd asked Owen if she should pack some snacks or drinks, but he'd told her he had it covered. She packed a tote bag filled with all the things she'd need for the day, determined to have fun, if for no other reason than to spite Erin.

Or maybe she wouldn't think about her sister at all today, and just enjoy the day with Owen.

Novel concept, Honor. A day out in public with your guy. Try having fun for a change instead of getting all up in your head like you've been doing.

She glared at herself in the mirror. "Ignoring your sarcastic thoughts, self."

She put a navy flowered cover-up over the top of her swimsuit, slipped on her canvas tennis shoes, and tossed her sandals in the bag. She had sunscreen, a scrunchie for her hair, hairbrush, lip stuff, detangling spray, bug spray and about a thousand other things weighing her bag down, but it never hurt to be prepared, right?

She was ready. She went downstairs and met her dad at the foot of the stairs.

"Going out today?" he asked.

"Yup. Out on the water."

"With Owen?"

She tensed. "Yes."

He nodded. "Good day for it. Be careful, bambina. Ti amo."

She exhaled in relief, so happy not to have an argument this early in the day, especially with someone she loved. "Ti amo, Daddy." She threw her arms around him and kissed his cheek, then headed outside, got into her car and drove over to Owen's house. He was already outside packing up his truck, while Bettie was out front lying in the shade under a tree. The dog came over as soon as Honor got out of the car.

Honor got down to give the dog some love. "Bettie, it's good to see you. You're looking lovely today."

Bettie rolled over for some belly rubs, and Honor had to oblige. At least until Owen whistled. The dog hustled onto her feet and scrambled up into the back seat of the truck.

Honor made her way over. "Is she coming with us?"

"Actually, she has a play date today. With Murphy."

"Is that right?"

"Yup. She and Murphy are going to a daycare for dogs. With a spa."

Her brows lifted. "A spa."

"Yeah. First they'll do some agility training and exercises, followed by swimming, then the whole spa treatment with the baths and massages and nail trimming."

"Huh. Maybe I'll go with Bettie and Murph."

"Funny. And, no. You're *my* date today, not Bettie's."

"Damn. I was really enticed by the manicure."

He slipped his arm around her waist, making her fully aware of just how long it had been since they'd seen each other, since she'd felt his touch. "I have other enticing things in mind for you today."

"Care to tell me about them?"

"Nope. It's a surprise."

"I'll try to contain myself."

"I do have to tell you that Brenna and Finn are coming with us."

"Really? That'll be fun."

"I was hoping you'd think so. And Mae and her date are coming along, too. Don't know him. Some new guy she's dating."

Her lips curved. "She's always dating a new guy. The more people, the more fun, right?"

"That's kind of what I thought."

She knew what he thought. That she'd be happier not to be alone, that she needed her sister—and a friend. He was right. Though she'd also have been perfectly happy to have some alone time with him. But their first date in public, with the support of family and friends? Even better. "Then why are we waiting? Let's get this party started."

He finished packing up the truck and they headed out.

They stopped at Barks and Recreation, an amazing indoor/outdoor facility that Honor wanted to spend some time exploring. Bettie's tail wagged enthusiastically when they met up with Finn and his dog, Murphy.

After a quick tour around the facility, which was totally amazing with its outdoor pool and agility course, along with all the indoor space for the dogs to run around, it looked like the pups were going to have a fantastic adventure. In fact, Bettie ran off without even looking back, which made Honor so happy.

Bettie was living her best life, thanks to Owen.

Finn said he'd meet them at the lake, since he had to swing back home to pick up Brenna.

"Hungry?" Owen asked.

"I could eat."

"I'm so glad you said that, because I didn't have time for breakfast and I need some fuel."

"Then let's stop somewhere and grab food."

They ended up at a small breakfast café outside of town. It was charming and filled with people, so they had to stand outside and wait for a table.

"I like this," he said, teasing the strap of her cover-up with his finger. "This color looks good on you. Then again, every color does."

"Thank you." She inhaled deeply, desperately happy to be with him today. She'd missed everything about him, from the deep timbre of his voice to the slight slant of his smile. She'd missed his smell, which was always clean and along the lines of wintergreen or pine. Soap, she was sure. Whatever it was, it hit her hot buttons.

They finally got seated and she perused the menu. It wasn't an extensive menu, but the items that were on it looked delicious. She ended up selecting a bowl of oatmeal and fruit along with toast, not wanting to overfill her stomach since they were going out on a boat.

Owen, on the other hand, ordered eggs, sausages, fruit and toast. When their server brought the food, she snatched one of his sausages. He merely smiled at her and ate his food.

The man even shared his food without complaint. What more was there to love about him?

How could she have let anyone come between them, even if that someone was her sister? She loved Erin, and they'd get through this, but there was going to be a reckoning at some point. Or at least a deep, emotional conversation. Then life would be back in order again.

Honor craved balance, and at the moment, everything was out of whack. She didn't like it.

"You were either hungry or deep in thought all through breakfast," Owen said, "because you hardly said a word."

They made their way out the door and toward the truck. "I'm sorry. It was probably a little bit of both."

"Something on your mind?"

She took his hand. "I was thinking how much I had missed being with you, and how irritated I am—mostly at myself—that I let this separation go on for so long."

He stopped and turned to face her. "Hey, you had some things to work through. And maybe those things aren't entirely . . . worked through yet. But we'll figure it out together, okay?"

"Okay." She felt better already.

He opened the car door and she slid onto the seat. Owen dipped his head inside. "For the record, I missed you, too." He brushed his lips across hers, then closed her door.

She sighed. Yes, she felt much better already.

It was a beautiful day, and by the looks of it, everyone else had the same idea—head for the lake. But Owen found a place to park, and fortunately Brenna and Finn showed up just a few minutes later—with the family boat.

"You brought the boat," Honor said to Brenna.

"Sure we did. Owen was going to rent a boat, but why would we do that when we already have one?"

"That makes sense." She knew he didn't ask her about the family boat because he was trying to surprise her, which was sweet. And also because of the current family situation, which spiked her irritation level. She could use the boat if she wanted to, even if Owen was going to be on it. The boat was available to any of them who wanted to use it. And, today, she definitely planned to use the hell out of it and enjoy doing it. Maybe she'd take a lot of pics and post them to her social media so Erin could see them.

When did she become so petty? It wasn't in her nature at all. She had to admit, though, given her current state of pique with her sister, just the thought of anything that might irritate Erin gave her a small amount of pleasure.

Petty. Definitely petty.

"You're smirking," Brenna said as they carried bags to the boat. "What's that about?"

"I'm ashamed to admit what I was thinking."

"Oh, now you have to tell me."

"I was thinking I'd take some pictures of Owen on the family boat and post them on social media, knowing how pissed Erin would be about it."

Brenna laid the bags in the galley, then turned to her. "That's so petty."

"I know."

Then her sister grinned. "Have I told you today how much I love you?"

Honor laughed. "No, but I'll take it. I love you back and I appreciate you standing by me."

"Hey, Erin's wrong. I get that she has a right to be irritated with you for dating Owen behind her back, but I don't understand why she's freezing you out. She needs to woman up and talk to you about what's bothering her about you and Owen being together. And until she does, I'm mad at her, too."

"Are you two still shit-talking your sister?" Finn asked as he laid fishing poles on the deck of the boat.

"It's our right as her sisters to talk behind her back," Brenna said. "Wherever she is today, she's likely doing the same thing."

"She's probably doing some relaxing spa thing and not thinking about either of you."

Honor looked over at Brenna. "Knowing Erin, Finn is probably right about that."

"Then forget about her, and focus on your own fun."

Brenna shot Finn a frown. "I hate it when you're right."

He grinned. "I know."

By the time they had everything stowed away, Mae and her date-of-the-day had arrived. This one was a tanned, blond, surfer-looking type with impressive shoulder and biceps muscles.

"Wow," Brenna whispered. "Where does she find all these gorgeous guys?"

"I think she attracts them somehow. She's some kind of hot-man magnet."

"And after one date she throws them away. Such a waste."

Honor shrugged. "You know what she went through with Isaac. Can you blame her for playing catch-and-release right now?"

"No, you're right. Having been burned once myself, I appreciate her game. And she's extremely good at it."

"Hey, everyone," Mae said as she came aboard. "This is Tanner. He's studying for his PhD in agriculture. He and his family have a ranch about an hour south of the vineyard."

Everyone introduced themselves. "I thought I recognized you," Finn said. "I've done some carpentry work at your family's ranch."

"Right," Tanner said. "I haven't had a lot of time to help out with ranching duties since I started working on my PhD. Between teaching and studying, I'm pretty busy."

"Let's get a beer. You can tell me about the program," Finn said.

Honor looked over at Mae as the guys wandered off. "Hot and smart? Where do you find these guys, Mae?"

Mae shrugged. "I don't know. Here and there. Tanner and I ran into each other at the farmer's market last weekend. We got to talking and realized we had some things in common, like attending the same college, knowing a few of the same people, that kind of thing."

Brenna rolled her eyes. "You really are like a magnet."

Mae laughed. "He's nice. But he doesn't have a lot of time to date, which is why I invited him here today. He could use a break."

"And look," Honor said, motioning with her head to where Tanner was already in deep conversation with Owen and Finn, "now he has two new friends."

Mae smiled. "Good. I don't think he gets out much. And you know what they say about all work and no play."

"Well, if anyone can teach him about the play part, it's you, Mae," Brenna said.

"Aww, thank you. I just want him to have a fun, relaxing day on the water."

"I want that for all of us," Honor said.

"And speaking of a nice relaxing day," Brenna said. "I made sangria. And sandwiches."

Honor sported a wide grin. "My favorite."

Mae joined her with a bright smile. "Mine, too. Oh, and I made the most amazing mango salad."

"I brought water and lemonade, being useless in the cooking department," Honor said. "Oh, and chips and dip."

Owen walked by. "I brought beer." He winked at Honor as he made his way to the stern. Her heart did a little leap and she smiled, this time not even attempting to hide her reaction to him.

How refreshing.

"We are so set for snacks and drinks," Mae said. "See? The day is already starting off with a bang."

Honor put on her sunscreen and her shades, and grabbed a seat since it appeared the guys were readying the boat for takeoff. Finn got the boat started, and they headed off across the lake.

She tilted her head back, soaking in the feel of the wind and the occasional spray of water. She'd been so wound up and tense lately with everything going on, it felt good to just . . . be.

They stopped long enough to get the tubes and skis out. Honor was more about lazily flying across the water in a tube, though she'd grown up waterskiing and was damn good at it.

Finn went out first on skis, and of course did great. He had amazing balance, riding the waves like he was born to water. Then again, he sort of had been, growing up in Ireland. But Honor was fairly certain waterskiing hadn't been one of Finn's recreational activities when he was a kid.

After he was done, he and Brenna went out on the tube together. She could swear that despite the boat's engine noise and the waves, she could hear her sister's screaming laughter.

"Those two," Mae said, laughing, "are so in love with each other."

Honor watched as Finn grabbed hold of Brenna before she could fall off the tube, then planted a long kiss on her. She sighed in happiness for her sister. "They definitely are."

"She's one of the lucky ones, for sure."

Honor looked over at Mae. "There's someone out there for you."

"Oh, I'm not looking for that someone. I'm still bearing the scars after that first 'almost.' Never again for me, thank you."

Her heart hurt for Mae. It had been over a year since Isaac had blindsided her friend, and she'd backed out on the wedding only a few months before they were supposed to get married. Honor hoped Mae would eventually heal and learn to trust again. Or maybe she just needed to find the right guy who could make her believe in love.

Of course, that would mean she'd have to go on more than one date with a man.

Mae and Tanner went out next and did slalom skis.

Brenna was combing through her wet hair as she stood next to Honor and watched the two. They were both in sync—and athletic, hopping over the waves as if they were nothing.

"They're both good at this," Honor said.

"Yes, they are."

"Maybe he's going to be the one to help her get over Isaac."

Brenna shook her head. "Nah, I don't think he's the one."

Honor switched her focus to Brenna. "Why not?"

"I don't know. Just a feeling. She's not ready yet, and like she said, Tanner has too many other things on his plate. She needs a man who's going to focus all of his attention on her. She needs someone who really wants her, who has the time to shower her with love and affection, to really sweep her off her feet, you know?"

"Hmm. You're right about that."

After Mae and Tanner climbed back onto the boat, Owen turned over the steering wheel to Brenna.

"You ready to do some tubing?"

She nodded. "Absolutely. Unless you want to ski first. I can wait."

"I thought I'd go with you."

"Then definitely yes."

They got into their life jackets, then climbed into the tube together. Honor grabbed the handles, while Owen held on to one handle, using his other arm to hold on to Honor.

"Wouldn't wanna lose you," he said.

Her heart did a little tumble just as Finn started up the boat, sending them sailing across the water.

And then her feet were flying in the air, her face was slapped with water, and it was the most exhilarated she'd felt in a long time. She kept gulping mouthfuls of water because she was laughing so hard, but she couldn't help herself. She was having such a good time, and it didn't hurt at all that the hottest man she knew was by her side.

They finally slowed and when the others started to pull them toward the boat, Owen leaned over and gave her a long, hot kiss. Right there, in full view of everyone. She got lost in that kiss, leaning into him, soaking in the heat of his mouth and the feel of his body touching hers.

"Hey, you two, get a room or take a dunk and cool off."

She laughed at Brenna's voice, pulling away from Owen, who gave her a promising smile.

"More of that later," he said.

By the time she climbed back into the boat, she realized it was going to take hours to get all the water out of her ears. Still, that euphoric, post-kiss feeling lingered.

She waited for someone to mention the kiss, but no one did, which made her so happy she wanted to do a celebratory dance around the boat.

Now if only she could get the rest of her family to realize that her being with Owen was no big deal.

CHAPTER
......
twenty-eight

It HAD BEEN a long, fun day out on the water, and Owen couldn't have asked for a better first official public date with Honor. It seemed like she'd had a good time. More importantly, she'd been relaxed, and he knew that was something she needed after all the turmoil of the past couple of weeks.

After skiing and tubing, they'd parked at a cove and everyone hung out and swam. Then they'd eaten and sat around and just talked. He only wished Erin and Jason had been there with them, but he wasn't about to say that to Honor. It was enough that Brenna was there supporting her. That his friends were there supporting both of them. That meant more to him than anything.

He stared out over the water and looked at Honor, her head resting on the back of the tube, her eyes shielded by her shades. She looked relaxed as she chatted with Brenna and Mae and Mae's date, Tanner. With the sun glinting off the lake, Honor looked like a golden mermaid, her feet casually dipping in and out of the water.

"You got it bad, friend," Finn said, grabbing his shoulder. "You're in love with her, then?"

He grimaced as he screwed open the top of his bottled water. "Maybe. Probably."

Finn sat next to him. "And now you're in the middle of this war between her and Erin. Yeah, you're fucked." Finn took a sip from his flask of whiskey.

"Thanks, Finn. That was so helpful."

"Glad I could help. But seriously, you want my advice? Stay out of any argument involving the sisters. They'll eventually work it out."

"Kind of hard to do that when I feel like I caused the argument in the first place."

Finn shrugged. "Maybe, and then again it could be part you and part somethin' else. Who knows when they get into a row. Either way, they've been through big arguments before. They know how to work through it. You gettin' in the middle of all of that will only make things worse."

He had a point, and it was the same thing Jason had told him.

"You make a valid point."

Finn laughed. "I'll drink to that. Now how about we get in the water and rile up our ladies?"

"I can get into that."

They dove in and Owen swam over to where Honor seemed to have drifted off by herself. She seemed utterly serene. She might even be sleeping, but he couldn't tell for sure since her sunglasses hid her eyes. All he knew was her feet had stopped flapping the water, and her arms lay still at her sides. So he crept up next to her very slowly.

"If you dump me off this tube, I will kick your ass," she said.

He laughed and rested his arms on the side of the tube. "I'd be interested in seeing you try to do that."

She lifted her shades. "You think I can't?"

"As feisty as you are? I'm pretty sure you'd give me your best."

She slid out of the tube and went under the water, coming up on the other side so they could both hold on for balance. "Kiss me," she said. "Since it feels so freeing to be able to say that without hiding in some corner."

He pulled her against him and pressed his lips to hers, pulling away just quickly enough to keep everyone from yelling at them to get a room. But it felt more like a tease, a taste of something he desperately craved and wanted to devour in its entirety.

"Later? You and me are having some alone time."

Her lips curved. "Most definitely making that a priority."

They hung out the rest of the day and everyone had an amazing time.

After they made their way back to the dock, Owen helped Finn pull the boat out and everyone started unpacking their things.

"Do you want me to help you clean it up?" he asked Finn.

Finn shook his head. "I'll do it at the house. It'll give Murphy a chance to cool off with the hose and water. He'll have a blast."

"Okay. Thanks for being the captain of the boat today."

Finn laughed. "Right, like that's a hardship."

They finished putting their gear into his truck, said their goodbyes, and headed off to his place.

"That was fun," Honor said. "I'm waterlogged and exhausted, but it was a blast. How about you?"

"Me? I had a great time. It was good to be out with people again."

"I thought so, too. It was also nice to be out with you."

He made the turn onto the highway. Once he merged into traffic, he said, "I was wondering if you'd be disappointed we didn't go out alone."

"Not at all. I think we've hidden out alone long enough. Today was perfect."

He was relieved to hear that. He'd thought that maybe a group event would make her feel more comfortable, especially if Brenna was there. He made a mental note to do it again. But first, he wanted some alone time with her.

They stopped to pick up Bettie from the spa. The attendant said she'd had a great day. She'd gone swimming, completed the agility course, got her spa on and then played with all the other dogs and that she was likely tired out from the day.

True to what the attendant had said, Bettie curled up on the back seat and promptly went to sleep. Once they got to the house, she looked annoyed at being woken up to go inside. She got a drink of water, went down the hall and climbed into her bed.

"Seems like she had fun today," Owen said.

Honor smiled. "Good for her. It seems like a great place."

"Yeah, it does. I'll have to take her back, maybe a couple of days a week or something so she can run off a bit of her energy. Though she does plenty of that here."

"Hey, someone has to manage the cattle."

He laughed. "True."

They took everything inside and Owen rinsed out the coolers, turning them upside down to dry in the driveway while Honor put things away in the fridge. When he came into the kitchen, she was washing some food containers.

"You want something to drink?" he asked.

"Just some water for me."

He fixed two glasses of ice water.

"What I really need is a shower," she said.

"Same here."

She leaned against the counter, took a couple sips from her glass and slanted a heated look at him. "We could save water by showering together."

He set his glass down. "I'm all about the environment. Let's go."

It took all the restraint he had in him not to drag her into the bedroom at breakneck speed. Instead, he took her hand and led her down the hall.

"You're awfully slow, ya know," she said, pulling him along.

He shrugged as they entered the bathroom. "I was trying not to appear too eager."

She slipped the straps of her cover-up down her arms, letting the dress pool at her feet. "I'm all about eager."

While she got out of her bikini, he turned on the shower and dropped his board shorts. He opened the door and a naked Honor stepped in. He followed, closing the door behind them.

She moved under the spray, wetting herself down from her hair to her toes.

"Oh, this feels good," she said.

He grabbed the body wash and poured some into his hand. "Step out of the spray and I'll wash you."

She turned around and moved out of the water and he lathered her up, enjoying the feel of her skin against his hands. He soaped up her neck and back, letting his fingers slide over her butt cheeks before bending down to soap up her legs and feet.

"Okay," he said. "Turn around."

She did, and he soaped up the front of her, standing to do her stomach, and breasts. Of course, he lingered there. How could he not when her nipples turned to tight points of arousal, causing his dick to harden. Not that he wasn't hard already, after having had his hands all over her.

She rinsed, then washed her hair while he stepped into the spray to get wet. After she finished with her hair, she poured some body wash on her hands.

"My turn," she said, circling his back, sliding her fingers over his shoulders, down his arms and around to the front of him.

He turned around, letting her have her way. Soap trailed down and she followed its path, but her eyes stayed locked on his as her fingers snaked over his stomach and then even lower, circling his cock.

He sucked in a breath as she began to stroke him. Unable to just stand there, he slipped his fingers between her legs, stroking the silken wet heat of her. And then he took her mouth in a blistering hot kiss, pushing her against the wall of the shower as he slid his fingers inside her and began to pump.

She moaned against his mouth and squeezed his cock, stroking faster, making his balls tremor with impending release.

He was close, so close, but he wanted to go with her, and he rubbed against her clit as he moved his fingers within her, feeling her tighten.

And then suddenly, she burst, her orgasm making her

rock against him in spasms. He deepened the kiss and came in uncontrollable spurts that left him dizzy and holding on to the wall for support.

He gentled the kiss, giving her small nips across her lips, her response little *mmms*.

"Yeah," he said. "Now I'm hot."

"You were hot before."

He laughed. They finished rinsing and he shut the water off. They towel-dried and then Honor disappeared from the bathroom. When he walked out to the bedroom, she was sitting naked on his bed, brushing out her wet hair.

"I hope you weren't planning to get rid of me," she said. "Because I'm staying the night."

He flipped the light off in the bathroom and walked toward her. "I've already gone too long without you." He climbed onto the bed, took the brush from her hand, and moved behind her, using it to gently brush through her hair.

"That feels good. I don't think anyone other than my mother has ever brushed my hair before."

"Not even your sisters?"

"Oh, God, no. They tried when we played make-believe, but they'd tug and pull and it hurt, so that was the end of that."

He smoothed his hand down the back of her head, swept her hair to the side and kissed the nape of her neck. "Aww. You poor baby."

"I was. Being the youngest sucked."

"Being an only child, I can't relate. But I can imagine it wasn't fun being picked on like that."

"No, it wasn't. Oh, that feels good."

He'd laid the brush to the side and had started kissing

her neck, moving to her shoulders. She twisted around and scooted back onto the mattress, reaching for him.

Then it was lips and tongues and his body covering hers, and a wild, untamed hunger for her that, for some reason, he could never seem to quench. Being apart from her the past couple of weeks only made the need for her that much more intense.

He ran his hands over her body, teased her nipples, following up with his mouth, the feel of her skin like the softest silk. He kissed her, licked her, tasting her body from her rib cage and down her belly to her sex.

She responded with moans and arches, telling him her need was just as great as his. He moved up her body and reached over to grab a condom. He quickly put it on, then lifted her leg over his hip and slid inside her, absorbing her gasp with his mouth.

She pushed on his shoulder and he rolled over, letting her ride on top.

Oh, hell yeah. The view of her on top of him, her hair all wild and damp, her nipples tight with desire, was his fantasy. The feel of her surrounding him, squeezing him, felt so damn good as she rocked against him and he wanted this woman every damn day and night until he died a happy man.

She rolled forward, then back, taking things slow, making him tense underneath her, feeling that swirl of orgasm just within his reach. And then she lengthened herself on top of him, squeezing his cock between her legs until he thought he might die from that pleasure.

And then she took them both right over the edge. He slid his hand into her hair and brought her lips to his, kissing her deeply while he rocketed through a powerful climax, taking in her cries of orgasm along with his until he had nothing left.

In the darkened bedroom, there was just her breathing and his and the feel of her heart beating against his chest. He smoothed his hands down her back, content to just feel her skin.

They fell asleep like that, waking—hell, he had no idea how much later. Bettie's whines let him know she wanted to go out, so he rolled Honor to the side and got up, disposed of the condom and went into the kitchen to let the dog out, then picked up the glass of water he'd left hours earlier and emptied it in a few quick gulps.

Honor came out, squinting as her eyes adjusted to the kitchen light. "How long were we asleep?"

He picked up his phone. "A couple of hours."

"I guess sun and sex will do that." She came over and laid her head against his shoulder.

He put his arm around her. "I guess so. Are you hungry?"

"Starving."

"I'll get dressed and make us something to eat."

She tilted her head back. "Or, we could go out."

"We could, couldn't we?"

"I'll go get dressed. How do you feel about pizza?"

"I feel very good about pizza."

She offered up a lazy smile and disappeared into the bedroom.

It had been a damn fine day, he thought as he let Bettie back inside, then fed her. Yeah, kind of a perfect day. And it was only looking up from here.

He went into the bedroom to get dressed.

CHAPTER

......

twenty-nine

HONOR WENT INTO this morning's meeting feeling more serene and relaxed than she had in a long time. Spending the day—and the night—with Owen likely had a lot to do with her state of mind.

She'd had fun, great sex, and it had felt so good to be out with Owen—actually out in public with him. And with her sister, no less. She couldn't thank Brenna enough for being by her side.

Nothing was going to ruin her happy buzz today.

She had already set up at the table, along with Brenna, Mae and Erin. Mom was on the phone so they were just waiting for her. It was quiet since Erin still wasn't speaking to her, but she refused to feel uncomfortable about it.

Mom finally came in. "Sorry. That call took longer than expected."

"No problem, Mom," Erin said.

Her mother looked them over. "You three got some sun."

Brenna grinned. "We took the boat out yesterday. Weather was perfect."

"I suppose Owen went with you," Erin said, looking directly at Honor.

"He did." She wasn't about to tell Erin how much fun they had and dig the knife in any deeper.

"And I don't remember getting an invitation to this outing."

And there went her happy buzz.

Brenna let out a short laugh. "Because you and Honor are besties right now, right, Erin? That would have been so fun. Or maybe you were just looking for an opportunity to toss our sister off the boat."

"Enough," Mom said. "Let's start the meeting."

Honor breathed a sigh of relief that they could turn their attention on anything but her. They had a full agenda of items including new wedding reservations, this weekend's weddings, and winery business, along with financials, so it took a while to get through everything.

"One last thing," Mom said. "I've had a couple of phone calls about something that I think could be an interesting business opportunity for us."

"What would that be, Mom?" Brenna asked.

"There's an entertainment company out of L.A. that is interested in coming out to look at the wedding venue and vineyards to possibly film a movie here. Or at least part of their movie."

"What?" Honor asked. "Why here?"

"They looked us up online and liked what they saw, and I guess they sent some scouts out to tour the vineyard and the wedding venue and really liked it."

"I don't recall having a movie company out here touring," Erin said.

"Neither do I," Honor said.

"They probably did it posing as a couple interested in a wedding or something," Brenna said. "That way we wouldn't be keyed in to the whole movie idea in case the location didn't interest them."

"Huh." Brenna had a point.

"Anyway," Mom said, "they want to do some further research and send another team, but they're extremely interested."

Honor frowned. "What would that mean for our business? Film crews take up a lot of time and space and we can't cancel weddings we've already scheduled."

"I explained that to them. They're willing to work around the weekend weddings and film only during the week."

"And what about the grapes?" Brenna asked. "They do realize they can't be stomping through our vineyards with their cameras and equipment, right?"

Mom gave Brenna a look. "Of course not, and I told them that as well."

"How's the money?" Erin asked. "Is this something that's potentially profitable for us?"

Mom named the figure that was quoted to her. "Not a final number, but one that was discussed."

Honor blinked. "Damn."

"Wow," Brenna said.

"I definitely like that number," Erin said.

Mae just smiled. "That would be good for the business. Plus, the marketing and promotional opportunities alone could be outstanding."

"I hadn't thought of that," their mother said. "But you're right, Mae."

"I just don't know," Honor said. "What about the disruption to our wedding planning, to prospective couples who want to come and tour the venue? The possibility of revenue loss there could be big. You know we book tours for our brides and grooms during the week. How long of a shoot are we talking about?"

"They weren't firm, but they said approximately six weeks to two months."

Her eyes widened. "Two months? Absolutely not. We can't shut down bridal visits for that long."

"I'm sure we could make other arrangements," Erin said. "Figure out a schedule. They can't possibly film all day and night. So whenever they're not filming, we can bring in prospective couples for tours."

"Oh, right. Like they know they're going to film from six a.m. to three p.m. on a Tuesday. Come on, Erin. You have to know moviemaking doesn't work that way."

Erin lifted her chin. "And you're suddenly the expert?"

"I didn't say I was an expert, only that I've seen how they make movies and I don't think it's on a set schedule."

"I believe Honor might be right about that," Mae said. "It could be troublesome."

"Oh, you would take her side."

"Hey," Brenna said. "No one's taking sides. We're talking through a potential business opportunity, and it's just too damn bad that not everyone agrees with you."

"Do you?" Erin asked.

Brenna paused for a few seconds. "I'm undecided right now."

Erin flung her hands up. "You'd do anything not to agree with me, because you're on Honor's side in all things, just like Mae."

"All right, I've had just about enough of this." Mom stood and she didn't look happy. "You have personal issues, and that's fine. But when we're in business mode, the personal issues stay outside. Is that understood?"

Erin gave them a smug look.

"That includes you as well, Erin," Mom said. "All of you."

Erin's smug look disappeared in a hurry. "I got it, Mom."

"Now if we could get back to the business at hand without hurling insults, I'd really appreciate it because I have a business to run. As, I assume, the rest of you do, too."

Feeling properly chastised, Honor nodded. "Taking notes as we speak."

They discussed pros and cons, and after they hashed it out, Mom got up.

"We won't make a final decision until we talk it over with your father, but we do have to let the production company know soon, so we'll pick this up again at our next meeting."

Mom left the room. Erin started to get up.

"Before you go," Brenna said. "I have something I want to discuss with all of you."

Erin paused.

"It's about Mom."

Erin sat.

"You know her birthday is next week. She always likes to downplay it, but I was thinking it might be nice to do a little surprise party for her."

"That would be fun," Honor said.

"She does love surprises," Erin said. "What did you have in mind?"

"We have the Parker/Sanchez wedding Saturday afternoon, and that should end by five. That would give us plenty of time after cleanup to decorate the barn and set up for a nice dinner party."

Honor liked that idea. "I can get in touch with one of our cake vendors who I know can make us an awesome birthday cake. And we'll need flowers, so I'll get a florist I know can deliver."

"Or we could just use the wedding decor from that day," Erin suggested. "And then all we'd need is flowers for the tables."

"Oh." Honor hadn't considered that. "That's a good idea."

"You don't think leftover decor would be tacky?" Brenna asked.

"Hmm." Honor considered that. "Maybe? What do you think, Erin?"

"I think Mom will be so surprised and happy, she won't even notice the rest."

"You're probably right," Honor said. "I'll still order some new ones for the table settings."

Erin nodded. "And I'll send out e-vites to their close friends, say it's a surprise, and see who can make it."

"I'll take care of catering," Brenna said. "And the wine, of course."

"But what about keeping it a surprise?" Erin asked.

"I already talked to Dad about that," Brenna said. "He's agreed to keep Mom off the premises while we get the barn set up and during the time the guests arrive."

"Then I think we're set," Erin said. She opened her notepad and started jotting down the things they'd discussed.

"Project Birthday is on," Brenna said, sporting a sly smile.

Even Erin offered a small smile, which Honor took as a positive sign.

Honor was so on board with this. And even better, the tension between Erin and her had lightened up somewhat. They hadn't actually resolved anything, but at least Erin was maybe starting to come around.

Baby steps, right?

This weekend's party was going to be amazing.

CHAPTER

······

thirty

OWEN WAS UP to his elbows in beer science. He'd had a few ideas and was working out the flavors. Dunk and Disorderly was coming along well, with a sweet, donutlike tinge to the ale. That one was a definite go. The Lime and the Coconut was going to take a little more refining. Or maybe he'd toss it entirely, because he had a few other ideas to play with.

The most fun thing about the brewery was coming up with new beer flavors. It was the thing he loved most about his job. Beer had been his passion ever since his first visit to a craft brewery, and all he could think about from then on was starting his own. After college he'd sat down and plotted out his plan, and then put everything he had into making The Screaming Hawk a reality. He'd been lucky to find a great location and awesome people to work with, and they had an outstanding group of regulars who seemed to love his beer. So far, so good. But the one constant in this business was reinvention, and that was the part he loved the most. Creating new beer flavors was flat-out fun.

His phone buzzed. He pulled it out of his pocket and smiled when he saw Honor's name.

Are you busy? Her text read.

He typed a response: Playing mad scientist with beer. You?

She replied with: I'm parked outside.

His stomach knotted up knowing she was there. Was this a bad or a good thing? Hopefully good. He opened the door and saw her car in the parking lot. She got out just as he made his way to her car. That knot in his stomach dissolved when he saw her smiling.

"Hey," he said, pulling her into his arms to kiss her.

"Mmm." She licked her lips. "That's a nice greeting. I didn't mean to disturb you, but I had to pick up some things from one of our suppliers nearby, so I thought I'd drop in and see if you were busy. Mad scientist, huh?"

"New beer flavors." He wrapped his arm around her and walked her inside where it was cooler. "Want something to drink?"

"I'll take an ice water."

He fixed her a glass of ice water, handing it over to her, then made another one for himself. "Busy running errands today, huh?"

"Yes. But I also had an ulterior motive for stopping by."

"Yeah?" He leaned against the bar. "What's that?"

"We're doing a small surprise birthday party for my mom Saturday night. I know you probably can't come since you're working here, but you're invited."

"I'll see what I can do. Your mom has been great to

me. I'd really like to be there. Provided some of the family members won't freak out about me attending."

"They won't. I'll make sure of it."

He hoped that was true. "Then I'll do my best to show up."

"Okay. I'll text you the details."

"You wanna hang out for a while?" He moved in close to her, breathing in her citrusy scent.

She laid her palm against his chest. "I wish I could, but I can't. I have a few more errands to run. And you have to go do . . . sciency beer things."

"It sounds so sexy when you say it."

"Because it is. Because you are. Look at what you do here."

"It's just beer, babe."

"Oh, it's so much more than that. You have a talent for designing flavor profiles that your customers love. That's an art, Owen."

He'd never considered it an art, just something he loved doing. But seeing that glow of appreciation in Honor's eyes? That meant something to him.

He walked her out to her car, pulled her into his arms and kissed her again, briefly, because if he gave her the long, deep kiss he wanted to give her, he wouldn't be able to let her go.

He opened her car door. "You should leave, because I like the way you look, love the way your skin smells, and your mouth makes me crazy."

"You can't talk to me with sweet words like that and expect me to walk away." She gaped at him for a long beat, and he wondered if she was going to grab him by the hand and walk him inside. "Dammit. Why is my schedule so full today? I have to go."

He grinned. "Sorry."

"Me, too." She gave him a quick kiss, a regretful look, and got into her car.

He watched her drive away, then turned and went back inside, counting down the days and hours until he could see her again.

CHAPTER

······

thirty-one

TRYING TO KEEP a secret from Mom was one of the hardest things ever. Since their mother was in charge of the overall running of the Red Moss Vineyards and Bellini Weddings, both financial and operational, she had her finger on the pulse of, well, everything. Which meant that putting on this surprise birthday party required all three sisters to do the wild dance of hide-the-party. It also meant lying. Honor was getting very good at that, unfortunately.

Thankfully, they'd enlisted Dad's help, so he'd kept Mom distracted during this afternoon's wedding festivities, and, more importantly, right after. Between Honor's sisters and Dad, she was certain the secret was well kept.

Dad had taken Mom out for a ride down by the lake, which was one of her favorite things to do. At first she'd objected, saying she needed to help with the wedding cleanup, but he'd insisted, and since they were still in that second-honeymoon phase it didn't take much to convince her to agree.

Huge relief. Once the wedding guests left, and the cleaning crew finished up, the sisters, along with Mae, swooped in to set up for the birthday party. They got the barn decorated in record time with purple and white tablecloths—Mom's favorite colors. Honor put out the flowers she'd hidden away that had been delivered earlier.

The caterers arrived to set up the food, and they put the cake on a round table. They'd left the beautiful twinkle lights up from the wedding earlier, because their mom loved those, and they'd be gorgeous at night.

Honor stood at the entrance to the barn and looked out over all the tables.

"Stunning, right?"

She looked over at Erin, who'd just come in. "Yes, it's beautiful."

Honor was happy to be able to have a conversation with Erin, even if lately they'd been short ones. And Erin wasn't exactly all hugs and warmth, but at least they could stand close to each other without Honor feeling waves of animosity pouring off her sister.

Progress.

"Mom's going to be so shocked," Brenna said, coming up to stand on Honor's other side.

"I really hoped we nailed the surprise," Honor said.

"No way she knows." Erin stepped out and they all pulled the barn doors closed. "Now I need a drink."

"I could go for a drink," Mae said.

"Me, too," Brenna said. "Let's go grab one at the house since we have people to greet our guests."

They made their way to the house and fixed glasses of lemonade since Erin wasn't drinking wine.

"Dad said he'd come in around the back when they

got home so Mom wouldn't see all the cars in the parking lot."

"Perfect," Brenna said, leaning back in the chair in the living room. She picked up her phone. "He said he'd keep her away for about an hour and a half to give us time to set up and for the guests to arrive, so they should be back in about ten minutes."

"I guess we should head over to the barn," Mae said.

"And I just put my feet up and it feels so good." Erin made a pouty face.

"You could stay here," Honor said.

She leaned forward and put her heels back on. "Not a chance. I'm not about to miss Mom's surprised face."

They went back over to the barn and slipped inside. The room was filled with family and friends, all being served drinks. Soft music was playing and it was absolutely beautiful.

Jason came over to Erin and tugged her against him. "It looks amazing, babe."

"You all did great," Finn said, coming over to stand next to Brenna.

"Thanks," Brenna said, then picked up her phone to read a message. "Just got a text from Dad. They're home."

Erin signaled the band to stop playing, then walked to the center of the room. "All right, everyone. It's time for the big surprise."

The room quieted down. Honor's heart kicked up a beat as she and her sisters went to the doors. When they heard Mom and Dad at the entrance, they pulled the doors open and everyone yelled, "Surprise!" Mom's hand went to her heart and her eyes widened, and Honor knew right then that they had truly surprised her.

"What is all this?" Mom asked as she walked in.

"Happy birthday, Mom," Erin said, and then there was a family group hug.

"I can't believe this," their mother said. "How did you do this without me knowing about it?"

"Your daughters," Dad said. "They're very sneaky. I helped."

"Yes, you sure did," Mom said, kissing Dad.

The music started up and Mom and Dad went around the tables to greet everyone.

Honor looked around for Owen but didn't see him. She hoped he'd show up—one, because she wanted him to help celebrate with them tonight, and two, because she really wanted to see him.

In the meantime, they had a party to put on, and tonight was going to be a blast.

OF COURSE TONIGHT had to be the busiest Saturday night they'd had in weeks, but Owen was lucky to also have the best people working with him, so he could take the rest of the night off. He made sure everything was in order before he slipped away. He took Bettie home, and fortunately, she was tired out from working with him outside all day, and from wandering through the crowds at the bar tonight having everyone worship her—as was her due. So when they got home she got a long drink of water, did her business outside and went straight to her bed with her favorite stuffed bunny.

Owen took the fastest shower on record, put on jeans and a button-down shirt and slipped into his cowboy boots, then flew out the door and into his truck. He looked at the clock, realizing the party had started an hour ago.

Damn. He wished he could have been there earlier, but there was nothing he could have done about that.

When he pulled into the parking lot, it was full, and there were lights shining outside the barn. He headed that way, walking up the steps and opening the door, smiling when he saw the Bellini signature décor of bright lights and amazing music, not to mention the smell of incredible food. Hopefully he hadn't missed dinner.

"You're late, man. I already ate all the food."

He threw a glare at Jason. "You'd better be lying."

"He's lying," Finn said, "because I ate all the food."

"And I ate the leftovers," Clay said.

He shook his head. "You're all assholes."

Finn laughed and put his arm around Owen. "Plenty of food left. And drink. And the party's just getting started."

He followed the guys inside to a table where Erin, Brenna, Honor, Alice and Mae were sitting, along with some guy he didn't recognize that must be Mae's date. Honor's parents were standing over there talking with them, too. His stomach dropped, because this was where he was about to be judged for dating Honor.

"Oh, Owen, I'm so glad you could make it." Maureen Bellini stood and came over to put her arms around him.

He exhaled in relief and returned the hug. "Happy birthday, Maureen."

"Thank you." She held his hands and extended her arms. "You look good. You took off work on a Saturday night?"

"I couldn't miss your birthday party."

She tilted her head and smiled. "Thank you. Did you eat?"

"No, I just got here."

"Go eat something. Have drinks. Enjoy yourself."

"I will, thanks."

Johnny came over and shook his hand. "Good to see you here, figlio."

Son. From the time he was a kid, Johnny had always called him that. It warmed him to hear that word again. Especially after everything he'd been through with the Bellinis. He was happy to know that Johnny and Maureen had both softened some on him dating Honor.

Maybe they'd just needed some time to get used to the idea. He hoped that was the case, anyway.

"Thanks, Johnny. I'm happy to be here. Vineyard looks great."

Johnny beamed a smile. "It does, yes? Another good crop this year. Come by and try some wine soon."

"I'll do that." When Johnny invited you to sample the wine, you didn't turn him down. He made a mental note to drop by next week.

"The Marches just stopped by," Maureen said, grabbing Johnny's arm. "Let's go say hello."

"All right. Go dance with my daughter."

"And eat some food," Maureen said.

He smiled and nodded and watched them wander off.

Honor came over and grasped his arm. "Hi."

"Hi, yourself. Have I ever mentioned how beautiful you look in yellow?"

She smiled. "Thank you. Have I ever mentioned how hot you look in jeans and a shirt? Or out of jeans and a shirt?"

He grinned. "Well, thank you for both compliments."

"Hungry?"

"Starving."

She led him toward the tables where the food was laid out. "Wait till I show you what I cooked up tonight."

"Oh, you made this, huh?"

She laughed. "Right. Actually, Brenna did the ordering. I just approved her selections."

He filled his plate with the amazing array of veggies, fish fillets, and rice, then took a seat at the table, where he met Damon, who was Mae's date tonight. He sat and listened to everyone talk while he stuffed delicious food in his mouth.

"I need to check on the food trays with the caterers," Honor said. "I'll be right back."

"Do you need help?" Mae asked.

"No, I've got it. You stay here and enjoy." She shot Owen a smile, then hurried off.

And then Erin sat down next to him.

Honor didn't say how things were going between them, so he had no idea how this was going to play out.

"Owen."

"Erin."

"I'm surprised you managed to slip away from the brewery tonight."

He took a swallow of water before answering. "I got a bar manager to cover for me."

She arched a brow. "You have more than one now?"

"A few, actually."

"So business is growing. How nice for you."

There was an edge to her voice, but he wasn't going to take the bait. "Thanks. How are you feeling?"

She rubbed her belly, which was surprisingly already showing a bit of roundness. "Like this pregnancy is moving right along. But it's all good, thank you for asking."

"I'm happy for you and Jason. You'll both make amazing parents."

"Thank you. We're still so shocked it happened so fast."

Jason sat next to Erin, coughed and mumbled, "super sperm."

Erin rolled her eyes, but Owen laughed. "Hey, however it happened, you two are having a baby."

"Seems like just yesterday we were all shooting water guns at each other," Jason said.

"And then sometimes you and Clay and Owen would throw rocks at us," Brenna said.

"Yes, until Dad caught you and made you work in the vineyard all day," Erin said.

"It was brutal," Owen said. "He made us rake and tend soil and it was scorching hot while you girls sat there and ate Popsicles in front of us while all we got was water."

Jason nodded. "And even worse, Maureen told our parents, so not only did we get punished with a day of labor, we got our asses kicked when we got home."

Clay winced. "I remember that. Wasn't pleasant at all."

Erin laughed. "You all deserved it. Bullies."

Jason cocked his head at her. "We were eight."

"Assholes, even then," Brenna said.

Mae's date, Damon, looked over at her. She shrugged. "Before my time. I didn't meet up with Honor until high school."

"Really sorry I missed that part of your lives," Finn said. "Ow, you elbowed me." He looked over at Brenna.

"You would have joined in, wouldn't you?"

"Lass, I would never."

Jason snorted, then gave Brenna an innocent look

when she glared at him, which made Erin laugh. And
then Owen got up to grab a beer while everyone was
laughing.

So far, things were going well. Maybe the worst had
passed between Honor and Erin.

He hoped so.

IT HAD BEEN such a fun night. The best part was that
Mom had been genuinely surprised. They'd had a great
crowd, and everyone had a good time. The food had
been delicious, the band had played all of Mom's favorite songs and she and Dad had danced for hours.

Almost everyone had left, with only the family remaining. And Owen and Finn, of course. Honor and
Owen had danced, too, and it had felt so good to be in
his arms. She'd finally been able to relax after all this
time. And, sure, maybe she'd had a little wine. More
than a little wine. Okay, a lot of wine.

She'd gotten her period two days ago, so she definitely wasn't pregnant. She should have told Owen about
that, but for some reason she hadn't yet. She didn't know
why. Maybe it was all the birthday party planning, or
maybe it was because the end of the pregnancy specula-
tion would also signal the end of their marriage, and she
wasn't ready for that just yet.

Was that unfair to Owen? Probably. But there'd just
been so much going on, and she wanted to enjoy a few
stress-free days before they had to sit down and officially discuss dissolving their marriage.

She looked across the room to see him sitting with
Jason, Finn, Brenna and Erin, which kind of surprised
her, but maybe that was a good thing. They were all

engrossed in conversation about . . . something. He'd
rolled up his shirtsleeves and she focused on his forearms, so muscular, the way those hairs on his arms felt
whenever she rubbed her hand across them.

She should go home with him tonight so she could
get his forearms totally naked. No, wait, they were already naked, weren't they? But other parts of him weren't,
and she'd definitely like to see those parts.

Good God, she was slightly inebriated, wasn't she?

Anyway, she went to check on a few things. When
she came back, everyone was laughing, but Owen wasn't
with the group. They were pointing at him as he stood at
the bar.

How dare they make fun of him behind his back? Say
what they want about her, but she was not going to let
them do this to the man she loved.

She marched over to the group.

"Okay, look. I get that Erin's pregnant and you're all
sensitive to that, but you could be kinder to Owen and
not laugh behind his back."

Erin blinked. "Honor. What the hell are you talking
about? He was just—"

"I come up here and find you pointing fingers at him
and laughing. Could you be any more cruel, Erin? I
mean, come for me if you want to, but leave Owen out
of this."

"Honor," Brenna said. "I think—"

Honor held up her hand. "I've got this, Bren. It's time
Erin and I have it out."

Erin stood. "Maybe it is time for us to have it out.
This has gone on for too long."

"Okay, enough. You three, come with me."

Honor looked up to see her mother's angry face staring down at her. She grimaced.

"Mom, I—"

"She started it," Erin said. "I didn't even do anything."

"And I don't want to hear it. Not anymore. Erin, Honor, come with me right now. Brenna, you come, too."

Brenna stood. "Me? What did I do?"

"Just come along."

"Well, shit," Brenna said, shooting a questioning look at Honor.

Honor could only shrug. Mom was using her angry voice, and when she did that, you didn't argue with her.

They followed their mother through the door and into a room they used for storage. She pulled out three chairs.

"Are you serious?" Erin asked.

"The three of you are going to sit here and work through this, and I don't want you coming out until you've all made up."

"This is ridiculous. I'm not going to—"

"Erin. Sit down." Mom gave her the look. Erin sat.

"When the three of you are all acting like friends and sisters again and have worked through this, then you can come out. I'll bring you some lemonade."

"What if I have to pee?" Brenna asked.

"You are not too old for me to go to your father."

Brenna took a seat and crossed her arms. Since it seemed like there'd be no escape, Honor sat as well.

"Now give me your phones."

Erin's head shot up. "What? You can't—"

"Mom, come on," Brenna said, interrupting Erin.

"This is kind of ridiculous," Honor added.

"No phones. No playing games or texting your complaints to anyone. Just the three of you, talking."

Honor rolled her eyes but handed her phone over. Erin and Brenna did the same, after a lot of grumbling.

Mom brought a pitcher of lemonade and three glasses, then closed the door behind her.

Dead silence. Honor finally got up and poured a glass.

"Anyone want some lemonade?" she asked.

"I'll take one," Brenna said.

She filled a glass and delivered it to Brenna, then turned to Erin.

"Erin?"

Erin waited a beat before saying, "Fine. I'll take one."

She handed the glass to her sister, then sat down and took a sip, enjoying the tart sweetness of the always perfect lemonade. She looked up to see Erin staring at her hands, rubbing her fingers over her nails. Brenna played with the bracelets on her wrists. They could be at this all night.

"This is so stupid," Brenna said. "It's like we're kids again."

Brenna wasn't lying about that. Their mother had always made them sit together in a room and talk out their problems. It typically worked. And if they wanted to get out of this particular issue, the only way to do it was for one of them to start talking.

"Okay, I'll go first," Honor said, shifting in her chair to face Erin. "Erin, I'm sorry for not telling you right away that I was dating Owen, and for whatever else you think I did wrong. If you'll just tell me we can talk it out."

Erin continued to focus on her nails.

"I'll go next," Brenna said. "No one was laughing at Owen, Honor. We were reminiscing about childhood antics and laughing, and then Owen got up to grab a beer and we were all still laughing. That's what you saw."

"Really?"

"Yeah."

"But maybe your guilt over dating my ex-fiancé made you read more into it," Erin said.

"It would if I felt guilty about it, which I don't. But I am sorry about accusing you."

Erin clamped her lips together after Honor's apology, and the room fell silent again.

"You know how Mom is, Erin," Brenna said. "She will actually keep us in this room until we work this out. Do you really want to give birth in here?"

Honor tried her best not to laugh.

Erin looked up. "Fine. You didn't tell me you were dating Owen. I just don't get it. Why did it have to be this big secret? Why didn't you tell me earlier?"

In that moment, Honor decided to come completely clean with Erin. She was so tired of lying. And maybe it was time for the truth to come out.

The whole truth. Then they could really clear the air.

"Okay, I'm going to tell you the whole truth this time. No more lying."

Erin cocked her head to the side.

"We were never dating. I mean, we're dating now, but what actually happened was, Owen and I ran into each other in Vegas. We were both there for conferences and ended up staying at the same hotel."

"And that's when you started dating?" Brenna asked.

She rubbed her temple. "Not exactly. See, we decided to have drinks and then dinner, only instead of dinner we ended up doing shots of tequila, which led to more shots, and the next thing we knew we woke up in bed together the next morning. Married."

She gave her sisters a little grimacy smile.

"You're married," Erin said. "To Owen."

"Yes."

"This whole time you've been married to Owen and you didn't tell anyone?" Brenna asked.

"Yes."

"Why?"

That slight headache that was burrowing its way between her eyes was growing ever stronger.

"Well, at first we thought it had been a huge mistake and we'd just get the marriage annulled, of course, so why would we even tell anyone about it, right? But we'd both been really drunk and couldn't exactly remember what happened that night, except we were both pretty sure there'd been sex. Only we couldn't remember if we'd used protection or not, and there was a possibility I could be pregnant, so to be safe, we decided to hold off on the annulment until I got my period. And then we talked to an attorney who told us our circumstances didn't qualify for an annulment, so we've started divorce proceedings while still waiting on that whole baby-or-no-baby thing."

Another smiley grimace while she waited for their replies.

"So not only are you married, but you could also be pregnant?" Erin asked.

"No, I'm not pregnant. I just got my period," Honor replied.

"And yet you couldn't tell us any of this?" Brenna asked. "Your own sisters?"

"We didn't tell anyone. I didn't want anyone to know."

"Because it's Owen," Erin said. "And you knew you'd made a huge mistake, right?"

Honor frowned. "No. That's not it at all."

Erin stood and started pacing. "Of all the irresponsible—I cannot believe you did this, Honor. How could you?"

Her voice had gotten loud. And then suddenly their mother was there.

"Aren't you supposed to be talking things out—"

"She's married, Mom," Erin said. "Honor and Owen have been married to each other since her trip to Las Vegas. She's been lying to all of us."

She felt dizzy and sick. She hadn't meant to spill it this way, to hurt Erin—everyone—this way.

Honor's mother looked over at her. "You got married in Las Vegas?"

She didn't feel very good, and suddenly Owen was in the room, his cool hand on the back of her neck, his gorgeous face in front of her.

"Are you all right?" he asked.

"I need some water."

He disappeared for only a few seconds and came back with a glass of ice water.

"Take some sips."

She did, and it helped, because her throat had gone dry. When she looked up, everyone was there. Her family, her friends, all staring at her as if she'd done the most terrible thing.

"I . . . I . . ." She had nothing.

And then she was being pulled up, out of her chair.

"She can't do this tonight," Owen said. "You can talk to her about it tomorrow."

"You have no right—"

"I have every right," Owen answered Erin. "She's not up to this, and I'm taking her home with me. We'll all talk tomorrow."

Honor leaned against Owen, grateful to be taken away from her family. All she wanted to do was hide, to shut out the accusatory voices of her sisters and her mother.

Owen helped her into his truck and buckled her in. She closed her eyes and let herself feel the lull of movement as he drove. If her eyes stayed closed, she was floating, and happy. She could shove out those last minutes as if they didn't exist.

"Come on, babe," he said, his voice soft as he helped her out of the truck and led her into the house.

And then her clothes were off and she felt cool sheets and a soft pillow. She reached out for him and he was there.

"Thank you," she said.

He kissed her lips, and then she fell asleep.

CHAPTER
......
thirty-two

OWEN PACED THE kitchen and drank his coffee, waiting for Honor to wake up.

It was nine a.m. He'd already been out to feed the animals. He'd fed Bettie and taken her on a walk through the pastures. Then he'd come back inside, figuring she'd be up by then.

She wasn't up. Not that he could blame her. Not after last night. He wouldn't want to face the questions her family had thrown at her, either.

He hadn't noticed she was drunk. Enjoying her wine? Yeah. But drunk? Nah. He didn't know what had happened, but somehow she'd told Erin that they were married. Had she done it deliberately, or had it slipped out unintentionally?

"Hey."

He looked up to see Honor standing in the doorway. She'd obviously washed her face and brushed her hair, having pulled it into a ponytail on top of her head. He was glad he'd thought to grab her purse before they left last night, knowing how important purse-things were to women:

"Hi. Want some coffee?"

"Yes, please." She walked into the kitchen and took a seat at the table, running her fingers over Bettie's fur as she stared outside.

He brought her some coffee and pulled up a chair next to her. "Do you feel okay?"

"No. I feel miserable. And stupid. I can't believe I told everyone that we were married." She looked over at him. "Can I just hide out here at your house? Like . . . forever?"

He smiled. "Yes." Actually, he'd like that, but he wasn't about to tell her that.

She curved her hands around the cup and took several swallows, then sighed. "Now I have more explaining to do."

"No, *we* have more explaining to do. You didn't do this marriage thing alone, Honor. We'll go together, explain it, and then it'll be done. All out in the open. No more secrets."

She nodded and stared at her coffee. "Okay."

"But first you need some food in you."

"That's not necessary."

"Yeah, it is. You can't go into battle on an empty stomach. Everybody knows that."

She gave him a half smile. "Of course, they do."

He made eggs, bacon and toast, along with some sliced cantaloupe, then poured some glasses of orange juice. He didn't expect Honor to eat much, but to his surprise, she cleaned her plate. She was either hungry or avoiding going home.

Maybe a bit of both.

After they cleaned up the dishes, she dried her hands and turned to him. "Do you need to take a shower or anything?"

"I already did that while you were sleeping. I used the other bathroom."

She sighed. "You could have come in and used your bathroom."

"I didn't want to bother you while you were sleeping."

She pushed off the counter and came over to him and laid her head on his chest. "I've made a mess of things, Owen. Including your life. I'm sorry for that."

"Hey." He peeled her away from him. "You have nothing to be sorry for. And you didn't make a mess of my life. Before we go to your place, you need to change your mindset. Be positive and upbeat. Be happy about where we are right now."

"Right. And where is that exactly, since we're supposed to be only temporarily married? With a divorce to come."

"Oh, yeah." This was kind of a mess, wasn't it? "I don't know. We'll figure it out together. In the meantime, we'll just explain what happened. Hopefully everyone will laugh."

She cocked her head to the side. "Really, Owen?"

"Okay, they won't laugh. But we'll get through it together, okay?"

"Okay. Might as well rip the Band-Aid off. I'm ready whenever you are. Let me just text Brenna to let her know we're on our way."

After she sent the text, they climbed in the truck and Owen brought Bettie along, figuring she'd be a balm for Honor.

Whatever happened, he'd be ready for it. And ready to support Honor.

They parked outside and Owen noticed no one was waiting in the yard with shotguns. Not that he expected that. Okay, maybe he did, at least metaphorically. So at least that was a relief.

He put his arm around Honor, felt the tension in her body. "It's going to be okay."

She gave him a tight smile. "It will."

They walked through the front door and down the hall, and there they all were, sitting at the table.

Bettie greeted everyone. They might be mad at Owen and Honor, but a dog was always welcome at the Bellinis'. She got lots of pets and then sat next to Johnny, who rubbed her head.

"Took you long enough," Brenna said.

"Sorry," Honor said. She started forward, then stalled. "I . . . need a shower and a change of clothes first. I'll be quick, I promise."

She looked to Owen. "I'll be right back."

He gave her a nod. "Go ahead."

She disappeared up the stairs.

"Oh, come on," Erin said. "I've got things to do."

"Erin," Maureen said. "Give her a minute."

"I've given her weeks."

Owen just stood there, not knowing what to do or where to go, which was so unusual since this place had always been his second home. Finally, Maureen asked, "Owen, would you like some coffee?"

"I'd love some, thank you."

"Well, I've got a few calls to make, so someone nudge me when the queen makes her grand entrance." Erin got up and left the room.

Owen tried not to wince at Erin's sharp tone, instead following Maureen into the kitchen. Louise was in there cooking up something delicious, as always.

"Hey, Louise," he said.

She gave him a bright smile. "Hi, Owen."

Maureen poured him a cup and handed it to him. "Thanks."

He turned and followed Maureen back into the dining room, feeling like all eyes were on him. He took a seat and Finn gave him a sympathetic look.

Bettie came over and lay down by his feet.

And then Jason walked in.

"What are you doing here?" Brenna asked.

Jason shrugged. "I don't know. Erin told me I needed to be here for this. I had a farm call nearby anyway, so here I am. Hey, Owen."

Owen nodded. "Jason." Well, this should be fun.

Honor came back downstairs, her hair damp. She wore a pair of shorts and a T-shirt and when she sat next to him, she smelled so damn good he wanted to hold her and kiss her and tell her everything was going to be all right. But the way everyone stared at them as if they'd done something wrong made him not so sure that was the case.

Maureen went to get Erin, and the two of them came back in and took their seats.

"Okay, Honor," Maureen said. "Why don't you tell us what happened in Las Vegas between you and Owen?"

Honor inhaled on a shaky breath, then let it out. "We ran into each other at the hotel. It turns out we were both there for conferences. So we had a drink in the bar, and we were going to have dinner together. Only one drink led to another drink—"

"Which led to shots," he added, smiling at her.

She smiled back. "Yes. Lots of shots."

Erin cleared her throat, which caused Honor to pull her attention from him and back onto her family. "Anyway, we woke up the next morning in a different hotel. Married."

It went silent after that.

"And that's it," Erin said. "You got drunk married. So why not just laugh it off and get it annulled?"

She chewed on her lower lip and hesitated. Owen put his arm around the back of her chair.

"Because there's the possibility that Honor might be pregnant," Owen finally answered. "We decided to wait it out since we might decide to stay married if Honor is pregnant. So we figured we'd keep it a secret at least until then, knowing everyone would freak out." He made it a point to look directly at Erin.

"Are you serious?" Erin asked. "I thought you said you weren't pregnant?"

Honor looked down at her lap. "I'm definitely not pregnant."

Owen looked at her, feeling as if he'd been punched in the stomach. "You're not? You didn't tell me."

She lifted her gaze to his. "I'm sorry. I just got my period a couple of days ago. I meant to tell you, but there's been a lot going on."

"Okay, then," Brenna said. "Now you can get your marriage annulled or get your divorce or whatever. Unless there's some reason you don't want to."

They continued to look at each other, neither of them saying a word.

"This is so ridiculous," Erin said. "Drunk married at the drop of a hat, keeping it all a secret like it's some game. It sure didn't take you long to marry this sister, Owen."

"Hey." Jason grasped Erin's hand. "What's this all about, babe? Why does it even matter to you that they got married? You've been at Honor ever since you found out they were dating. Do you still have feelings for Owen or something?"

She shook her head. "That's not it at all. I'm just trying to protect my sister."

"It seems to me that you're angry about her being with Owen, which makes me think you're not over him."

Now Erin shifted in her chair. "No, that's not it at all."

"Isn't it? Maybe you should start thinking about how *you* feel instead of butting into other people's feelings." He got up and walked out, leaving Erin staring after him.

When he left, Erin got that angry look on her face. Owen had definitely seen that look before.

This was not going to go well.

HONOR COULDN'T BELIEVE this was all happening. It was the last thing she'd wanted. She felt like she was hurting everyone she loved.

"Erin, I'm sorry you're hurting, but believe me when I tell you we didn't deliberately set out to cause anyone pain."

"Are you in love with him?" Erin asked.

"What?"

"With Owen. Are you in love with him or is this some game you're playing?"

"Of course it's not a game."

"You didn't answer my question. Are. You. In. Love. With. Him."

Honor saw all the expectant looks on the faces of her parents and Brenna, and the angry, hurt look Erin directed at her. She shifted to Owen, who gave her the sweetest, half-apologetic, half "I'm here for you" smile.

Of course she was in love with him. She had been for years. Wasn't that part of the reason she'd made a mess of every relationship she'd had during her adult life? Because she'd wanted Owen. Even when he was engaged to Erin, deep down she'd wanted him, knowing she'd never have him.

Now? All she had to do was say that yes, she was in love with him.

But seeing that pained look on Erin's face made her pause. She'd already caused her sister so much heartache. Could she really dig the knife in deeper, now, when Erin seemed so vulnerable?

"I . . . I don't know."

Owen's face fell. "I, uh, think I have to go do some things." He stood and walked toward the door.

She hurried after him, stopping him on the porch.

"Owen, don't. I just . . . didn't know what to say. We're in this huge group and my family is all staring at me. I didn't know what to say." She was repeating herself and she knew it, but she couldn't get the right words out, the ones she'd wanted to say but couldn't. Because those words should be said for the first time when it was just the two of them. And when everything wasn't so confusing.

"It's okay. I get it. We both knew this was temporary and now it's over."

"No, it's not. Don't say that. Look, I get that it was

tough in there—for both of us. But we can work through it, right?"

"I've caused nothing but pain for you and your family. This is all my fault—again, and I need to stop the cycle of hurt."

She frowned. "I don't understand."

"I can't continue to be the source of all this turmoil between you and your sister—with you and your family. I can't keep putting you or your family through it."

She couldn't believe he was taking this all on himself. "Owen, it's not you. It's—"

"What are you going to say? That it's Erin? No, Honor. It's me. I'm the problem, and this time I'm removing myself from the equation so your life and Erin's life and your relationship with your family can get back to normal."

She crossed her arms, the need to protect herself so powerful it made her want to run inside and lock the door so she could lock away all this hurt. "So you won't stay and fight with me. For me."

"I think we know how we both feel about this."

"Oh, you know how I feel?"

"You made it pretty clear in there."

The problem was, she hadn't. And that was on her. But Owen just had. He wasn't willing to fight for her. To choose her.

"Fine. Walk away. No, run away again, Owen. It's what you're good at, isn't it?"

She refused to acknowledge the look of pain that flashed across his face. Instead, she stood with her chin held high as he walked down the steps to his truck and drove away.

She'd hurt him. Badly.

She sat on the steps and stared out at the vineyard, not knowing what to do next. She'd screwed up so many things, had hurt people she cared deeply about.

Why hadn't she just told her sisters about the Vegas marriage as soon as it had happened? Maybe Erin would have reacted differently and they would have all laughed about it.

And why couldn't she have admitted just now that she loved Owen? What was she so afraid of? She didn't want to hurt Erin any more than she already had.

Or maybe she was afraid that Owen didn't love her back.

Her mind was jumbled and her head hurt.

She didn't know how long she'd been sitting out there, but she heard the front door open and hoped it wasn't Erin, because she didn't have the emotional bandwidth to go through another battle with her sister.

Instead, her dad sat down next to her.

"I'm sorry, bambina," he said, running his hand over the top of her head like he'd always done when she was little and feeling sad. "Things didn't work out like you thought they would."

She leaned against her dad. "I've messed everything up, Daddy. I don't know what to do. I've hurt Erin, and now I've hurt Owen. And then he hurt me back."

He put his arm around her. It took him a while to say anything, which was typical of her dad, who was always one to ponder his words before speaking.

"Owen—you love him, yes or no?"

This time, despite the painful argument they'd just had, she didn't hesitate. "Yes, I do."

"Why didn't you say so in there?"

"I don't know, Dad. I think all the pressure, everyone staring at me. I was scared. I didn't want to hurt Erin more than I already have."

"Does he love you?"

"I think he does."

"Hmm."

He went quiet again, but she didn't mind. It was enough that her dad was there with her, giving her the comfort she so desperately needed.

"Your sister has always had big feelings," he said.

"I know."

"But that doesn't mean your feelings don't matter, cara, because they do. Being the youngest doesn't mean you aren't important. You matter just as much as Erin. I don't want you to ever forget that."

Her heart swelled with love for her dad. She threw her arms around him and hugged him close. "Grazie, Papa."

"Now, you have to figure out how to make peace with your sister, and tell Owen you love him."

She pulled her knees to her chest. "I don't know how to fix all of this."

He grasped her chin in his hand. "You have always been the peacemaker. You'll find a way."

After her dad left, she thought about it, wondering why it was up to her to fix everything when she wasn't the only one who'd broken it.

Okay, that was only partially true. Her fight with Erin was on both Honor and her sister. But with Owen? Yes, she'd definitely wrecked that relationship mostly by herself, and it was on her to repair it. If that was even possible.

They'd both said things to each other that hurt. And he hadn't chosen her, hadn't stayed to fight with her. Instead, he'd walked away. Again.

But still, she was in love with him. And even though that idea scared the hell out of her, her feelings weren't going to change.

So now what was she supposed to do?

CHAPTER
······
thirty-three

OWEN WAS CLEANING out the chicken coop when he heard a truck pull up out front. Bettie let him know they had company by using her official vicious bark. She was a marshmallow, but at least she sounded mean. He pulled the rag from his back pocket to wipe his hands and headed through the backyard to check things out. By then Jason was already in the yard petting Bettie.

"Some guard dog you are," he said to Bettie.

Jason laughed, then stood. "She also led me right to you. All while wagging her tail."

Owen looked down at Bettie, who was currently on her back, wagging her tail, begging for belly rubs. "Yeah she's a hell of a watchdog. Come on inside and we'll get something cold to drink."

"Sounds good to me."

Jason followed him into the house, along with his traitorous dog. After Owen washed his hands, he got some iced tea out of the fridge and poured two glasses, handing one to Jason, who was currently sitting at the table, leaning over to examine Bettie's ears. Bettie looked up at Jason with something along the lines of adoration on her face.

"Can't turn off the veterinarian mode, can you?"

Jason looked up at him. "Hey, I was just petting her."

"Uh-huh. So, how are her ears?"

"Clean. You're doing a great job with her."

"You had any doubt?"

"No. But I do like to check."

Jason was an excellent vet, one of the many things he liked about his friend. "You're a good guy. And I appreciate how much you care about Bettie."

"Hey, thanks. Speaking of caring, and friendship and all that shit, I have a serious question to ask you."

Owen took a seat at the table. "Okay, shoot."

"It's about Erin."

"All right."

He paused, and Owen could tell it was taking some time for Jason to come up with the right words.

"Hey, buddy," Owen said, figuring that maybe he should be the one to start. "We've been friends for almost our whole lives. There isn't anything you can say to me that'll change that."

Jason nodded. "Okay. Do you have any unresolved feelings for Erin?"

He leaned back. "No. Not at all. Why?"

"I don't know." Jason dragged his fingers through his hair. "I'm trying to figure out where all this shit with Erin has come from. You know, her being pissed off about you and Honor being together. And she keeps telling me she doesn't want Honor to get hurt. But I think it's more than that. I think the majority of it has to do with you."

"With me?"

"Yeah. I don't know if she still has feelings for you that she can't talk to me about, or if it's something else. But she won't speak to me about it. So I thought I'd start with you and see if there was anything you felt."

He leaned forward. "I'll tell you right now, Jason, that I am one hundred percent in love with Honor. Erin is part of my past. I don't feel anything for her other than friendship."

Jason blew out a breath. "Okay, thanks. That's good to know. I mean, I didn't think there was anything between the two of you, but at the same time, I think there is, at least on Erin's part."

"Do you doubt that she loves you?"

"No. And she's told me that over and over."

"And do you believe her?"

"Yeah. But I still think there's something in her head—maybe in her heart—that's unresolved between the two of you."

"Then we need to resolve it, so the two of you can move on with your lives. Do you think it'll hurt or help things if I go talk to her?"

"At this point, I honestly don't know, but we can't keep fighting about you."

Owen nodded. "Then I'll talk to her. If nothing else, maybe she'll get pissed off at me and the two of you can get back on track."

Jason laughed. "Thanks. Let's hope that's not what happens."

"I do think it would be a good idea if you were there when we talked. That way you know exactly what's on her mind."

"You're probably right. Why don't you drop by the house tonight? The brewery is closed, right?"

"Yeah. Just text me and let me know what time."

"I'll do that. Now, how are things going with you and Honor?"

He was hoping that topic wouldn't come up. "They're not. We broke up. Or at least I think we did."

Jason gave him a sympathetic look. "I'm sorry, man. But you love her, right?"

"Yeah."

"So, fix it."

"I don't think it's that simple."

"It never is. But if you love her, you don't want to lose her, right?"

"Right. But I hurt her."

"Exactly. So you both hurt each other. One of you needs to swallow your pride and take the first step."

Owen blew out a breath. "Yeah. You're right. Thanks, man."

"Hey," Jason said with a half shrug. "I'm always right. If only my wife knew that."

Owen laughed. "Yeah, I'm sure she doesn't buy into that line of bullshit."

"You got that right."

After Jason left, Owen went back to working outside. But thoughts of Erin crept into his head. He knew she didn't have feelings for him. They'd settled that long ago, back when he'd confessed the reason he'd bailed on their wedding. They'd had long conversations while he'd been undergoing cancer treatments and he was confident that they'd covered everything.

But maybe he'd missed something, and he owed it to Erin to let her talk it through. And maybe then she could finally put the past away.

Even more importantly, he needed to talk to Honor, and that was going to take some thinking and planning. Because he couldn't just rush over to her house and blurt out that he loved her. That wasn't going to be enough. He'd hurt her, and he had to tell her all the reasons why. And then some serious groveling would be in order, because she was right. He had walked away, and she deserved better than that.

Now he had to prove to her that despite all his flaws, he was still the right man for her.

But one thing at a time, and the first thing on his list was fixing the situation with Erin.

After he finished up with the yard work and the animals, he did chores like laundry and paying bills, then cleaned up and went to the grocery store. It had been a good, productive day, which he'd needed to get his mind off what was coming tonight.

Jason had texted and told him to come over around eight, so he grilled some chicken breasts and made a salad, watched sports for a while, then took Bettie out for a wander around the property before it was time to head over to Jason and Erin's house.

It was hot and humid and his shirt was sticking to him, which didn't do much to help his confidence, but he figured he was going to let Erin do the talking anyway. He went up to the door and rang the bell.

Jason answered. "Thanks for coming."

"Thanks for inviting me."

He stepped in and followed Jason to the living room, where Erin had her legs curled up on the sofa while she was watching TV. When she saw him, she frowned. "What are you doing here?"

"I invited him," Jason said. "It's time you two talk."

She lifted her chin and glared at Jason. "Owen and I don't have anything to talk about."

Jason sat on the ottoman in front of the sofa and took Erin's hands. "I actually went to Owen today and asked him if he still had feelings for you, because I'm so damn worried about us."

Erin sat up. "What? Why would you do that?"

"Because I keep asking you over and over again what's bothering you about Honor and Owen being together, and you won't give me a straight answer. And I think you have some residual feelings for Owen. I want you two to talk it out so we can move forward with our lives."

Owen hung in the background, feeling embarrassingly like a voyeur into what should have been a very private conversation between husband and wife. And when he saw tears shimmer in Erin's eyes, he knew he'd hit the mark about him being involved somehow.

"Fine," she said. "Owen and I will talk. But you'll stay, okay?"

He took her hand. "Yeah, I'll stay."

Jason looked up at Owen and nodded, so he came forward. Jason got up and sat next to Erin, and Owen took the spot on the ottoman where Jason had been sitting.

"There's nothing you can say to me that I haven't already thought about myself, Erin," he said. "But there's no reason to take it out on Honor, if I'm the one you're pissed at."

She sighed. "Honestly, Owen, I just don't know. My reaction to seeing you two together made me red-hot angry."

"Let me make a suggestion. Maybe it's me you're mad at, because you never got the chance to express that anger when I was sick."

She started to say something, then cocked her head to the side and just stared at him.

"Babe," Jason said. "You okay?"

She reached over and patted Jason's leg. "Yes, I'm fine. You know, Owen, you might be on to something there. We had talked so much when you were sick, and I thought we had resolved everything. Everything but how utterly pissed off I was about you dumping me and disappearing just days before our wedding."

Now they were getting somewhere. Now her real feelings were coming out. "Which was a total dick move."

"Yes, it was. How could you do that to me? You said you loved me, and even if things between us hadn't been ideal, we had been friends since childhood. You don't treat someone you care about that way. I'm so mad at you for that, Owen. You hurt me."

"I know. I'm so sorry, Erin. What I did was shitty and reprehensible, and no one who claims to care about someone should ever do that."

"You're right. They shouldn't. You shouldn't have. Even a phone call would have been better than that lame-ass email you sent me. You were a coward and a bastard and I hated you."

Whoa. It was really coming out now, but she had every right to let him have it, so he was going to sit there and take it.

"I'm so sorry. You're right. It's an unforgivable offense and I offer up no excuses other than what I told you that day we talked. I was afraid and consumed with dealing with treatment. I didn't think of you or my family or anything other than trying to survive. Which is no excuse for the way I treated you. I should have respected you enough to tell you the truth."

"Yes, you should have. Even if we had broken up right then, at least I would have known what was going on, instead of thinking there was something wrong with me."

"It was never you. It was me. All me."

"You broke my heart. And falling in love with Jason doesn't erase that."

"No, it doesn't. And I will always feel awful for the way I handled it." He dragged his fingers through his hair, inhaled a deep breath, those old feelings of guilt wrapping themselves tightly around him again, making it hard for him to breathe. But Erin had every right to express herself. "You have no idea how often thoughts of what I did—how I handled things—creep into my head. I still carry a lot of guilt for how I treated you, how I ended things between us. I don't have regrets about any part of my past except for that. If I could have one do-over in my life, it would be the way we broke up. I'm so sorry, Erin. I will always feel like shit about that."

She almost smiled. "That makes me feel marginally better."

"Good."

She shifted to face Jason. "And I'm sorry for letting you think for one second that you aren't the absolute love of my life. You are my one and only love, the only man I want to raise a family with. You have my entire heart, Jason."

Jason leaned over and kissed her, and Owen stared out the window, giving them that moment.

"Okay," Erin said. "Thanks, Owen. I needed to get that out."

"You deserved to let it out and I'm sorry it took this long."

She shuddered out an exhale. "When I saw you with Honor, I was angry. Not because I was jealous or had feelings for you, but angry, and I didn't know where it was coming from. Now I know, of course, but before, I didn't. And then in my mixed-up head I thought I was trying to protect Honor, hoping the two of you would fail so you couldn't hurt her. And I'm sorry about that, because it was wrong."

She shook her head. "Oh, God. I have got to talk to my sister. I've really messed things up with her. And so have you, Owen."

"Yeah, I need to talk to her, too."

"Aren't we doing family dinner tomorrow night at your parents'?" Jason asked.

"Yes." Erin looked over at Owen. "Please come to dinner. We'll both talk to Honor."

"I don't know. I don't think I'm very welcome at your family's place right now."

"You let me take care of that," Erin said. "Please say you'll come."

It could work in his favor. Maybe she wouldn't throw him out if he could get Erin on his side. "Okay. I'll be there."

He got up and so did Erin. And then she hugged him.

When she pulled back, she said, "Owen, I forgive you. Let's put the past where it belongs, and leave it there for good."

"I'd like that."

"I'd for sure like that," Jason said.

Erin went over and leaned against Jason. "Only the future now, babe."

"For sure."

Owen was so happy for his friends, and happy to finally be free of the pain and guilt over what he'd done to Erin. Now he could move on. And moving on meant a future with Honor. If she'd forgive him.

He'd find out tomorrow night.

CHAPTER

. . . . . .

thirty-four

HONOR HAD SPENT the entire workday locked in her office, avoiding contact with her family. If she didn't have to see or talk to anyone, then she wouldn't have to fight with anyone. And right now, all she craved was some peace. Fortunately, everyone had left her alone, with the exception of Mae, but Mae wasn't pissed at her, so that was okay.

She looked up when she heard Mae's knock on the door and called out for her to come in.

Mae slid her laptop down on the desk. "Are you going to hide in here all day, or come out for air sometime?"

"I'll leave the office. Eventually."

"Erin's in a good mood today. Just FYI."

She looked through her office doors to where Erin sat talking on the phone. She was actually smiling, which Honor hadn't seen lately. "She's probably in a good mood because she hasn't had to see me."

Mae frowned. "I don't think that's it. And you two are going to have to talk eventually."

"Will we, though? I have a very comfortable office, and she usually goes home by six."

"Not tonight, though. Brenna reminded me it was family dinner night and asked if I'd stay. And Erin said she was looking forward to dinner, and Jason was going to be there, too."

Crap. Honor loved family dinner. There was always a huge spread, and Louise had told her they were having a seafood boil tonight. Which meant crab and shrimp and potatoes and corn on the cob. Plus, homemade bread. Honor's stomach was already growling just thinking about it.

The hell with it. She wasn't going to let Erin or anyone in the family keep her from enjoying one of her favorite meals.

"I will leave my office cave for family dinner."

Mae grinned. "Excellent. Maybe you and your sister will actually manage to have a conversation."

"Yeah, and pigs will fly across the dining room table tonight, too."

Honor and Mae got down to work putting the finishing touches on this weekend's weddings, which took her mind off having to sit at the table with her sister. By the time they were finished, it was close to dinnertime. Mae left to tidy up her own office, and Honor headed upstairs to freshen up. When she started back downstairs, she paused, then frowned.

Was that Owen's voice she heard? Her heart did a small leap.

No, it couldn't be. What would he be doing here?

She inched down the stairs, and then, like she had when she was a child, she peeked between the stair slats.

Sure enough, there was Owen, standing in the dining room, beer in hand, talking with Jason.

And Erin.

And everyone was smiling. Erin wasn't even stabbing Owen with a knife.

Had she fallen asleep upstairs and this was all a dream? Had she stepped into an alternate universe?

The only way to find out is to actually go into the room, girl.

She wrinkled her nose and mentally shushed her internal voice, which was, of course, right as usual. She stood and walked nonchalantly into the dining room.

"Oh, Owen. You're here."

Way to be obvious, Honor.

She and her inner voice were going to have a harsh conversation later.

"Yeah. I got an invite and who would want to miss seafood boil night?"

"Right."

She wanted to ask who invited him, because as far as she knew no one in the family was speaking to him. Except everyone in the family was speaking to him, apparently. Her mom smiled at Owen as she brought the plates in. And Dad had chimed in on the conversation Jason and Erin were having with him.

And then Brenna and Finn walked in.

"Hi, all. Sorry we're late," Brenna said. "Hey, Owen."

What in the seventh level of hell was going on here?

Honor went to the sideboard and poured herself a very large glass of sangria, took several swallows, then turned to face the group gathered there.

"I have a question."

"What's that?" Brenna asked.

"Why is Owen here?"

"Oh," Erin said. "I invited him."

What? Had she lapsed into a coma and missed a year of her life or something? Except Erin was very obviously pregnant so she didn't think that had happened. "You invited him. Excuse me but what did I miss?"

"Well, if you'll let me explain, Owen and I talked last night and got some things figured out. So I thought it might be nice if he came to dinner. And maybe you two could work some things out, too."

"Oh, is that right? How nice of you to make all these arrangements without my consent, Erin."

"Honor, I—"

She held up her hand to silence Owen. "You and I are not speaking. And last time I looked, Erin, neither were we. So it would be really awesome if someone filled me in."

"Well, maybe if you wouldn't spend all your time hiding in your office and ignoring requests for meetings, someone might just be able to have a conversation with you."

Honor gaped at Erin. "Hello, pot. Meet kettle. Who's the one that's been cold-shouldering me, refusing to speak to me, for, I don't know how long? And you're mad because I spent the day locked up in my office?"

Erin started to argue, then blew out a breath. "You're right. My bad. Can we please talk?"

"Fine."

Erin motioned for Honor to come sit at the table. Warily, she complied. She thought maybe everyone else would leave, giving Erin and her some alone time. But, no, true to form for her family, everyone else took a seat, too.

Including Owen. She didn't know what to make of him being there. Or of the fact that he and Erin were now on speaking terms.

"Owen and I had a conversation last night. One that was long overdue and cleared some things up for both of us. For me, especially."

"How—" She pulled back the snarky comment, deciding it was best to listen. "Go on."

"I realized that when I saw you two kissing, and then you told me you were dating, and eventually you told me you were married, I was upset. Not because you were together, but because the closure I thought I had gotten when Owen and I had talked when he was sick wasn't the closure I needed."

She frowned. "Why?"

"Because Owen was sick, and I couldn't get mad at him. And I really needed to be angry with him. I *was* angry. And hurt. Only I didn't get a chance to let that out."

Now the lights were coming on. "Oh. You were holding all that in because of Owen's cancer treatments."

Erin nodded. "Yes. So seeing him with you brought all of that back—don't ask me why. I guess because it was you, and I was being protective in my own screwed-up way. I didn't want to see you hurt. Only I did end up hurting you—the last person I would ever want to do that to. I'm so sorry, Honor. The way I treated you was unforgivable. If I'd known what was going on in my head, if I hadn't been so confused about my feelings, this never would have happened. I can't apologize enough for my horrible behavior."

Her heart squeezed. "It's okay."

Erin shook her head. "It's not okay."

"She said she feels so bad about it that you could choose our baby's name," Jason said.

Erin pinned Jason with a look. "I never said that."

Jason smirked.

Honor laughed. "Well, that's totally unnecessary." She squeezed Erin's hands. "I'm sure that was a very confusing time for you. And I forgive you. We're sisters."

Erin's eyes filled with tears. "I love you, Honor."

"I love you, too."

They reached for each other, and it felt so good to hold Erin against her again. She'd felt so lost without her all this time.

"Good God, I'm glad that's over," Brenna said. "You two are exhausting."

"Brenna," her mother warned.

"What?" Brenna asked. "We're all thinking it."

Honor ignored her, continuing to bask in Erin's warm embrace. When they pulled back, Honor asked, "Did you get the closure you needed?"

"I did. It was actually Owen who suggested I had pent-up anger and hurt. We talked it out—mainly I vented and ranted and he sat and took it. Now it's firmly in the past, where it belongs."

Honor looked over at Owen, who was watching her intently.

"And speaking of bright futures . . ." Erin looked over at Owen, who stood and moved into the center of the room.

"Right. Honor, can you come over here so we can talk?"

She wasn't sure she was ready for this conversation,

especially in front of her family. They'd both said terrible, hurtful things. Rehashing those would be painful. And she wasn't certain of the outcome. Was he here to tell her that he wanted the divorce? Her heart couldn't take it if that was the case. Maybe that was why he wanted to do it with her family here, to help ease the blow.

One way or the other, it would all be over tonight. Finally.

Except she didn't want to lose him. Her heart belonged to him. How was she going to make him see that before it was too late?

She got up and walked over to him, feeling exposed and vulnerable and more than a little bit on display. But when he took her hands in his, everyone else fell away and it was just the two of them.

"You were right when you accused me of walking away from you. I never should have done that, because since the day you became my wife, I've been by your side, and that's the only place I ever want to be. Walking away from you was by far the biggest mistake I ever made, and one I don't ever intend to repeat."

She took a deep breath.

"There's a lot I have to be sorry for. First to Erin for the way everything went down between us. She and I have talked it through, but I'm going to apologize to the family again. I didn't just hurt Erin. I hurt all of you, and I'm sorry. I know you said you forgive me, but I hope you mean that, because I'm in love with Honor."

He turned to Honor. "You are the one I want, the only woman I will ever love with my entire heart. And now I'm going to stop apologizing for the way I feel because how I feel when I'm with you, Honor, is like magic. I feel like I'm whole again. You and I were meant to be, and maybe all this had to happen so we could be together. Unconventional? Sure. A little crazy? Definitely. But it's been fun and I wouldn't change a thing about you and me.

"I want to stay married to you. I want to be married to you for the rest of our lives, if you'll have me, because I love you."

Honor's heart was beating so fast she was afraid she might faint. He'd said everything she'd hoped he'd say. And oh-so-much more. She was so filled with love for this man.

"I love you, Owen. I should have said those words the last time we were together, in front of my family, and I'm sorry I didn't, because my love for you has been clear in my heart for a very long time. And there's no excuse for why I didn't, other than a little bit of panic, fear of hurting Erin more and the eyes of my entire family on me. I wanted the *I love you*s between us to be a private moment, but you know how the Bellinis are. Always in each other's business."

"Hey," Brenna said. "You're right, of course, but hey."

Honor laughed. "It's okay. At least Owen knows how we are. Anyway, if you'll have me, Owen, I would very much like to continue being your wife."

She thought maybe he'd kiss her and then the family would celebrate. But he surprised the hell out of her by getting down on one knee and producing a velvet box.

"I don't even remember where those cheap wedding rings came from that we got in Vegas," he said, opening the box and revealing an incredible diamond-encrusted wedding band that took her breath away. "But you deserve much more than that."

He took the ring out and placed it on her finger, then stood. "Will you be my wife, Honor Bellini?"

She pulled him close. "I am your wife, Owen Stone. Forever."

And then he kissed her, a hot, passionate, curl-her-toes kind of kiss, right there in front of her whole family, who might have been clapping or cheering or throwing food at them for all she knew. But she was so wrapped up in Owen that she was blissfully unaware of anything other than kissing her husband.

There really were such things as happily-ever-afters. Who knew?

EPILOGUE

......

"So, YOU FINALLY showed up for a wedding."

Owen slanted a look at Jason. "Funny. And I did show up to marry Honor the first time. Though the details are a little fuzzy. Besides, I couldn't get married—officially married—without my best friends standing up for me."

And they all had. When Honor's mom asked if they wanted to do an official wedding ceremony, they'd said no at first. But then Honor suggested that maybe it wasn't a bad idea, since no one had been present at their first wedding—including themselves, since they'd both been so toasted neither of them could remember anything. So they decided to do a family-and-close-friends-only event, and to keep it simple.

Of course, with the Bellinis involved, *simple* and *wedding* didn't fit in the same sentence. Which was why Owen currently waited in the grooms room wearing a tux.

"At least you know we'll make sure you're sober for this one," Clay said.

Finn came in with a bottle of whiskey and a handful of glasses. "Who wants shots?"

Owen groaned. "Definitely not me."

"Oh, come on," Finn said, lining up the shot glasses on the table. "One shot only, to toast to your future."

He could do that. After all, he had his boys with him, and they'd never let anything bad happen to him.

He picked up the glass, remembering that night that seemed like an eternity ago, when in reality it hadn't been all that long.

"To Owen," Finn said. "The luckiest son of a bitch I've ever known."

Owen grinned and they all took their drinks.

Finn was right about that. Owen felt incredibly lucky. He'd survived cancer, had accidentally married the woman of his dreams, and despite all the drama and misunderstandings and total fuckups, he got to marry her again today in front of her family and his.

Could life get any better? He didn't think so.

There was a knock on the door and Mae popped her head in. "Five minutes, guys."

"Thanks, Mae," Owen said.

He was ready. More than ready to step into his future with Honor.

"YOU ARE SO beautiful, cailín leanbh."

Honor took in a deep breath and smiled at her mother. "Thanks, Mom. I feel like I might faint."

Her mom grasped her by her shoulders. "No, you will not faint. You are strong, in love, and you're about to walk down the aisle to your husband."

"Right." She nodded, needing that pep talk.

"I don't know why I'm so nervous. It's not like this is a big deal. We're already married. And I've done so many weddings before. I could do this with my eyes closed."

Erin came up behind her and smoothed out her hair. "But this is your wedding, Honor. Trust me, I know. The feeling is different."

She'd wanted to go small scale. Just a little garden thing, with a barbecue after. Just the immediate family, to make Mom happy. That was the way the planning had started, but then things had escalated, and then one day when she'd been out shopping with Mom, Erin and Brenna, she'd found the prettiest dress in a store in Oklahoma City that would absolutely not go with barbecue. Her sisters insisted she try it on.

It was a strapless silk taffeta. Not super fancy or anything, but it was beautiful, needed only minimal alterations. The moment Honor put it on, she wanted to burst into tears. The fact that she could tell her mom and sisters were also holding back waterworks told her all she needed to know.

This was her dress. And Mom had told her that Grandma's pearl necklace would look amazing with it. That sold her completely.

Today she stood in front of the full-length mirror, her hair pulled up, Grandma's necklace around her neck for something old, the beautiful sapphire blue earrings Erin had bought for her for something new, Brenna's bracelet adorning her right wrist for something borrowed, and the blue garter surrounding her thigh for something blue.

She was so ready to go marry her guy. The one she'd spent the past six weeks living with at his home—now their home—with their dog. It had been idyllic and perfect and she couldn't be happier.

Now to make it official. Well, it was already official, but it would be nice to remember this wedding.

"I can't believe you're getting married while I'm pregnant," Erin said, running her hand over her now very obvious belly.

"Yeah, but you're glowing and beautiful," Brenna said. "First trimester might have sucked for you, but you're rocking the second like a champion."

Erin beamed and pulled Brenna in for a squeeze. "Thank you. I feel amazing. And thank you, Honor, for choosing the most beautiful bridesmaid gowns."

"They are quite lovely," Mae said. "You have an eye for color, Honor."

Honor grinned. "Hey, I know what you all look good in. And God knows we've all seen plenty of hideous dresses."

"Amen to that," Brenna said.

Since they all had different coloring, with Erin having midnight-black hair and Brenna being a redhead, she chose a dark-burgundy-colored dress for her sisters. There was one thin shoulder strap, and another with ruched fabric. The flow of the dress was amazing, especially the slit partway up. Both her sisters looked like goddesses.

"You're all beautiful," Mom said. "Now let's go get married."

Honor laughed. "Okay, Mom."

She met her dad outside, his eyes sparkling with happiness. "You are beautiful."

"Grazie, Papa." She kissed his cheek, the photographer took pics and they were off to the arbor.

Her stomach knotted with nervousness as music started to play and she waited while Erin and Brenna made their way down the aisle. Mae was in charge of the wedding today and she was doing an impeccable job.

"Okay, Honor," Mae said, giving her an easy smile. "Time to go."

Now it was her turn. As soon as she saw Owen at the arbor, all the tension in her body fled. He looked tan and tall and gorgeous standing there in his tux, and all she could think was how the stars had aligned and somehow she'd gotten lucky enough to have this man as her husband.

Her dad handed her off to Owen, and they stood in front of the pastor and said their vows, the ones where they promised to take care of each other, to love each other forever. And she realized at this moment just how important this wedding was to her, because it made their marriage feel real.

Sure, she knew they were legally married. She had the piece of paper from the chapel in Vegas to prove it. But now they were really married. They'd said the words, sober and from their hearts and souls. And that meant everything.

"I now pronounce you man and wife. You may kiss each other."

Her heart did a little leap when Owen cupped his hand around her neck. He paused, gave her a smile.

"Forever, my only love," he whispered.

"Forever," she whispered back.

He pressed his lips to hers and sealed the deal.

And then there were cheers and applause and they turned to face their families and friends.

Time to celebrate.